THE HARSH BITE

CODENAME: SPITHRA

APEX TACTICAL SERIES

CANDICE WRIGHT

For everyone who turned up to see me at RARE London.
Thank you for all the love and support.
You popped my book signing cherry.
I hope it was as good for you as it was for me.

CHAPTER ONE

Astrid

"This is a stupid idea," I mumble as I contemplate turning around. If it hadn't taken me so long to find the place, I might have, but stubborn is my middle name, and a bigger part of me wants to see this through. Besides, as much as I like to project an *I don't give a fuck* vibe to the world, I'm not sure how many more souls my conscience can carry before I break.

I take the turn I passed three previous times—before I realized I'd been going around in circles—and drive slowly up the unmarked road. When I say road, I mean the dirt path made by all the brave vehicles that have gone before me. I cringe at the pinging sound of gravel and rocks bouncing off my new SUV. I ignore it for now, putting it in the pile of tomorrow's problems in my brain. A pile that is already overflowing. Instead, I take a deep breath and blow it out.

The road goes on for miles, and I'm starting to think I've gone the wrong way yet again when a building finally comes into view. I'm not sure what I was expecting when I set out on this journey, but it sure as hell wasn't this.

A sign greets me as I pass through a wooden archway with *APEX* carved into the wood.

"Thank you, sweet baby Jesus."

Now that I know I'm in the right place, a weight lifts from my shoulders. At least until I reach the top of the hill and get a better look at the place.

When I was told about the team of men—or more precisely, ex-soldiers—living out here calling themselves Apex Tactical, I'll admit I rolled my eyes. I pictured an old ranch or a hunting cabin where a bunch of washed-up old soldiers who couldn't hack it in the military came to play with their guns. Asking around about them, I found that assumption rather quickly dismissed, but I still couldn't seem to shake the image I had in my head of the ranch.

Now, I'm more than happy to admit when I'm wrong, and boy, was I wrong. This ranch is not just any ranch. It's like your friend saying her boyfriend likes to box a little, and then you find out her boyfriend is Mike Tyson.

As I drive toward the parking area, I swear I see a flash of red out of the corner of my eye. But when I turn, I don't see anything.

I focus back on what looks like the main building and smile. It looks like something out of a movie. I mean, I guess you could call it a ranch if the ranch had been given steroids. For a start, the place is huge. I didn't do any research on the building itself, and knowing how hard the damn place was to find, I doubt I'd have found anything. What I can see, even from here, is that it's been restored—keeping a lot of the original features —and painted a warm, earthy red. Two large black doors with smooth steel handles stretch from the bottom of the entry to the top. A sandstone walkway leads up to it from the parking lot. There are various low-maintenance shrubs lining the path, giving it a homey vibe. Floodlights, which aren't on yet, will probably cast the place in a warm glow once the sun sets.

I pass the large garage to the left of the house and park my car near the front of the building. Turning my engine off, I climb out and stretch, working out the kink in my back from driving for so long. I shut the door, the noise loud in the quiet of the place, and pocket my keys.

Now that I'm here, I feel a wave of unease wash over me. It doesn't take much for my emotional pendulum to swing from one mood to another. This place is too quiet, and the stillness of it feels unnatural. I wipe my sweaty palms on my jeans, ignoring the feeling between my shoulder blades that tells me I'm being watched, and give myself a pathetic pep talk as I walk toward the front door.

"You've got this, Astrid. If they don't listen, well, that's on them, not you. All you can do is your best. Hang in there." I pause when I realize I'm quoting from those stupid kitten posters that are dotted around my therapist's walls. Well, ex-therapist now, I guess.

Therapy has always been a minefield for me. You go in, and they treat you like you're crazy, and when they find out you were right all along, they're the ones who start acting like nut jobs. Now I just go for my own amusement. I play my part pretty well, I think. If the world believes you're losing your mind, they tend to leave you the hell alone. Given the burden I carry, alone has always suited me just fine.

When I reach the door, I lift my hand to knock, hesitating when I see the doormat that simply reads, *Fuck off.* Before I can decide if this is a really stupid idea or not, the door swings open, and I find myself staring down the barrel of a gun.

Well, I guess that answers the question about this being a stupid idea. I can't even find it in me to be scared. I'm just pissed at not listening to my better judgment. I knew this would happen, though I'll admit I usually open my mouth and speak before someone points a gun at me. I take a deep breath, ready to launch into the awkward explanation of who I am and why I'm here, when I'm grabbed from behind and a sack is pulled over my head.

Any thought of being calm and rational goes out the window at this point.

I swing my elbow back into someone's gut, pleased with myself when they let out an *oof* sound. I lift my leg and stomp down on their foot with the heel of my boot. I don't stop to see if the person in front of me will shoot. I duck and hope that if they do, they'll take out the asshole behind me. I stumble down the path, reaching up to pull the sack off, but I'm grabbed from behind once more, and this time my arms are pinned to my body, rendering them useless as I thrash in their hold.

"Let me go!" I scream, but they ignore me as they drag me kicking and screaming through the door.

"Shut the hell up," one of them snarls, which makes me fight harder until I'm dumped in a hard chair and the bag is yanked off.

I move to stand but freeze when I see four large men standing in front of me, two of which I realize are twins. I ignore that fact in favor of concentrating on the other two, the ones who have guns pointed at my head. The two are polar opposites of each other. The one directly in front of me has fair hair that's long on top and shaved short at the sides. His eyes are soft green with a hint of blue, and they crinkle from the smirk playing at the edge of his full lips. The other has dark hair that's long enough to skim his jaw. His eyes are a deep midnight blue, and the scowl on his face screams *fuck off*. And while his arms and neck are covered in ink in shades of black and gray, giving him the ultimate bad-boy look, I don't see any tattoos on the other guy.

My eyes drift to the twins, who are also dark-haired. Both are taller and broader than the two with the guns. Though they aren't the ones threatening me, they carry a sense of menace and authority.

"Who the fuck are you?" one of the tall, dark, and deadly twins snaps. I'd answer if I could, but my tongue is stuck to the roof of my mouth, and my heart is beating so hard I wouldn't be surprised if it jumped out of my chest like a scene from *Alien*.

When he realizes I'm not going to answer, the long-haired guy who looks like an extra from the show *Vikings* I like so much walks over to me and presses his gun to my forehead.

"We've just decorated, so I really don't want to splatter your pretty little head all over the walls, but that doesn't mean I won't. Did you come here alone?"

I think about lying and saying I came with a bunch of deranged serial killers who are super protective of me, but somehow, I don't think that would go down well. And I suspect they would know I was lying anyway.

"Yes," I admit. "I came alone."

"Search her." This order comes from the other twin, who, until now, has been quiet. His voice is every bit as cold and hard as his face. The Viking next to me shoves his gun into a holster at his back before he reaches for my arm and yanks me up.

"Alright, Jesus fucking Christ, all you had to do was ask me to stand up," I snap, my arm stinging from where he grabbed me.

With my pale coloring, which is about as close to being a ghost without being a transparent shade of white, I tend to bruise like a peach. I'm sure I'll have a lovely ring of finger-prints circling my arm by tomorrow. That's if I'm still alive by then.

The behemoth ignores me and spins me around before leaning down and talking quietly into my ear. "If you move, Slade will shoot you."

I stand still and close my eyes, swallowing hard as I lock my legs and grit my teeth. Slade is obviously the tattooed man with the gun still pointed at me. Good to know. I like to at least know a person's name when they threaten to kill me.

The Viking dick forces my arms up and out on either side of me, then kicks my legs apart. He slides his hands up and down my arms before moving them across my body and down my hips. He draws them up and down each leg, checking my ankles before standing up once more and moving his hands to my rib cage.

As they glide upward, I snarl at him, "If you touch my boobs, I'll kick you between your legs so hard you'll be able to lick your own balls."

He hesitates, the sound of a snort coming from behind us, before his thumbs swipe under the edge of my bra. I tense and ready myself, but thankfully he doesn't push his luck.

Instead, he takes my arm again and whirls me back around. "Mouthy little thing, aren't you?"

"Well, the role of big prick was already taken," I snap back, my default setting returning to sarcasm with a hint of bitchiness.

"Sit." He doesn't give me a chance to do anything other than sit when he all but shoves me back into the chair.

I rub my arm where he grabbed it, glaring up at him, but his stoic gaze never wavers. I turn toward the demon duo when I hear a cell phone chime.

The slightly taller one pulls his phone from his pocket before reading a text and nodding. "E confirms she's alone. She's been casing the place, circling around four or five times."

I roll my eyes. "I was not casing the place. Who even says things like *casing the place?*" I mutter, thinking this man must have watched *Ocean's Eleven* one too many times.

"We have you on camera—" he starts, but I cut him off.

"Trying to find this place, yes. I'm sorry, I didn't realize getting lost was a crime."

He tilts his head, studying me as his brother pulls out his own cell and fiddles with it.

"Who are you, and why are you here?"

"Honestly? I have no fucking clue what I'm doing here. I'd like to go home now. I have reached my bullshit limit for the day."

He looks away from me, dismissing me as if I'm nothing but a nuisance, before he says something to his brother that I don't hear and then jogs off.

His brother steps toward me, making me tense. "You know who we are?"

I roll my eyes and cross my arms over my chest. "Apex Tactical."

They all tense at my words.

"What?"

"And who am I?"

"Either Tweedledee or Tweedledum. I can't tell which of you is which, though."

"Cute. I guess you think that makes you Alice." Slade chuckles as he lowers the gun.

"Fuck no. I'm not interested in anything you guys are selling. I just have a message I want to deliver, and then I am on my way."

"A message?"

I drop my head and sigh because what's the point? They aren't ever going to believe a word I say. They've already made up their minds about me.

"Who's that?"

I lift my head when I hear a woman's voice and open my mouth to reply. But the asshole beside her speaks before I do.

"Don't get any closer, Salem. We don't know who she is or who she works for."

"I don't work for anyone. That's what I've been trying to tell you," I snap, jumping up from the chair I'm sitting on as the Viking man steps closer to me.

I swallow and sit back down, letting my head drop and my hair cover my face as I give myself a second to get my shit together. "I knew I should have kept my mouth shut. But did I listen to myself? No. And now I'm going to die at the hands of a bunch of hot GI Joes." I almost want to cry at the injustice of it all, but I refuse to give these assholes the satisfaction.

"Can you tell us your name and what you're doing here? I'm sure you won't believe this, but nobody is going to kill you. These guys are just a tiny bit protective of me."

I lift my head and stare at her, wondering what it might be like to wear rose-tinted glasses like she appears to be. These guys would sooner snap my neck than let me anywhere near her, even if I came here to warn her.

Shit, I still have to talk to her, or all this was for nothing. I bite my lip and feel myself deflate, knowing this is only going to end badly. I look around, hoping to find a way to escape, but I know I won't get far with everyone watching my every move.

"My name is Astrid, and I'm here because I listened to a crazy man who clearly wants me dead," I admit, vowing to wring Penn's neck if I ever see him again.

"Stop speaking in fucking riddles and tell us how you found Salem," Slade—the asshole with the gun in his hand—snaps, making me jump. He might not have it pointed at me anymore, but I can still see it.

"Slade," Salem says his name firmly.

I try to mask my emotions, not wanting them to see how fucking freaked out I am right now. But I can't get my hands to stop shaking.

"You said something about a crazy man. Does he have a name?" Salem asks me in a softer tone than she used with Slade.

I stare at her for a moment before swallowing. "He calls himself Penn Travis, but I don't know if that's his real name or not." I don't know anything about the man at all.

She takes a step closer to me. "You know Penn?"

"Not well. He…uh, helped me out of some trouble," I answer vaguely, not wanting to open that whole can of worms.

Slade snorts. "Shocking. You have trouble written all over you."

My temper flares, eroding my fear and common sense. "Kiss my ass, dickhead."

Salem laughs, but I keep glaring at Slade.

"Astrid?"

I turn to look back at Salem when she calls me. Her eyes stare into mine, and I have a flash of the vision I had of her. I swallow down the urge to vomit as I busy my shaky hands by playing with the hem of my top.

"Why did Penn send you here, and how did he know where I was?"

"He didn't know where you were. That's why it took me so long to find you. He heard tales of a woman they called Bruja in Mexico. He wrote it off at first until the rumors said she could heal with her hands. By the time he got there, she was gone." Or at least that's what he told me. I'll admit, I wasn't sure if he was pulling my leg, but I owed him, so I threw caution to the wind. And look where that landed me.

"He tried to find me?"

She isn't denying that she can heal with her hands. Does that mean… "It's true? You can heal with your hands?"

She doesn't answer, so I sigh in defeat. Might as well get this over with. "He told me something happened, and months later, he tracked you to a clinic. He thought he had cleaned the problem up, whatever that means, until he bumped into me." I take a breath and am about to tell them how the only information he could give me was the name Apex when I'm interrupted.

"I'm confused. Cleaned what up?" one of the twins asks. "And who the fuck is this Penn person? How does he know you?" he asks Salem.

"Penn was a man I met when I was a kid. He showed me how to use my gift. Taught me about the duality it had to offer."

The other twin steps closer to Salem and looks into her eyes. Something unspoken passes between them before he speaks.

"Think he was the one to blow the place up?"

She shrugs. "I don't know. I haven't seen the man in twenty years. Why would he do that?" Salem asks, looking confused.

"Why indeed?" he questions calmly. But the other twin seems pissed.

"There were innocent people in that place. So if it was this Penn person, he's not exactly a good guy here, Salem, which means we can't assume his protégé is either."

"Hey, I'm not his protégé. I've met the man a total of two

times. Once when he saved me, and once when he asked me to find you."

"Son of a bitch. This screams set-up to me," Viking asshole pipes up. "Let me guess. You're supposed to let him know when you've found her and where? Are you wearing a wire or a tracking device?"

"What? No!" I yell. God, why did I come here?

I stare at Salem, willing her with my eyes to hear me out so I can get the hell out of this place. "I didn't come here to cause you harm. I didn't even know you existed until Penn saved me."

"You keep saying that. But what exactly did he save you from?"

I wrap my arms around myself. "Does it matter?" I say quietly, but she doesn't say anything.

I look at her again. "You're gifted. Just like he is. Just like me," I whisper, knowing she won't admit it but deciding I have to give her something, and if there is the slightest chance, then maybe, just maybe, she'll believe me.

The tension in the room reaches fever pitch as Salem steps closer.

"When I touched Penn, I had a vision of you." I stare straight at her and tell her the truth.

"What did you see?"

"You were fighting someone. I don't know who they were. They were wearing a mask that covered their face and hair, and there was smoke all around you."

"The clinic?"

I shake my head. "I don't see the past, only the future. I don't know when it happens exactly, but I remember the fairy lights that you see at Christmas twinkling on your face when you fall." I hold myself tighter, waiting for their reactions.

"What else did you see, Astrid?"

I close my eyes and feel a tear run down my face. Getting her to believe me is only half the battle, the other half lies in saving her.

"I see you die. That's why I'm here, to try and stop the vision from happening."

The room goes silent.

"How often do your visions come true?" she whispers.

I don't look away from her, needing her to know the truth no matter what. But I can tell by the look on her face that she knows the answer. My visions always come true. And another tear slips down my cheek.

CHAPTER TWO

Slade

I slide the gun into my pants pocket, but I don't take my eyes off the woman in front of me. If she thinks I'll let my guard down just because she's female, she has another thing coming. I've seen women do evil, unspeakable things. I'll never be the type of man to underestimate one. I stare at her as she stares at Salem, her expression one of sadness, but I'm not buying the bullshit she's spreading.

"Let me guess, the best way for you to help is to stick close? What's your aim here—to drive a wedge between Salem and the rest of us? Or is it simply to get her alone?"

She looks up at me. If she had the ability to spit fire, I'd've been incinerated on the spot.

"I get that you don't like me for whatever reason, but believe it or not, I'm not Salem's enemy. You, on the other hand, I have no problem smacking around a little."

Someone behind me snorts, but I ignore them, glaring at Astrid.

"Look, I don't care if you believe me. You won't be the first to turn me away, and you won't be the last. I get it. It all sounds so fantastical. But is it really more unbelievable than having the ability to heal someone?"

Nobody says anything to that because we know she's right.

"I've said what I had to say. I can walk away with a clear conscience, at least. You know to be careful, and if I see anything else, I'll let you know. But I'd rather text you, if that's okay. Because as much as I've been made to feel so darn welcome, I think it's time for me to go."

"Yeah, I don't think so," Oz states. I look over at him and see him shaking his head.

"Oz," Salem says softly.

"No, Salem. We don't know her. We sure as hell can't trust her. Zig, tell them."

Zig, who up until now has been trying to dissect Astrid with his eyes, turns to look at Salem.

"Oz is right. She can't go until we know if she poses a threat or not. Until then, she stays here."

"What? No." Astrid jumps to her feet, but Jagger's hand on her shoulder pushes her back down into the chair.

"Slade, take her keys and search her car before moving it into the garage," Zig orders.

"You guys are out of your mind," Astrid snaps.

"Keys." I hold out my hand to her, but she slaps it away.

"Fuck you. Fuck you all." She stands and tries to run, but I grab her and spin her so that her back is to my front.

I shove my hand into the front left pocket of her jeans, knowing where her keys are from the outline of them. I pull them out and pass her off to Jagger, who steps around the chair to grab her.

"Watch her, or she'll run the first chance she gets."

"Guys, this isn't right," Salem complains as I head toward the door.

I hear Astrid struggling, but I ignore it and listen for Zig's reply in case he changes his mind.

"We won't hurt her, Salem. But she stays. We won't take risks when it comes to your safety. We've come too close to losing you too many times."

I head outside, leaving them to it, and whistle when I see the car she drove here. I didn't pay much attention when we grabbed her or to the keys in my hand. I expected a beater, but apparently not. This girl either has a rich father or a sugar daddy to be driving around in a Porsche Cayenne Turbo GT. Unless, of course, it's stolen.

I pull out my cell phone and call E.

"Yeah?"

"You run the plate?"

"Doing it now. Give me five, and I'll call you back."

He hangs up, and I shove the phone in my pocket and make my way to the back of the car, looking inside. Popping the locks, I open the backdoor and find a bag on the back seat and a couple more in the trunk, including a suitcase and a messenger bag with a laptop. I leave them where they are for now, closing the door and opening the driver's side, and climb into the front seat. I start her up and pull her around to the garage, which is now open and ready for me to drive right in. I park, getting out as Greg walks over.

"Shit, nice ride."

"Yeah, not cheap, that's for sure. She has a bunch of shit in the back that needs checking over."

"Hawk and Creed should be back in a minute. I'll fill them in and get them to go through it all. Any electronics?"

"A laptop. There's probably a cell in there, too, because Jagger didn't find one when he patted her down."

"She might not have one."

I chuckle at that. "Given the car, I highly doubt that. It's probably a top-of-the-line one in a blinged-out pink case."

"Wow. You really don't like this girl much, do you?"

"I don't know her, and I don't need to to know she's trouble."

Greg cocks his head, and I know I'm not going to like what he's about to say.

"She could be telling the truth. Like you said, you don't know her. A year ago, if you told me that you met a woman who could heal people, I would've assumed you hit your head or started taking drugs. I guess what I'm saying is that I'm not ready to write her off just yet. And the thing is, if she is telling the truth, then she drove all the way here for no other reason than to help Salem. And look what we're doing to her for her efforts. You think if she has another vision, she'll be as forthcoming with it?"

He walks away, leaving me to think about what he said. The

thing is, he's not wrong. I'm not sure why I'm being such a dick, but there is something about that girl—

My cell rings. I pull it out and see that it's Evander, so I swipe to answer. "What did you find?"

"Car is registered to Astrid Montgomery. Address is out in Beverly Hills, believe it or not. She's twenty-two years old and has a couple of arrests for disorderly conduct, assault, and vandalism. She was a minor at the time, so she was let off with a warning and community service. Her parents are some kind of philanthropists. They spend a lot of their time flying around the world, helping those less fortunate. They are both trust fund babies, and from what it looks like, their marriage was an arranged one."

"What is it with rich people? Do they really think they can just buy love?"

"I don't think love factors into it. They would have been thinking about legacies and inheritances. Of course, that doesn't mean that love can't come out of the arrangement. Thousands of cultures around the world have arranged marriages, and they make them work."

"Right, whatever. I don't really want to get into the pros and cons of this right now. Anything else on Astrid herself?"

"Nothing of interest since she was a teen. Seems she went from somewhat of a wild child to a recluse."

Something happened. I don't have anything to base it on other than a gut feeling, but then what do I know? Kids do stupid shit all the time. Maybe she was just acting out to get mommy and daddy's attention. The question is, did she grow out of it, or is she still seeking attention in all the wrong places?

I shake my head and snort at how different our teenage years were. It's hard to drum up much sympathy for a pretty little rich girl crying in the front seat of her Porsche when, at the same age, I was sitting in a prison cell, wondering if I'd make it through the night.

"Slade?" Ev says my name, and from his tone, I'm guessing he's said it more than once.

"Sorry, just thinking. What does she do? And if she's really gifted, how would she have kept it under the radar? Sounds like the family is pretty high profile."

"Yeah, but that can work in her favor too. Money can go a long way to paying off people and making them recant or forget things."

Anger hums in my veins, making it hard not to draw parallels between this situation and my own.

"As for what she does, I can't find anything. Her family moved a lot when she was a kid. She went to more schools than an army brat, but for the most part, it looks like she was home-schooled. I can't find any traces of a formal education after that."

Yeah, well, the CIA tends to recruit them young, when possible, and train them.

"Maybe she helps her parents out with their charities?" Ev suggests, as if he can hear the direction my thoughts have gone.

"Helped them spend their money more like it. Focus on that for now. I want to know what she's been doing since she graduated. Young, rich, pretty girls don't just disappear from the society pages. Keep me posted if you find anything else."

"Will do."

He hangs up, and I shove my cell phone in my pocket as Hawk and Creed walk through the door.

"Ev give you the heads-up?"

"Yeah. Are you buying her story?" Creed asks, looking the car over.

"Not even for a second. Here." I toss him the keys. "Search her stuff. She has a laptop in the back, probably a cell phone somewhere in there, too, since we didn't find one on her. Search for trackers and shit as well."

"On it."

I turn and leave them to it, needing to get my eyes back on this girl. It's the only way I can be sure she's not up to something.

When I walk into the main living area, Oz and Salem are gone, but Astrid is sitting back in the chair, her head tipped down so her long white-blonde hair covers her face as Jagger looms over her. Greg watches with a cautious expression on his face.

Zig looks up when he sees me. "Everything good?"

"Ev is doing his thing. Hawk and Creed are going through her things now."

I watch Astrid as I speak and see her body tense, but she keeps her mouth shut for a change.

"Alright. The question is, where do we put her for now? She'll run, given the—"

"She can stay with Jagger and me. She won't get away from us."

Again, I expect her to protest, but she says nothing as she lifts her head. Ironically, it's her silence that makes me more

20

wary than before, when she was hissing and spitting like a pissed-off cat.

"You sure?" Zig looks from me to Jagger, who shrugs.

"I'm game. I always wanted a pet."

Astrid's face pales, but she says nothing. Though I don't necessarily like scaring women, if I think fear will keep her from doing something reckless, then I'm not above using it.

"Jesus Christ, guys, rein it in a little. You're scaring her," Greg snaps.

"Good. She should be scared. Because if she's come here to hurt Salem, then there is nothing she can do or a place she can hide where we won't hunt her down," I state.

The room goes quiet. Threatening females goes against the grain for all of us, but we know what's at stake here. We won't hurt her. She just doesn't need to know that. Greg looks at me and shakes his head. I can see he wants to step in and say something else, but Zig gets the final word.

"Go and get her settled. Impress upon our guest how important it is for her to follow the rules while she's here." He says the word *guest* the same way he might say *hostage*.

I fight back a grin and offer him a nod before walking over to Astrid and looking down at her. "Let's go."

She doesn't stand up, but she lifts her head and looks up at me. I expect her gaze to be hostile, or at least fearful. But when I stare into her eyes, I see nothing. It's as if the lights are on but nobody's home. I swallow, not liking how it affects me. To cover my unease, I wrap my hand around her bicep and tug her to her feet.

Jagger looks at me with a cocked eyebrow. "So how is this

going to work?" he asks quietly as I pull her out of the room onto the deck.

"Simple. We watch her until we can prove her story one way or another."

"I meant, where's she gonna sleep?" he says dryly.

"She can take your room. We'll rotate watching her. I have a feeling whoever stays with her won't get much sleep because the second we close our eyes, she'll run."

"I wouldn't worry about that. It's hard to run with handcuffs on your wrists."

She stumbles at Jagger's words but still says nothing. I'm not gonna lie, it's beginning to piss me off. I look at Jagger, who shrugs.

"Tough girl, huh? Let's see how tough you feel after a few days with us."

CHAPTER THREE

Astrid

I keep my mouth shut as I let Dickhead One and Dickhead Two lead me outside to one of the smaller buildings out back. I look around subtly, not wanting them to think I'm checking everything out. But of course, I am. The second I see an opening, I'm taking it. I'm so over doing the right thing and being the better person. It doesn't get me anything but heartache and grief. It's not like I didn't expect their suspiciousness, but this is taking things too far.

The large building we're leaving seems to be where most of them gather. The rest of the buildings scattered around look like small homes. If the building materials and equipment I see are anything to go by, I can guess that the extra housing is new. I wonder what they all did before. And if they lived off-site, why did they all decide to change that now? For Salem, perhaps? I'd feel a little green with envy if they weren't all such fucking psychos.

We stop at a building that's a little farther back than the others. It's a smaller replica of the main house and smells like new wood and fresh paint. I wait while Jagger opens the door and stands back so Slade can usher me inside. Stepping into the open-plan living area, I'm thankful that it doesn't have that murder-cabin vibe. As much as I've dreamed over the years of swapping my life with a heroine from one of my beloved books, it would be just my luck to find myself in a horror story, making stupid decisions like running upstairs in my underwear with a killer hot on my heels.

A cough breaks me out of my wayward thoughts, something my brain tends to do when I'm in situations that make me nervous. I might not be able to leave, but I can let my mind drift away. It's something I've done since I was a kid.

The room is light and airy, with pale sage walls and light oak floors that run throughout the space. But there is a distinct, unused feel to it. I can tell they live here—I can smell hints of their aftershave, and there is a coffee cup sitting on the kitchen counter—but it's void of all the little things that make a house a home.

The sitting area has a dark charcoal sectional sofa that contrasts well with the paint color, and the nubby area rug makes the room feel cozy and warm. A large ottoman with a magazine tossed on top of it sits just in front of the sofa, ready for when people want to kick back and watch movies on the large television mounted on the wall opposite the sofa.

On the other side of the room, there is a small dining table with chairs in the same light oak as the floor. The tabletop is made of a dark, almost burnt-looking piece of driftwood, with edges that look as if they have been smoothed over time from being thrown around in the ocean.

The kitchen area at the far back of the room has white, glossy cupboards and dark wooden counters stained the same color as the tabletop, while the kitchen island is all white and has four tall high-back chairs upholstered in a charcoal suede that matches the sofa.

"This is where you'll be staying. If you need anything, tell us, and we'll see about getting it for you," Jagger tells me, coming up from behind me and acting hospitable all of a sudden.

"I'll take a carving knife, a gun, and my freedom, please."

"You could try to hurt us, Astrid. I'd like to prove just how futile that would be," Slade snaps, his deep voice cracking like a whip.

I swallow, refusing to be intimidated by these assholes. They might have the upper hand right now, but I know how easily the power balance can shift.

"What's the matter, little girl? Cat got your tongue?"

I turn my head and look at Slade, who seems to be having way too much fun baiting me.

"Why do I think you want me to claw your face off? Is it so your pretty outside can match your ugly inside? You might fool everyone else, but I can see past that smile of yours and see there is something fucked-up inside of you. There's a part of you that wants to hurt me, and for what? Trying to help? You can paint me as the bad guy all you want, but I've done nothing but come here and try to help. All you have done is remind me that there is no such thing as a good deed or good guys."

That shuts him up, and an uncomfortable silence descends on the room. I have to fight the urge to fidget, not wanting either of them to see me squirm.

"Let me show you the room you'll be using." Jagger takes my hand, making me jolt as he pulls me away from Slade. I look down at it and frown, but I don't pull away. I didn't expect the gentle way in which he reached for me after the way I've been handled so far. It's disconcerting and makes it harder to keep my anger from fading.

I let him lead me through the room to the door on the far left. When he opens it, it reveals a hallway with four more doors, two on the left and two on the right. The closest one on the right leads to the bathroom—which Jagger quickly shows me—the one opposite it leads outside, and the remaining two at the far end of the hall are their bedrooms. My heartbeat picks up, knowing I'll be staying in one of their rooms.

Even though I pretended not to be paying attention to them earlier, I know one of them will be in the room with me while I sleep, watching over me so I can't run away or pull off the nefarious plan they're convinced I've cooked up.

"This is Slade's room." He holds the door open and shows me the room. Before I can take much in, he closes it and leads me to the last door on the left.

"This one is mine. You'll be staying in here for the time being. There are clothes in the dresser and closet if you need anything until your stuff gets here. The bathroom is through there." He points, but I'm still taking in the large bed beside the window with its deep green covers and navy-blue throw. On the cherry wood floor is a navy rug, and in the corner, next to a floor-standing lamp and a small end table, is a reading chair with another navy throw tossed over the back of it. The walls are a rich cream with abstract artwork in various shades of green and gold hanging in solid black frames.

It might look effortlessly masculine, but I can tell a woman had her hand in making it look this way. For a start, I've never in my life met a man who bought a throw.

Jagger watches me, my eyes skimming over the dresser and the door to the closet before I make my way over to the bathroom. I glance around the black and white tiled room, noting the shower is ridiculously huge. It's clean and tidy, and everything is minimalist, unlike my bathroom at home, which is cluttered with creams and makeup and shit I don't need, though I swear I do.

"You want something to eat?"

I turn my head and look up at him, blinking. "Funnily enough, no. Being held captive tends to mess with my appetite."

"Been held captive often, then?" Jagger chuckles darkly as he steps closer to the bathroom.

I back away, keeping some distance between us. "More times than I care to admit. So, why don't you tell me how this is going to play out? Are you two doing the whole good cop/bad cop thing on me? Because if you are, I'll save you the trouble and tell you right now it won't work. I won't trust either of you. Why would I when you're holding me hostage?"

"You're not a hostage. We're just holding you until we find out the information we need," Jagger states, crossing his arms.

"So, you're holding me against my will until you get what you want. Hate to break it to you, but that's the very definition of a hostage. And just saying, I've told you what you need to know. You're just not listening."

Laughter has me whirling around to see Slade standing in the bedroom doorway. He stalks toward me with the lethal grace of a panther. "So brave." He grins, reaching out to touch a strand of my hair, but I slap his hand away.

He chuckles again, and something about it seems a little unhinged.

"It's a good act, but I've seen better. Plus"—he leans down, his lips a hair's breadth from my cheek, making my heart thud loudly in my chest— "I can smell your fear," he murmurs before stepping back. That mask of indifference slips back down over his face.

I glare at him, my hands fisted at my sides. "Of course I'm scared. I'm not insane like you. Besides, I'm a woman locked up with two strange men who look like they'd have no problem hurting me. In fact, I think you'd enjoy it. But sure, let's just pretend that I'm the one at fault here."

I give up arguing with them. What's the point? Everyone is so quick to make up their mind about me. I'm sick and tired of trying to convince people that I'm a good person. If they want to think the worst of me, then fuck them, that's what I'll give them.

"Slade," Jagger says, but Slade continues to stare at me for what feels like forever before finally turning to his friend.

"Go put some coffee on and see if E has found anything else while I make sure Astrid is settled."

Slade cocks his eyebrow at that. "You gonna help her change?"

Jagger narrows his eyes at Slade, who seems to shake himself out of it. He doesn't apologize for being a dick, though. I suppose I should find comfort in the fact that he's an asshole to everyone, but I don't. I'm a firm believer that kindness doesn't cost a thing. Though, saying that, I'm happy to give out sarcastic quips for free too. Hardly surprising after a lifetime of dealing with people who were mean just because they could be.

No matter how many times we moved when I was a kid or how many schools I went to, it always came down to the same two groups: the bullies and the bullied. Because of my…quirks, I tended to end up in the later one. When people realized I just didn't give a fuck anymore, they mostly left me alone. There was a limit to what they would do. They might not like me, but they knew my family was richer than most of theirs combined, and in the world of the elite, money was power. They could hurt me with their nasty words, hold me down and beat the snot out of me, but I'd heal. What my lawyer could do to them —and not just them but their whole families—was bankrupt them. To the socially vapid vampires I went to school with, that was a fate worse than death. Unfortunately, anyone who wanted to befriend me was fair game. I wasn't willing to make someone a target by association, which left me pretty much alone. Sure, being alone could be soul-destroying at times, but I refused to ruin someone else's high school experience by being tarred with the same brush as me. I left people alone, and they left me alone.

And then the incident happened, and everything changed.

I shake that thought away, not wanting to take a trip down memory lane, especially not now.

When Slade leaves the room, Jagger focuses his attention back on me. I'm not a tall girl. At five-three, I'm shorter than most of my counterparts. Add in that I have curves, meaning a whole lot of tits and ass, and I've always looked very different from the tall, model-type girls I went to high school with. But standing next to Jagger, who is easily six-four and built like he eats small children for breakfast, I feel positively tiny.

"Don't take his attitude personally. He doesn't like strangers."

"Isn't everyone a stranger until you take the time to get to know them?"

His lips twitch as he lets his arms drop to his sides. "It's different with Slade. He doesn't just see strangers; he sees potential enemies. He's watchful, and like you said, he can be a bit of a dick. But he isn't usually cruel. Once he's warmed up to you and he knows you've got nothing to hide, you'll see that he's a good guy."

I snort at that. "Sure, whatever you say."

Sighing, I take a step closer to the window just as a strange whirring sound makes me jump and a shutter begins to drop over the window.

I turn to Jagger, who looks at me before he shrugs. "Like I said, he doesn't trust easily. Give it time."

I shake my head and fold my arms, putting a barrier between us. "With all due respect. I don't have to do anything. I owe you guys fuck all. If anything, today was just the reminder I needed."

He steps closer and stops. His hands twitch as if he wants to reach for me, but he holds himself back. "A reminder of what?"

"That people aren't worth it. I should have stayed in my lane. That's on me. I've learned my lesson. Don't worry, I'll be the model prisoner, and as soon as you've dug your way through my life and deemed me innocent, I'll go. And if I ever get a vision about any of you again, I'll keep my damn mouth shut."

CHAPTER FOUR

Jagger

She juts out her chin. The pure stubbornness of it makes me want to bend down and bite it. I'm not sure what it is about this woman, but her sheer defiance does something to me. My cock has been hard ever since she started throwing her attitude around.

I like my women on the submissive side in the bedroom, but I don't want a yes/no woman. I like to bend them to my will. I like them to have fight in them because it makes their submission so much sweeter. Astrid is full of sass and snark, but beneath that, there is something vulnerable. She is good at masking it, but I've seen it poke through before she drops the mask back into place.

I let my eyes move over her, taking the time now that we're alone to soak her in. She's got the most spectacular tits I've ever seen. And I have to fight the urge to rip her T-shirt off just so that I can see them better. Thankfully, I resist. Not sure that would have made the best impression, especially with the whole hostage thing we have going on.

We might not mean her any harm, but she can't know that. I drag my eyes from her chest down to her shapely hips and thick thighs before they move up to her flushed face.

"You done?" she asks with bite, but her fingers are fiddling with the edge of her T-shirt.

I take a step forward, crowding her, relishing the sharp intake of breath. "Do I make you nervous, Astrid?"

"If by nervous you mean sick, then sure."

I grin and lick my lips, her eyes following the movement of my tongue. "I think you're curious." I move closer until there is only a sliver between us. "I think you're wondering how I taste."

"Close. I was wondering if you take drugs because something is not right with your brain."

I lean in, my mouth a whisper from hers. Her breath skates over my lips as I speak. "If you're hoping your attitude will turn me off, you'll be sadly mistaken. I like my women with a little spunk in them."

"Please tell me you don't mean that literally. I'd hate to have to rip your balls off, rendering your baby batter useless."

I pull back and take a step away from her before I think *fuck it* and throw her down on the bed. I've never had such a visceral reaction to a woman before.

"I'll leave you to get settled in. Wash up, borrow whatever you need, then come out and have something to eat. You might not be hungry, but you should really eat." I frown, wondering when she last ate.

She folds her arms over her chest, letting me know that if I push harder, she'll do the opposite of anything I ask of her, just in spite.

With a sigh, I turn around and head for the door. With my hand on the knob, I look over my shoulder. "For what it's worth, I'd like to know more about you. And not because I don't trust you. You intrigue me."

"Wow, I'm honored."

"Really?"

"No," she deadpans before turning her back on me.

I laugh and pull the door closed behind me. I find Slade sitting at the kitchen island with his cell phone in his hand.

"Anything new?"

He looks up at me before pointing at the now-full coffee pot. I walk over to it and pour myself a cup before leaning against the counter to face him.

"Hawk and Creed didn't find anything in her stuff that raised any red flags. The electronics are with E, though. They'll take a little longer to go through."

"I'll head over and pick her clothes up then."

"Don't bother. She can do without them for a day or two."

I raise my brow in question at that, knowing he must have a reason.

"I want her to feel uncomfortable."

I blow on my drink and look at him over the rim of my mug. "It's more than that. I know you, Slade. What's your plan here? I know you have one, but we're a team in this, so I need to know."

He looks up at me and tosses his phone on the island. "If she feels like she has the upper hand, then she has no reason to talk. And something tells me she won't tell us dick right now. So, we need to find her trigger and trip it. I want to make her nervous, wary. Then, when she feels like she might snap, I want to befriend her and coax her into telling us more."

"You want to seduce her."

He shrugs. "I'd rather not have to torture the information out of her."

Something sours in my stomach at the thought of playing her. But is it really playing when I want her this much?

"I'm not against it, but I think we need to tread carefully. If we treat her like the enemy and it turns out she's telling the truth, then we'll blow any chance we have of getting her on board as an ally."

He doesn't look bothered by my words, though, making me curious.

"You don't for a second believe that she's on the up and up, do you?"

"I'm not ruling out that she has a gift. I'm not saying I'm one hundred percent buying into it. But after everything that went down with Salem, we'd be stupid to dismiss it completely. What I have a problem with is her sincerity. You don't think it's a bit convenient that she's here, claiming she had a vision? If it was anything else, we'd have told her to fuck off already, but she's played on our one weakness."

"Salem," I answer, seeing where he's going with this.

"Exactly."

I take a sip of my coffee and think about what he's saying.

He's right to be cautious. It's the smart thing to do. But that woman in there intrigues the fuck out of me, and it's been a long time since any woman managed to get a reaction out of me beyond a hard-on.

"She doesn't exactly come across as—" He cuts me off with a shake of his head.

"That's what makes her the best person for the job, though, right? She's pretty enough to gain our attention, but not in an over-the-top, obviously sexual way. She's not too eager to please or firing off too many questions that would raise red flags. She is actually going about it the opposite way. Making snarky, hostile digs that give her a standoffish vibe that could almost make a man believe she's not interested in the answers— almost. When she was talking to Salem, she was solely focused on her. It was like the rest of us didn't exist. She is here for her, no doubt about it, but I'm not sure I believe it's just so she can give her a warning. I mean, why bother? I'm not trying to be a dick, but she doesn't know us. She doesn't know Salem. She had no godly clue what kind of situation she was walking into. Unless, of course, she did."

"You think we have another rat feeding her information?" I tense at that.

"No, I think Cooper was our only leak. But that doesn't mean she wasn't getting info from him at some point. And now that he's dead, she might have come to see if she could get the information herself."

"I suppose it makes as much sense as anything else right now." I blow out a breath and place my coffee on the counter. "Alright. Let's see how it plays out then."

I move to the fridge, check out the contents, and wince. There isn't much here. We eat most of our meals in the main house.

"Not much here to feed her. We'll have to get some food if you don't want her eating at the main house with the others."

"I think it's best we keep her here for now. Isolating her will only add to her unease."

"She still needs to eat."

Slade climbs from his seat and heads to the fridge. He rummages around inside before moving to the cupboard above his head. He tosses the things he grabs on the counter, then opens the top drawer for a knife.

I snort at the ingredients. "A peanut butter and jelly sandwich? That's the best we can do?"

"We're not a hotel. If she's hungry, she'll eat."

I look at him as he assembles the sandwich. I pick my mug back up and finish my coffee. He's acting odd, even for him. "What is it about her that sets you off?"

"I don't know what you're talking about."

"Bullshit!" I scoff, placing my empty mug in the sink before turning back around to look at him. "I know what you're saying, and I'm not saying I don't agree with you. But there is a difference between being suspicious and downright hostile. There is something about this woman that sets you off. Why?"

He ignores me as he puts the sandwich on a plate and cleans up, but he should know better than to assume I'll drop it.

With a grunt, he shoves the plate into my hands. "How about you take this to her?"

"Take it yourself. Shouldn't be a problem, right?" I shove the plate back and walk away.

He mumbles something under his breath before stomping down the hallway. He doesn't bother knocking on the door. Instead, he shoves it open, and seconds later he yanks it closed. He glares at me before moving over to the sofa and throwing himself down on it.

"She, okay?"

"She's fine, if the look she gave me is anything to go by. I suggest we make sure all the knives are hidden."

I chuckle, sitting next to him after grabbing the two controllers for the PlayStation and tossing one at him. "You need to chill. Like you said, for however long it takes Ev to dig into her life, we're stuck together. You need to figure your shit out."

"My shit is just fine. Don't worry about me. Worry about yourself. Don't think I don't see the way you've been looking at her."

I don't deny it. I look at him and roll my eyes. "Tell me that you don't want to fuck her too."

He doesn't answer, which, of course, is an answer in itself.

CHAPTER FIVE

Astrid

I eye the food on the floor before turning away from it in disgust. Aside from the fact that the giant asshole couldn't be bothered to walk the ten steps to put it on the dresser, reminding me that I'm little more than a prisoner right now, the sandwich itself has peanut butter in it. I can smell it from here. Since I'm deathly allergic to peanuts, I think I'll pass. Though it might be worth keeping a little of it back just in case I need a way out. As dramatic as it sounds, I swore the last time I was used as leverage, I wouldn't be someone's pawn ever again. I'm afraid of many things but dying isn't one of them.

I sit on the edge of the bed, my body aching from standing tensely in the same spot for so long. They want me to take a shower and make myself comfortable. But if they think I'm going to make myself vulnerable by stripping, they're crazy.

Rubbing my hand over my face, I feel exhaustion tug at me. The last few weeks have been draining. Hell, the last few years have been. If, I mean, *when* I make it out of here, I need to take a good long look at my life and make some changes.

I've tried using my gifts to help people. I've tried keeping my mouth shut and dealing with the horrendous guilt in the aftermath of staying silent. I've rebelled and conformed and tried to be everything people wanted me to be, but it was never enough. I'm finally at the point where I realize I never will be.

Spending time away from people has been the best thing. Loneliness is always going to be better than persecution, but I hadn't been ready to give up on the human race just yet. Coming here, though, reminds me that you can't give up on someone when they gave up on you first. No. I'm done here. When I get out, I'm going to get a dog, I think. A golden retriever or maybe a rottweiler—something that will eat anyone that comes to my door.

I want to live in peace, and having a dog will mean I have someone to shower all my love on. A tightening around my chest makes my breath hitch, and I feel tears prick my eyes as a feeling of utter hopelessness weighs me down. The tears start to fall, and I feel weak for not being able to hold them back, but the harder I try, the faster they fall.

I crawl into the center of the bed and curl into a ball, ignoring the way my jeans dig into my stomach. If I were at home, my pants and bra would have been off the second I walked through the door, but that's not an option here. Just something else for me to hate them for. Eventually, my crying tires me out, and I drift off to sleep.

Later, when I wake up with a crick in my neck and my stomach rumbling, I realize someone came in while I was sleeping and took my boots off. I can't even pretend to be surprised that it didn't wake me when I usually sleep like the dead. Still, knowing that one of them was in here while I slept makes my stomach roll. Thankfully, my clothes are still on.

I sit up and rub my eyes. Looking around the room, I try to guess how long I've slept, but with the shutters drawn over the windows blocking the light, it's impossible to tell. I climb off the bed and quietly walk across the room, noting that the sandwich from before is now on the dresser. I have to assume it was Jagger that came in here because Slade doesn't seem to give a fuck about me or my comfort. I'm sure he'd have been quite happy for me to eat it off the floor like a dog.

I walk over to the door and press my ear against it, but I can't hear anything. I bite my lip and chew on the idea of going out to investigate, but I bet they're out there waiting for me to do just that. Instead, I make my way to the bathroom and turn the light on. I close the door and go to lock it before realizing the door doesn't even have a lock on it.

"Fan-fucking-tastic," I mutter to myself as I move over to the sink and stare at myself in the mirror. My hair looks like a rat's nest, and my cheek has creases from falling asleep leaning on my hands. I look pale, but then I always look pale. My eyes are aggravated from falling asleep with my contacts in. As much as I'd like to leave them in, I know I can't.

As quickly as I can, I use the facilities and wash my hands, splashing some cold water on my face before cupping them and using them to drink the cool, refreshing water. Once I'm finished, I leave the bathroom and walk across the room to the door again, each step feeling like a mistake. But hey, what's one more to add to my collection?

I turn the handle, surprised to find it unlocked, and step out. Taking a deep breath, I walk down the hallway until I reach the door that leads outside. I look toward the living room, which had been my original destination, before my hand closes over the knob of the backdoor.

It's stupid. I have no shoes on, no car keys, no purse. But I can't help it. I might never get this chance again. I turn the knob, and when the door opens, I throw caution to the wind and pull it wide. The second it swings open, an alarm sounds, forcing me into gear.

I sprint outside as if my life depends on it. Who knows? Maybe it does. I ignore the pain in my feet and just flat-out run, having no idea where I'm going. It's far darker than I anticipated it would be, and with no streetlights out here to guide my way, it isn't long before I trip and land hard on my hands and knees. I bite back a scream as something cuts into my palm before stumbling to my feet and taking off again.

I barely make it a few steps before I'm tackled to the ground, my head hitting something with a thunk. Everything spins, and I hear yelling, but the roaring in my head makes it impossible for me to make out who it is. Still, I fight against the body pinning me to the ground. Suddenly, the weight holding me down is gone, and I suck in a deep breath to scream, but it barely comes out as a whimper as my head throbs in time with the pain in my hand.

"Jesus fucking Christ," a voice snarls before I'm scooped up and held tightly in someone's arms.

When I realize I'm being carried back to the very place I ran from, I start fighting again. But his hold tightens, making it impossible for me to break free.

"You stupid woman," he snaps at me, my brain finally recognizing the voice now that it's shifting out of escape mode. I should have figured it was Slade all along, given how hard he tackled me to the ground.

"Get the first aid kit," he says, but this time he's obviously not talking to me.

As he carries me through the door and into the living area, I wince as the brightly lit room sends a bolt of pain through my brain. He falters for a second, and I bury my head under his chin, trying to shield myself from the light. Hearing footsteps, I crack open my eyes and turn my head to see Jagger with what I'm guessing is the first aid kit in his hands.

"Sit her on the island," he tells Slade, who walks me into the kitchen and does just that. As soon as he lets go of me, he steps back, and I move to jump off the counter.

Sensing what I'm about to do, he leans forward, his angry expression making me swallow hard. "If you move, I'll spank your ass so hard that you won't be able to take a single step without feeling it."

Shocked by his words, I freeze.

When he moves aside to let Jagger in, I grip the edge of the island, crying out when I put too much pressure on my injured hand. I squeeze my eyes shut, trying to hold back my tears at the shooting pain. I'm not going to lie, I'm a big old baby when it comes to pain.

Just stubbing my toe can leave me curled up in a ball. Badass, I'm not, but that doesn't make me a coward. I don't regret taking the chance to escape. It's not in my nature to give up without at least trying—and usually failing—first. Maybe this will be the time I learn my lesson.

"Open your eyes, Astrid. Let me look," Jagger asks me.

Reluctantly, I open them, and he softens when he sees the tears I'm trying to keep at bay.

"You banged your head pretty hard."

"Sure, we can call it that, or we can call it having my face smashed into the ground by Mr. Happy over there. I guess it's kinda the same thing."

"You shouldn't have run," Slade grumbles.

"You knew I would," I reply quietly. "How could I not?"

"We said we wouldn't hurt you," Jagger reminds me.

"And yet here we are."

That shuts Jagger up, but not Slade. He snorts, grabbing a square of gauze from the first aid kit, and then lifts my hand before pressing it against my bleeding palm.

"You tripped."

"Riiight. Just like when a woman with a black eye claims she *tripped*."

He growls at me and pushes harder on the gauze, making me yelp, proving my point.

"Slade," Jagger snaps.

Slade lets go and steps back, his expression an odd one. He

looks almost remorseful, but that can't be right, can it? "Why run? You knew you wouldn't get far, and now look at you."

"Why wouldn't I run? I'm being kept against my will. It's a little early in my captivity to be expecting Stockholm syndrome from me."

Jagger pauses before huffing out a laugh. "I never know what's going to come out of your mouth next."

"Yeah, well, since I'm not allowed to leave, I'm sure I'll be a fountain of entertainment for you."

He presses some gauze to my head, making me wince. "I don't think you're going to need stitches. How's your vision? Do you feel nauseous at all?"

"And before you answer, no, we won't be taking you to the ER. We have a doctor that does house calls and who is loyal to us," Slade throws in.

I resist cursing him out. Slade makes me forget I'm a pacifist and instead makes me want to embrace my homicidal urges. I stare at him and zone out for a second while I picture myself stabbing him in the eyeball with a fork.

"Astrid?" Jagger's voice snaps me out of my thoughts.

"I'm fine."

"And you'd tell us if you weren't?"

"Not a chance in hell," I admit, making him sigh.

"I need to clean that"—he points to my hand— "so it doesn't get infected," Slade states before moving back to lift the gauze.

I shrug. "If I get an infection and die, it will get me out of your way. Win-win, right?"

He sighs like I'm annoying him and tends to my hand.

I squeeze my eyes closed when he pours some kind of liquid over it. I bite my tongue so hard I taste blood, wondering if the fucking sadist just poured acid over my cut. He pats it dry, applies a thin layer of antibiotic ointment to it, and finishes with a bandage.

"There," he announces, and I open my eyes. "Keep it covered for tonight, and I'll take a look at it tomorrow."

Whatever. I hope the asshole steps on Lego.

"Alright, your head looks good now too," Jagger says, applying a small bandage to my forehead. "Where else are you hurt?"

"I'm fine. Just take me back to my cell."

He shakes his head and looks me over, his eyes dropping to my knees. I don't need to look to know my jeans are torn and my knees are bleeding. I can feel the blood running down my legs.

"Your knees."

I open my mouth to speak, but Slade jumps in.

"Don't say you're fucking fine." He grits his teeth as I slam my mouth closed.

"You need to take your pants off," Jagger tells me quietly.

I laugh in his face. "Yeah, that's not going to happen."

"Don't flatter yourself, Astrid. You don't have anything we want. Let him check you out so we can be done with your bull-shit," Slade snarls.

Okay, I admit it. It's not nice to think that these guys find me so damn unappealing. Don't get me wrong, this isn't a movie, so it's not the start of some epic romance, but I'd be lying if I said his disgust didn't sting a little.

"I don't care, asshole. This is my body, not yours. You have zero say in what I do with it, and that includes me taking off my clothes."

"Is that so?" Slade replies, his voice taunting.

Suddenly, I'm not feeling quite so sure about myself. Before I can say anything else, Slade tugs me off the island and spins me around, wrapping one arm around my chest and the other around my throat.

His lips press to my ear as Jagger looks at him with a scowl.

"You like making things hard, don't you?" He presses against me, ensuring I understand his words' double meaning.

I freeze in his arms, not sure what I should do.

"Slade, come on, man," Jagger growls, but Slade doesn't loosen his hold on me.

"Take her pants off and check her knees. Then she can scurry back to your room and hide."

Jagger's jaw clenches, and for a second, I think he'll tell Slade to fuck off. But then he steps forward, and his hands drop to the button of my jeans.

"Don't," I whisper, and his hands stop. His eyes move to my mouth before they lift to my eyes.

"I'm just making sure you're okay."

"Liar."

He swallows and lowers the zipper of my jeans before he drops to his knees, his eyes never leaving mine. There's fear snapping at me, but it's not all I'm feeling. And that's the thing that terrifies me right now.

He hooks his fingers in the belt loops and tugs my jeans down over my ass, slowly sliding them down my legs.

"There now, that wasn't so bad, was it?" Slade purrs in my ear, but there's a hint of malice in his tone.

I've never wanted a person to get hit by a bus more than I do right now. Saying that, I'm not picky. I'll take him getting struck by lightning or getting mauled by a bear if that's an option. Anything to get the douchewaffle away from me.

"Step out of your pants, Astrid. The sooner you do, the sooner I can clean you up, and this will all be over."

I grit my teeth and do as he asks. He might be the lesser of two evils here, but he's proving that he won't go against Slade, so I'm very much on my own.

CHAPTER SIX

Slade

This woman could test the patience of a saint. As much as I want to throttle her, I can't deny that having her ass pressed against me isn't having an effect. The woman has curves for days, and every time she opens her mouth to sass me, I'm assaulted with images of shoving her to her knees and thrusting my cock down her throat.

"Help her back onto the counter." Jagger glares at me.

Oh yeah, he's pissed, but I don't care. Given a chance, this woman would have him wrapped around both his finger and his cock. When he moves back, I spin Astrid around, hook my hands under her armpits, and lift her off her feet and onto the island. While she's flustered, I shove her legs open and step into the space between them. I might not trust her, but that has no bearing on how much I want her. And that just adds to my anger.

"I see you want to flex your claws, kitten. But your efforts are wasted on us. So, how about you spare us the attitude? That way, we can get on with our jobs."

She turns her head and looks away from me, focusing on a spot on the wall opposite us. Figuring that's the best I'm going to get, I step back, and Jagger shoves me aside and tends to her knees. I keep my expression neutral as I take in the cuts and scrapes but tighten my fists at my sides, not liking the sight of her blood.

"Alright, you're done. You want some painkillers?" Jagger stands and tucks her hair behind her ear.

"No," she replies, but she keeps her gaze on that damn spot.

"Back to the bedroom for you, then. Jagger, once you've put this shit away, you'd better head over and let the others know that she attempted to escape."

"It's not like she made it far," he argues, but I fold my arms across my chest.

"Doesn't matter. It just proves she can't be trusted."

"Christ, I hope you know what you're doing," he mutters, shoving everything back in the first aid kit before tossing the bloody stuff in the trash.

Once he's finished, he stares at me, his eyes drifting to Astrid for a moment before coming back to me. "Let me get her settled first."

"I've got it. Go."

If Astrid wasn't here, he would probably have punched me

by now. Though if she wasn't here, we wouldn't be in this mess to begin with.

"I'll be back," he says to Astrid before heading out.

She goes to slide off the counter but curses when she puts weight on her hurt palm. Moving to her, I lift and lower her to her feet. She takes a big step away from me and bends to pick her pants off the floor, but I reach for them and yank them away.

"Hey, give those back."

"They need to be washed. If you hadn't run away, this wouldn't be an issue. Now you're covered in mud and expecting to crawl into Jagger's bed? How is that fair to him?"

Yeah, I'm a bastard playing her like this. I just don't give a fuck. She wraps her arms around herself and dips her head, letting her hair fall around her face. I don't like her hiding from me. So I step closer, happy when her head snaps up.

A flash of fear passes through her eyes, but she masks it well.

"I'll need your T-shirt too."

She looks down to find it covered in mud and blood. "Can I have my bag first, please?" She forces the *please* out through gritted teeth.

"Sorry, it's not ready yet. But I'm sure I can find you something."

"Don't bother. Jagger said I could use his stuff."

She whirls around and storms to the bedroom. Tossing her pants on the island, I follow behind her. When get to Jagger's room, she walks in and tries to close the door behind her.

I shove my hand in and push the door open. "Oh no. You

broke any trust I had in you, so until I think you won't run again, I'm going to be your shadow."

"Oh my God, I said I wouldn't run. Lock the fucking door if you don't believe me. Honestly, if you're going to hold someone prisoner, that should be the first thing you do. I think you left it open on purpose, knowing I'd try it. Anyone in my shoes would have. You just wanted a reason to punish me."

I crowd her, making her back toward the bed. "Ah, Astrid. You being here is reason enough. I don't like you in my home, and I sure as shit don't like you bringing trouble to my door."

"What the hell would you have done?" She throws her hands up in the air before dropping them quickly when she realizes she's flashing her underwear.

"I'd have kept my nose out of other people's business."

She scoffs. "Bullshit."

I grin savagely at her before wrapping my hand around her arm and dragging her into the bathroom.

I release her and turn the shower on before stepping to the side and crossing my arms.

"Shower," I order her.

She shakes her head. "Not while you're in here."

"It wasn't a request."

"Fuck you. I'm not getting in until you leave."

"Is that right?"

I step forward and bend, wrap my arms around her thighs, and toss her over my shoulder.

She yelps before smacking me on the back. I ignore her and walk into the shower, closing the door behind us. I lower her to her feet and block the door with my body.

"What the hell is wrong with you? Get out!"

"Nope. Now strip."

"No. Not just no, but hell no."

"Fine. I'll do it for you."

"What? No." She stumbles away from me, but she has nowhere to go.

She presses herself against the wall as I invade her space and grip the hem of her T-shirt.

"Stop it. Get away from me."

I yank the T-shirt up and force her to raise her arms before I tug it off. I toss the T-shirt to the floor before pinning her in place and reaching around her to unclip her bra.

"Please stop," she begs. This time, she lets her fear show as tears run down her face.

I grip her jaw and tip her head back. "I'm not going to hurt you. I just want you to take your clothes off so I can wash them. We both got muddy, and we both need to clean up before bed. Stop making this something it's not."

Her mouth drops open in shock, and I have the insane urge to kiss her. I hold back, though, instead using her shock to unhook her bra and slide the straps down her arms. I pull the bra free and toss it away as she wraps her arm around her chest. She swallows when my hands drop to her waist, and I hook my fingers in her panties. Slowly, I slide them over her hips and down her thighs. I don't pretend not to check her out. Her stomach is slightly rounded, her hips are flared, and fuck me sideways, her pussy is bare.

I lick my lips and tear my eyes away as I wait for her to lift each foot. I toss the panties onto the growing pile of discarded clothes before standing up and stripping out of my own shirt.

She gulps before saying my name warily. "Slade, I don't—"

"We're just getting clean," I remind her, my voice thick. "You're the one just standing there staring."

She spins so fast she almost slips. I steady her before continuing to undress. She reaches for the shower gel and quickly lathers herself up as I strip out of my jeans. I move in closer behind her, getting a perverse thrill out of freaking her out. I reach around her, my chest pressing against her back as I grab the shampoo. She sucks in a sharp breath, but I ignore it as I pour a small amount into my palm and start to massage it into her hair, careful to avoid the cut on her head. Her breathing becomes shallow as she freezes, not knowing what to do with herself. She doesn't say anything, wisely knowing I'll only shoot down any of her protests again.

"Rise. We don't have any conditioner, but I'll get one of the guys to pick some up for you when they do a run into town."

She nods rapidly before stepping directly under the spray of water. I shampoo my hair before using the suds to wash my body. Soap is soap at the end of the day.

Once she is free of suds, I pull her back and reverse our positions. I close my eyes and rinse the soap from my hair and body, not surprised when I hear the shower door open and the cool air hits me. I don't rush, but I can't help the smirk on my face when I hear her gasp at the lack of towels.

Turning the water off, I wipe the water from my face and step out. Astrid stands in the corner, as far from me as she can get, shivering and looking kind of pathetic. A pang of remorse hits me when I see how drawn and wary her face is, but I brush it off. I'm not about to start questioning my methods now.

"Stay here. I'll get you a towel."

I walk out of the bedroom and into mine, grabbing a towel for myself, which I wrap around my waist, and an extra one for Astrid. I use it to pat the excess water from my skin before I grab a pair of boxers and a T-shirt from my dresser.

Heading back to Jagger's bathroom, I pause in the doorway when I find Astrid standing in front of the mirror with her head bowed, her hands clutching the sink so hard her knuckles are white.

"Here." I hold the towel out for her, but it's like she doesn't hear me. "Astrid?"

She lifts her head, and I'm struck dumb at the vivid violet color of her eyes. How had I not noticed them before? I glance down at the counter and see a pair of contacts sitting on top of it.

"I've never met anyone with purple eyes before. Why hide them?" I ask, my suspicion pushing me to question her.

She reaches for the towel, but I don't let go of it, waiting for an answer.

"I get a lot of attention because of my hair, but people are always weird about my eyes."

I release the towel, and she wraps it around herself, but because I'm a dick, I gave her one that doesn't cover nearly as much as she'd like.

"I have OCA, otherwise known as oculocutaneous albinism. My hair is naturally white, it's not a stylistic choice. The purple color of my eyes is another side effect. My eyes are actually blue, but because I have very low levels of melanin, you can see the blood vessels, which is why they look violet. Can I get dressed now?" she asks me quietly after delivering her speech in a monotone voice.

I hand her the T-shirt. Before I can say anything else, she pulls it over her head and yanks it down before tugging the towel off and using it to twist her hair up on top of her head.

"I've heard of albinism, but I'll be honest, I know next to nothing about it."

"Not many people do. I was born with it, so I don't know any different." She shrugs, clearly uncomfortable, but that's what I wanted, right? Though, for some reason, I'm not such a fan of her being uncomfortable about a medical condition that's beyond her control.

"Not that it stopped kids from being assholes," she mutters under her breath, gasping when I drop the towel and slip my boxers on.

"So, it only affects the color of your hair and eyes?"

"And my skin. This isn't due to a lack of vitamin D. I give Casper the Ghost a run for his money. But because of my coloring, I burn easily, so I have to be careful in the sun. Same with my eyes. They are super sensitive to bright light, and my vision was pretty shitty. But I've had corrective surgery, though I still need glasses."

"But you're not dying, right?"

She scoffs and folds her arms across her chest. "I should be so lucky. No, my life expectancy would have been the same as the next person right up until I came here. If I'd known how this was going to turn out, I would have gone swimming with sharks instead. That seems like it would have been a safer option."

I lick my lip and grin. "I wonder if sarcasm is a side effect."

"I'm actually pretty fucking nice, but assholes always bring out the worst in me."

I step closer, unable to resist. Part of me wants her to end up being a fraud, so I have a good reason for punishing her.

But the other part wants nothing more than to yank her into my arms and kiss her.

Fucking hell, this woman is going to be the death of me.

CHAPTER SEVEN

Astrid

The way he's looking at me makes me shrink back. He shakes his head as if to clear it before clearing his throat.

"Do you need to use the bathroom or anything?"

"I'm fine."

"Good. Then I'll tuck you in."

The urge to punch him in his stupid handsome face is so strong I have to take a deep breath and count to ten before blowing it out.

"I think I can manage," I say between gritted teeth.

I move and walk past him into the bedroom, and he grabs my wrist and spins me to face him.

"Did I make it seem like an option?" He backs me up until my feet hit the bed and I topple down.

I scramble across the bed, fighting to hold the T-shirt down so that I don't expose myself, which is ridiculous. He's already seen it all, but there's something far more intimate when a bed is involved.

"Now, don't look so scared, pet. Your virtue is safe from me."

I'm not sure if he's telling me he's a good guy or if I'm just not his type. Frankly, I don't care as long as he keeps his hands and dick to himself.

"What about my tongue?" He smirks, which is when I realize I said all that out loud.

My face flames, but I simply lie down and move as far across the bed as I can and face the wall. If I can't leave, the least I can do is ignore the asshat. I hear a drawer slide open, but I don't turn. I keep myself as far removed from him as possible until I feel the bed dip.

I'm mid-turn when I feel my arm being tugged and hear the telltale sound of handcuffs clicking as they snap into place around my wrist. I open my mouth to scream, but he presses his free hand over it, using the other to snap the other end of the cuff to the ornate metal bed frame.

"You can scream all you want. The rooms are soundproofed."

My chest rises and falls rapidly as I try to suck air into my lungs, but it's not helping.

"Be good, and you'll earn privileges. Piss me off, and I'll show just how much of a bastard I can be." His free hand skims up my thigh as the other continues to cover my mouth. "After all, the T-shirt is mine. I could just take it back. And the bed is Jagger's. You could always sleep on the floor."

I tune him out—his words blurring into one another as I

dismiss his monologue—while I try to calm the panic threatening to make me pass out. I don't like being confined, but I can handle it—barely. It's one of the things I got help with from the legion of therapists I saw, but handcuffs... Well, that's a different story altogether.

He climbs off the bed and heads for the door. I want to beg him to remove the cuffs. Plead with him that I'll be good if he just takes them off. But I bite my lip hard, knowing it'll just give him more ammunition.

I wait until he leaves and closes the door behind him before I give in to the tears. I sob into the pillow, glad for the soundproofing right now. I don't want him to have the satisfaction of knowing how much his brand of torture is affecting me.

My chest feels tight, and my breathing comes in short pants while spots dance before my eyes as I find myself caught between then and now. Normally, I'd talk myself through a panic attack, reminding myself that I'm not back there, I'm home and safe. But that won't work this time. Right now, I'm as far from safe as I can get.

So instead of fighting the darkness when it pulls at me, I give into it, needing a break from the fear that's making my muscles seize and cramp. My body already throbs from my failed escape earlier. If I ever want a second chance at getting away from this place, I need to heal, and right now, that means sleep.

I KNOW exactly where I am when I wake up. Oh, how I would have loved two minutes of blissful ignorance between the end of my dreams and my eyes fluttering open. But no. I'm not that lucky and this is no dream. It's a fucking nightmare, and unfortunately, it's real.

I go to move and groan when I remember my arm is cuffed. Testing my restraint, I jolt in surprise when I realize my wrist is free. I roll over, fully ready to get up and test the door again, but I'm hit by two things at once—pain from my aching body and a large arm reaching for me.

I yelp when I'm yanked against a hard chest. I struggle to get free, but that struggle hurts my already tender body, making me whimper. The hold on me loosens a fraction before I hear the rustle of blankets, and then the light from a cell phone is turned on and spun my way. I gasp as the light hits my eyes.

"You look like shit. Let me go get you some ice and painkillers," Slade states before getting out of bed in nothing but the boxers he slipped on earlier.

"What the hell are you doing in bed with me?"

"Keeping an eye on you."

"Your eyes were closed," I snap.

"I'm a light sleeper. There is no way you'd get past me without waking me up."

"So then sleeping in the chair should be fine."

"I'm not sleeping in the fucking chair," he grouses as he opens the door to the bedroom and pauses on the threshold, looking back at me.

"Yo, Jagger."

I don't hear anything, and then a few moments later, a

groggy Jagger emerges from Slade's room in nothing but a pair of white boxer shorts. Fuck me, don't these men own pajamas?

"What?" Jagger grumbles, squinting as Slade flicks the hallway light on.

"Stay with Astrid. I need to get her some ice and pain meds."

Jagger's whole body tenses, and his head snaps in my direction, though I doubt he can see me very well in the dark.

"Is she okay?"

Is that concern I can hear in his voice? If it is, I can work with that. I'm pretty sure I remember reading somewhere that it's best to endear yourself to your kidnappers so they think of you as a person and not a thing. If I can make them care about me, maybe they'll let me go.

"She's sore, which, given her idiotic escape earlier, is hardly surprising," Slade replies.

Yeah, I won't bother trying with that man. I'd have better luck with Satan.

"I've got her," Jagger replies, heading my way. I scramble to sit up and bring my knees to my chest.

I'm shaking, and I'm not sure if it's left over from my panic attack, the cold, or from something else entirely, but suddenly this whole endearing-him-to-me thing sounds like the most ridiculous idea ever. He moves to the corner of the room and turns the lamp on, bathing the room in a soft, warm glow.

When he turns to look at me, his jaw clenches, so I can only assume Slade was right, and it looks as bad as it feels. "Christ, Astrid."

He walks toward me and climbs onto the bed. I watch him warily as he lifts his hand and gently tips my jaw up with his thumb before skating his other thumb over the apple of my cheek.

"You're going to feel that for the next few days, but the ice will help."

I swallow, not sure what to say when he moves to the other side, so he's between me and the wall and slides under the blankets.

"Come on, get in."

I shake my head. "I need to use the bathroom."

It's an excuse, but I need a goddamn minute to get my shit together before I have a heart attack.

His lips twitch, but he doesn't stop me as I scrabble off the bed—ignoring the pain—and hurry to the bathroom, closing the door behind me. I steady myself against it for a minute before cursing because I really do have to pee, and I don't want to do it with him on the other side of the door. Biting my lip, I know Slade won't think twice about coming in here. I turn on the faucet, running the water before hurrying to the toilet and relieving myself, setting a new land speed record. I flush and hobble over to the sink, my knees throbbing—possibly even more than my head.

As I wash my hands, I look in the mirror and groan at my reflection. Fuck, I do look like shit. Worse than shit, actually, whatever that might be. The bruising on my face stands out in stark contrast to my pale skin, and my eyes look like I'm suffering from the hangover from hell. My right one is swollen, as is my cheek. I must have hit the ground harder than I thought. I look down and inspect the rest of my body and sigh. There are bruises around my biceps and wrists, and my knees are red, but at least they are beginning to scab. I clench my fists, and the skin on my injured hand pulls painfully tight.

"Shit."

The door swings open, making me jump, and Slade strolls in and frowns at me. I hate feeling fragile around him. Something in my expression must tell him that I'm barely hanging on by a thread because he doesn't snap at me like he normally would. Instead, he walks over to me and lifts my hand, carefully removing the bandage to inspect it.

"The bleeding has stopped, and it's started to scab. So, I don't think it will need the bandage anymore. You'll have to be careful, though," he tells me before gently checking the cut on my forehead. Satisfied that it's healing just as well, he throws both bandages in the trash and turns to look at me once more.

Without another word, he wraps his hand around my wrist and leads me back into the bedroom, walking me over to the bed. I sit on the edge of it and accept the glass of water he hands me.

"Here. Take these."

I look at the pills in his hand and look up at his face.

He sighs and takes my empty hand and forces my fingers to open. "They are just regular over-the-counter painkillers. If I wanted to hurt you, I would have done so already."

I don't point out that half of these injuries are because of him. I take the pills and shove them in my mouth—before I can question my idiocy—and swallow them down with the water.

Once I'm finished, I hand it back to him and fiddle nervously with the hem of my T-shirt as he places the glass on the nightstand next to what I'm guessing is the ice pack.

He sees me looking at it and lifts it, placing it gently against my cheek. "It's frozen peas, but it's better than nothing. Now climb in. Some of us have to be up in a few hours."

"I can sleep in the chair," I offer quickly, my words bleeding into each other. He shakes his head and stalks over to the chair. I breathe a sigh of relief before realizing he's only turning off the lamp.

When he stalks back to the bed, I'm left with no choice but to move over.

I stay on top of the covers, or that's the plan. Jagger, who I thought had drifted off to sleep, yanks the covers back and tugs me until I'm lying down with the blankets covering my bottom half.

"Just sleep. Nothing is going to happen to you tonight."

"So, I'm safe tonight, but tomorrow I'm fair game?"

I don't even have a chance to get my thoughts together before Slade climbs in on the other side of me. He throws his arm across my waist as Jagger reaches out to make sure the ice pack is in place.

I blink and stare sightlessly up at the dark ceiling and wonder for the millionth time, why the fuck me?

CHAPTER EIGHT

Jagger

I watch her as she tries to relax and almost feel sorry for her. She has no idea what's ahead of her. When I came home after giving the others a rundown of what happened, I never expected to find both Slade and Astrid asleep in my bed. I stood in the doorway like a creeper, watching them for a second, and felt something profound snap into place.

Oh, Slade might talk a good game when he's awake. But when he's asleep, his walls are down. He had no idea he was curled protectively around the woman he professes to dislike so much. Truth be told, I think she scares him far more than he scares her. Hell, she scares me too, and I don't have half the trust issues that Slade does.

I contemplated sitting in the chair and watching over them, but I didn't want Slade to think I don't trust him with her. He'll push her, of that I have no doubt, but he won't cross the line. How I treat him is as much a test of our trust as all the rest of it. Being thrown in prison, especially the way he was, fundamentally changed something inside him. I don't know the ins and outs of what went on behind bars, but I know it wasn't good. So, yeah, some of Slade's reactions are excessive, but they are done out of reflex. We don't push him on it because he shuts down and disappears for days on end. I'd rather him be here where I can at least keep an eye on him than fuck knows where, doing fuck knows what, while he tries to forget the shitty hand he was dealt.

I'd closed the door and headed to Slade's room before stripping down to my boxers, forgoing a shower before I climbed into bed. The next thing I knew, Slade was calling me.

Now they have both fallen back to sleep, and I find myself feeling restless. Lying on my back, I stare into the dark room and think about my talk with the others earlier.

"Why did she try to escape if she has nothing to hide?" Oz had asked, leaning back in his seat at the table.

"Why the fuck wouldn't she try to escape? Lord knows I would have taken my shot the second I saw an opening," Greg replied. He's the most vocally opposed to this, but he won't stand against us.

"Is she okay?" Zig asked, looking at me as I ran my hand through my hair.

"She's pretty banged up. Slade sacked her like the former all-star football player he is."

Crew winced. "Ouch. You gonna get Salem to heal her?"

Crew and Wilder came back late, so hadn't met Astrid yet. All they knew was what they'd been told.

I looked at Zig, but he shook his head. "No. It might be exactly what she's after. Proof that Salem is gifted. We don't know if Astrid is. We only have her word for it, and I, for one, won't believe shit until I have proof."

Hawk gritted his teeth and looked away.

"It's just some bumps and bruises. She'll be sore tomorrow, but she'll be fine," I told him. I get it. I don't like her hurting any more than he does. I helped to patch her up, so I know her injuries aren't as bad as I first feared.

"Maybe this way she'll think twice about running next time," Oz said.

"For fuck's sake, Oz. What's gotten into you? You're being an asshole," Greg growled.

"I don't like having someone here who could be a potential threat to Salem. She's been through enough."

"I get it. I do, but Astrid hasn't done anything to earn your ire. So, why don't you get a handle on it before you do or say something you'll regret? Where is Salem anyway?"

"She's lying down. She has a headache." Oz rolled his eyes.

"I didn't think she got headaches much. Not unless she overdoes it on healing, anyway." Wilder looked confused for a second, but when he saw Oz glaring at him, he snickered.

"Oh, I see. You're getting the cold shoulder, huh? I guess Salem isn't a fan of how we're all playing this?"

Zig lifted his beer and took a swig of it. "It brings up a lot of unfortunate feelings for her," he admitted.

"That's hardly surprising. She was held captive herself, and now we're doing the same damn thing to Astrid," Greg huffed.

Oz stood and slammed his palm on the table. "It's not the same."

Greg stood too and sneered, having reached his limit. "No, you're right. It's not. Salem was held captive because of her gift, whereas Astrid is being held because she can't prove hers. You'd all love for this with Astrid to be nothing more than an elaborate hoax. If she is who she says she is and really saw Salem get killed, then you'll have to face the fact that you're holding prisoner the one person that holds the key to saving your woman's life." And with that parting shot, Greg shoved his chair aside and stalked off.

"Fuck," Oz cursed, wiping a hand down his face. "It's not that I want it to be like this, but I can't—I won't—put Salem in danger."

"I know. I feel the same way. But I can't say I believe her to be guilty or innocent right now. I don't know her. None of us do. We made a decision, though, and now we need to let it play out until we can determine the truth about why she is here. She won't run again. She'll be lucky if Slade lets her take a piss alone after tonight's escape attempt."

"Jesus, if she makes it through the night without stabbing him, I say we should declare her a saint," Hawk blurted, making me chuckle.

"He's not that bad."

Creed raised his eyebrows at that.

"Alright, I'll admit he can be intense. But he's protective, that's all. He likes Salem, and he knows what's at stake here.

Out of all of us, he's the least likely to be fooled by a pretty face."

I roll over and sigh, realizing I underestimated Astrid's impact. Most of the guys here are into ménage relationships. Some have been in serious ménage relationships, like Creed and Hawk. Some are just open to the idea. But Zig, Oz, and, to an extent, Luna, and her MC guys kind of normalized it all. Now we don't even blink at the concept of relationships with multiple people in them. I can't say I leaned one way or the other until Slade was released from prison.

We've never spoken about it, but a pact was born in silence, stemming from the trauma Slade experienced and my fear of losing him again. I might not want to fuck Slade—that's not who we are—but there is a connection that exists solely between the two of us.

Since he got his freedom back, he only lets his guard down enough to fuck if I'm there to watch his back. For me, the only time I can get out of my head enough to let everything go and just relax is when he's in the room with me. The guilt I still feel about how everything went down keeps me up at night. If I had been with him when this all happened, I could have—

I roll over and growl into the pillow. Could have, should have, would haves are for pussies. He's here now, and that's all that matters. Watching him lying there at peace does something to me. I can't tell if I'm grateful or jealous. Perhaps a mix of both. She can give him what I can't, and that's precious in itself. But precious things get broken, and I don't think Slade can survive another hit without shattering.

What is it about this fucking girl?

She's beautiful. I'll give her that. It's not the kind of beauty we're usually exposed to, either. Slade and I tend to go for easy girls. That makes us sound like dicks, I know. But we were not looking for anything serious, and barflies tend to want nothing more than a little fun with a couple of men from the wrong side of the tracks before settling down with Mr. Right. We're always willing to oblige.

Astrid is about as far from a barfly as you can get. Aside from the fact that she stinks of money, she has an air of class about her, a poise that some women are just born with. Her looks, though, are what set her apart. Her beauty lies in her uniqueness. Her long white hair, porcelain skin, and violet eyes that shone in the lamplight earlier, make her look like a fairy tale character. I had the strange urge before to slip her hair behind her ears to see if they were pointed. No joking, she would not look out of place in a Tolkien movie.

Her face might scream fairy tale, but her body is the devil's work, created to make a man think of nothing but sin. I wonder how many have fallen to their knees for her. She's tiny and curvy, and she makes my dick hard every time I'm in the same room as her.

The irony isn't lost on me that while Slade has found peace in her arms, I'm over here with nothing but chaos on my mind. The woman has me twisted in so many knots I worry that when it's time for her to go, I won't know how to unravel the bonds between us.

Taking advantage of the quiet, I slide my hand into my boxers and grip my hard dick, stroking it up and down as I picture Astrid on her knees looking up at me with those haunting eyes. I tug hard and squeeze tighter, liking the bite of pain. I imagine Astrid biting her lip as Slade eases up behind her and cups her breasts, kissing a path down the slope of her shoulder.

Friend or foe, I already know it's not going to matter. Slade and I won't be satisfied until we have her spread out between us.

I fuck my hand faster and faster until I shoot my cum all over my stomach. I take a moment to catch my breath before I climb out of bed and use the bathroom to clean up.

Blowing out a breath, I stare at my reflection, almost wishing the image staring back might try to talk some sense into me, but no such luck.

This time, when I lie down in bed, it doesn't take me long to drift off to sleep, with pretty violet eyes haunting my dreams.

CHAPTER NINE

Astrid

When I wake up, I tense, feeling a warm body beside me. I turn to look at Jagger and find him still asleep. He's lying on his back with one arm tucked under the pillow and the other across his chest.

I look to the other side of me and find the space where Slade slept empty. I blow out a breath, unable to hold back my relief as I sit up. Slade is intense, and I don't think I have it in me to deal with his particular brand of assholeyness before I'm properly caffeinated.

Looking back at Jagger, I have the bizarre urge to lie back down and snuggle into him.

That thought brings me up short. Snuggle into him? He's a kidnapper, not a fucking teddy bear. *We do not snuggle with kidnappers.*

Okay, yeah, I need caffeine now, preferably administered by the gallon intravenously.

When Slade appears in the doorway, I sigh. Forget the coffee and just give me tequila.

"You're awake."

Perceptive, this one. "It seems so."

"Do you need more painkillers?"

I want to say no to him so badly, but I can't. I feel like a warmed-up bag of shit this morning. I need drugs more than I need to use my bitchiness. "Please."

He nods and disappears, returning a few minutes later with a couple of pills and a fresh glass of water. I reach out a shaky hand and take the pills from him, popping them into my mouth and swallowing them down with the water. I hand the glass back to him and watch as he picks up the glass from the night-stand and takes them both to the kitchen.

I bite my lip and look toward the bathroom, wondering if I can pee quickly before he comes back.

The answer is no. A moment later, he returns, walking over to the dresser for the plate with the peanut butter and jelly sandwich on it. He turns, eyeing me with a twitch of his lips before he takes that out with him too.

I don't waste another second. I jump out of bed and hurry to the bathroom, biting back tears at the pain in my body. I pee and wash my hands—this time I avoid looking in the mirror, knowing it will, at the very least, look as bad as it feels. And it feels fucking awful. I hurry back out of the bathroom and collide with Slade, who is waiting just outside the door.

I yelp in shock on impact—his hands grabbing my arms to

steady me—and bite back the moan of pain. His expression flickers with concern for a moment before he masks it. Lifting my hand, he looks at my palm and nods happily at how it's healing. Letting me go, he checks out the cut on my head before he drops into a squat in front of me.

I stumble backward and gasp. "What are you doing?"

"Checking out your knees. What did you think I was doing?"

There's a taunting tone to his voice, but I keep my comeback from spilling out, feeling too off balance to enter into a sparring match with this man.

He reaches for me, grabbing my hips and tugging me closer. Once he has me where he wants me, he runs his fingers over my tender knees before looking up at me.

"How do these feel?"

"Sore and swollen."

"Well, they are definitely that. You'll be slow-moving for the next few days." He smirks, looking pleased.

"Yeah, I bet you just love that, don't you?"

He doesn't answer. He stands up and leans over me. He uses it as an intimidation tactic. Not even trying to hide his hostility from me. But beneath the hate, there is something else —curiosity.

"You want to shower?"

I blink, my eyes moving away from the five o'clock shadow he's rocking to his eyes.

"Alone?"

He dips his head and whispers in my ear. "Now, where's the fun in that?"

"No shower then, thanks." I huff and pull away, walking back over to the bed.

He looks from me to Jagger. "In such a hurry to get away from me. Tell me, pet, is it because you like Jagger more than me?" He mock pouts. "Or is it because you want me so fucking bad that it terrifies you, so you do what all prey does when it's cornered: run?"

His words ignite a fire inside me.

"I'm nobody's prey," I snarl before yanking the edge of the blanket and climbing back into the bed, throwing him a pitying look.

"I saw you both in your boxer shorts. Let's just say I'll stick with Jagger."

He scowls at me and opens his mouth to say something. I can't help but dig my claws in a little farther.

"I know, I know, it's cold." I deliver my comeback in my most condescending voice. He might be a fucking dick, but he has nothing on the society girls I went to school with. Their words were as sharp as their French-tipped nails, each one designed to draw blood.

Instead of anger, I'm surprised to see amusement.

"It is cold," he agrees, tugging the blanket up around me. "It sure would explain these, huh?" He thumbs my hard nipple before he winks and turns away. I fume, hating that he gets the last word.

Besides, it's not like them being hard has anything to do with Slade or Jagger. They're sensitive. Sure, the guys are good-looking—if you like that ruggedly handsome, could pick you up and toss you over his shoulder, bad-boy type of thing. Wait, where was I—? Oh, right. Hard nipples. I look over at Jagger quickly to see if he heard any of that. Thankfully, he's still asleep. Unfortunately, when Slade tugged the blanket, he pulled it off Jagger's chest, leaving it exposed for my viewing pleasure.

My nipples tingle in response, making me silently curse. God damn traitorous Stockholm syndrome suffering boobs! I need to stay the heck away from these guys. I will not be that girl who lets a man find the answers to his problems in her vagina. I don't have a therapy pussy that will fix whatever issues these two asshats have while being petted. I will not—

"Hey."

I yelp and scramble away and fall right off the bed.

"Motherfucker." I lie in a crumpled mess and pray he rolls back over and goes to sleep.

He doesn't, though, because the universe hates me. His head appears over the edge of the bed, an amused smirk on his face. "What are you doing?"

"Looking for my dignity."

"Need a hand?"

"No, that bitch is long gone." I sigh, making him laugh.

"I mean, do you need a hand up?"

"Oh, right. No. Just leave me here. I'm scared if I move, it will hurt."

He frowns before crawling off the bed and standing over me. Warm golden skin, abs that look like a fucking mountain range, and, oh, look—an outstanding area of natural beauty. Wait, is that tree growing? Eek.

I slam my eyes shut—ignoring the fact that my pussy wants to do the cha-cha slide—and give thanks that my nipples don't light up when I'm turned on. And now I'm mad again. It seems like I only have two settings lately: murderous bitch and hoe bag.

When I hear him laughing, I crack open an eye and stare up at him.

"What?" he asks when he takes in my expression.

"Your smile," I say, feeling like a loser.

"What about it?"

"Nothing. You should just do it more often. You have a great smile. Not that the whole package isn't great." My eyes widen as I realize what I've said. "Not your package, package. I mean this whole—" I wave my hands around to encompass his chest, doing a rather lame impression of Mr. Miyagi from *The Karate Kid*, before I just give up.

I turn and attempt to roll under the bed, where I can curl up in the fetal position and wallow in my humiliation in peace. But I'm stopped when he bends down, grabs my hips, and yanks me up off the floor.

Unprepared for the move, I flounder like an electrocuted fish until I'm set on my feet. I shove my hair out of my face, refusing to look at Jagger and hoping that the ground will open up and swallow me whole.

"Hey, it's all good," he attempts to reassure me. Or I think that's what he's doing. It's lost on me when he steps forward, and his big old dick pokes me in the stomach.

"Your twig is poking me."

He bites his lip, trying to hold back his laugh as I shake my head.

"I don't know what's wrong with me. I think I must have hit

my head harder than I realized."

He reaches out and traces the cut on my forehead with the pad of his thumb. "I think you're gonna be fine."

"Yeah, no. I don't believe you. I'm pretty sure I have brain damage."

"Really, and why's that?" His voice dips lower, making my stomach feel like I've just driven too fast over a hill, all while his twig and berries are pressed against me.

"Because I'd rather go out there and sit with Slade than have to finish this conversation."

"Now, don't be like that. I kind of like this flustered version of you. It's cute."

"Oh, good. I can die with the remarkable achievement of being cute under my belt. Man, my parents would have been so proud." Shit, I didn't mean to say that.

"Would have been? Don't you live with them?"

Wow, it didn't take them long to investigate me, did it?

"I haven't seen them in a really long time, and no, I don't want to talk about it."

"That's okay, for now, at least. There are other ways to get to know a person."

How can someone make a simple sentence like that sound like such an innuendo?

"Yeah, I'm gonna pass. I feel like I fell asleep and woke up in an alternate universe or something. How long do I have to stay here for?"

He takes a step back and crosses his arms. If I didn't know better, I'd say I've offended him in some way.

"As long as it takes. Why? Are you in a rush to be

somewhere?"

"Would it matter?"

"No."

I throw my hands up in frustration. "Then why ask? You don't care, and answers like that make me want to scream."

"Look, I get that you're pissed. But surely you can see where we're coming from. You have no idea what Salem has been through. So, I understand you don't get why we're as protective of her as we are, but there is a good reason for all this. If you have nothing to hide, then why does it even matter? It's a few days out of your life."

I bite back the urge to scream in his face. Instead, I take a deep breath.

"I do understand, to a degree. I expected disbelief and hostility—even anger—because I'm used to those things. What I wasn't expecting was to be kept prisoner. Now you can justify it however you like, but when you turn the lock on a door that I have no key for, you become my captor, not my friend. And I have a surprisingly low tolerance for bullshit when it comes to strangers who think they can dictate what I do with my life.

"I can see you trying to keep the mood light between us. And unless I'm really off my game, I can feel the attraction too. But what this is right now is all it will ever be. My attraction to you is nothing more than me admiring something shiny. So, I'm just going to follow my mother's advice and look but not touch."

"You think you have it all figured out. But like you said, we're all strangers here. We owe Salem. But you... Well, we don't owe you anything."

I snort and turn away, heading toward the bathroom,

needing space to breathe. I stop in the doorway and turn to face him.

"I drove halfway across the country to save the woman you all profess to love so much. You owe me everything."

CHAPTER TEN

Slade

I take the headset off and pause the game when Jagger comes storming into the room and sits down beside me.

"Something wrong?"

"No."

"Right." I stand up and head to the kitchen to pour us both a coffee. I wait for him to walk over and take a seat at the island before sliding it over to him.

"She just gets under my skin, that's all."

I sip my coffee as I wait, knowing there's more.

"I want her."

"I know."

"She knows it too, but she isn't willing to go there. Not after all this."

I shrug. "Can't say I blame her. Not sure if the roles were reversed, I'd be interested either."

He scoffs. "Yeah. We both know that's bullshit."

"It doesn't matter anyway. It's not about me."

"Oh, it's not? So, when I do fuck her, you want no part in it?"

"So, it's *when*, not *if*?"

He jolts at that, not realizing what he'd said. "I guess so. If I can get her to come around."

"Yeah, come around your cock."

"Don't even pretend you don't want her."

"I don't even like her."

"And you have to like her to fuck her?"

"You want me to fuck her like I hate her? Who am I punishing, Jagger, her, or you? Because you seem way too pissed-off over being rejected by a girl you've known for all of five minutes."

Jagger's chest heaves as he gets his anger under control. I don't speak, giving him a chance to settle down as I continue to drink my coffee.

"I'm pissed because I want her, but this whole situation is fucked. And I don't want to do this without you, but I don't know what's going on in your head. One minute you can't stand her, and the next, you're wrapped around her like a fucking pretzel."

"I don't think I can be held responsible for what I do when I sleep, Jagger. Jesus."

"That's the thing, Slade. You don't sleep. At least, not until last night, that is."

"Don't read into that shit," I warn him. The last thing I need is for him to start acting like Astrid is some miracle cure for the messed-up shit in my head.

He scrubs a hand over his face before taking a big gulp of his coffee and placing it back on the counter. "I'm going for a shower, then a walk. I've gotta clear my head. There are also a few things I've gotta check on with the construction team when they get here."

"Fine. I'll keep an eye on our little pet. But you owe me."

"Yeah, story of my life," he mutters, walking away as he heads to my room to shower.

I finish my coffee, marveling at the chaos one woman can cause, before I pull out the stuff to make a fresh peanut butter and jelly sandwich. It's clear from the look of disgust on her face this morning when I took the old one away that she is not a fan, but she hasn't asked me for anything else. If she wants something else bad enough, she'll speak up. And when she does, I'll make a bargain with her.

Not sure how she takes her coffee, or if she drinks it at all, I pour a cup for her and add some half-and-half before placing it on a tray with the sandwich. I throw on an orange and carry it back to the room.

The shower is on when I enter, so I slide the tray on top of the dresser and walk to the bathroom, pushing the door open a little. I watch her through the frosted glass door as she lathers her body up. I can't see anything but a blurry image of her, but I don't need to see her to remember what she looks like. Every time I close my eyes, I picture her sexy-as-fuck body slick with water from the shower.

My dick is rock hard in my boxers, but if I touch it right now, I know I won't be able to beat back the urge to bend her over the counter and fuck her until she screams my name. I throw on a pair of Jagger's sweatpants and snag a T-shirt with a bottle of beer on the front of it and head back out to the living room to call E.

I check my watch and see it's still early. Not many of the guys will be up unless they have a job, but E, like me, has always been an early riser.

He answers on the first ring, his voice sounding clear and wide awake.

"You ever sleep?"

"About as much as you do. You don't have the market cornered on demons, Slade," E reminds me, and he's right. Prison messed with my head, but most of the guys here have had to work through some kind of trauma at least once or twice. In E's case, shit started when he was a kid.

"Did you find out anything else about Astrid?" I get straight to the point.

"If you're wondering if I know for sure the reason why she made the trek out here, the answer is no. I didn't really expect to find one. That's not how it works, and you know it. What I do know is she gets her groceries delivered and pays her bills on time. She spends most of her money on books, and aside from that, she's truly boring. I can't find any signs of a job. I can't find signs that she ever had one."

"Her parents must fund her lifestyle," I mumble.

"They might fund her financially, but they sure as hell don't shower her with attention. I guess raining money down on her is a way to ease the burden of guilt for effectively abandoning her."

"Abandoning her?"

"They haven't been home in years, as far as I can tell. They sure as fuck don't call her."

"Not even a wish-you-were-here postcard?"

"I don't get the impression they wish her anywhere near them. You know, a lot was said about me when I was growing up. Judgments made because I lived in a fucking trailer, but rich people are the fucking worst. My mom might have had next to nothing, but I never doubted her love for me. These people don't seem like they would piss on Astrid if she were on fire."

"If they're never around, I doubt they'd even know she was on fire to begin with."

Just more proof that money can't buy love.

CHAPTER ELEVEN

Astrid

I stare at the plate and resist the urge to throw it across the room. The fruit sitting on top of it makes my mouth water, but I can't risk eating it now that it's come into contact with the sandwich. I blow out a breath and move to the dresser, rummaging around until I find a large T-shirt, some boxers, and a pair of sweatpants.

The pants are huge, but they have a drawstring waist, so I tie them as tightly as I can and roll the waist over a few times. They are still too long, but they will have to do until I get my stuff. Next, I make my way over to the closet. I look through the clothes on the hangers and grab a light gray hoodie. It's not that I'm cold, but I like the thought of being able to hide behind an extra layer of clothing. With a sigh, I walk back over to the bed, and as I sit on the end, my stomach growls.

I feel a wave of melancholy roll over me and tuck my hands into my sleeves. I've never been a particularly lucky girl. I'm pretty sure if I didn't have bad luck, I'd have no luck at all. It's fine. I've accepted it. But sitting here with a window barricaded by shutters, I can't help but wonder, how the hell did I let myself end up here?

I cross my arms over my chest, ignoring my stomach and the smell of the coffee over on the food tray. God, what I wouldn't give for just a sip right now, but I can't. Just like the orange, I can't risk it. Fuck. I need—What I need is a plan. Running is not an option. After my first attempt, they'll be extra watchful. That leaves me with even fewer options than before, and I didn't have any to begin with. I don't think my endearing them to me plan is going to work. Slade hates me and Jagger... Well, Jagger clearly wants in my pants, but I don't think that has anything to do with me as a woman. I'm just pussy that's handy.

I'm surprised that knowledge stings. Stockholm syndrome aside, I'm not going to deny the man is hot. They both are. I guess I should be grateful there is at least some appreciation involved. Usually, I'm reduced to my flaws. It's easy for a person to dismiss you if all they allow themselves to see are negatives. Well, this girl is an expert on shit like that. The only way Jagger will get in my pants is if he does my laundry.

"Okay, the pity party is over."

I stand up and head for the door. I pull it open and head in the direction of the living area. I look longingly at the door that leads outside but resist the temptation this time. When I make it to the middle of the large room, I find Slade sitting on the sofa playing *Call of Duty*. I watch him for a second before taking advantage of the fact that he's wearing a headset and sneak over to the kitchen.

Spotting the fruit bowl on the counter, I snatch a banana and peel it quickly, just in case he catches me and takes it away. I eat the whole thing in four bites—not tasting a thing in my rush—before reaching for an apple. I take a big bite and moan as the sweetness of the apple explodes on my tongue.

When the game on the screen pauses, I do, too, feeling like a kid caught with their hand in the cookie jar. When Slade turns his head, his eyes narrow on the apple in my hand before he stands. In a fit of rebellion, I eat as much of it as I can as he strolls toward me. My mouth is so full I can hardly chew, but I feel oddly proud of myself. Take that, asshole. Of course, I don't say that out loud, not wanting to risk his wrath by spitting pieces of apple all over him.

"What's the matter, pet? Is the food we're giving you not good enough to meet your high standards?" he mocks. I couldn't answer him if I tried, so I don't. I continue to chew my food, hoping I don't choke because he'd probably just stand there and watch me die.

He takes the core from my fingers and tosses it in the trash. He waits for me to finish eating before he speaks again. "You done?"

I nod warily.

"Well, now, taking things without asking isn't nice. What are you going to do to make it up to me?"

He crowds me as I frown. What the hell is he implying? When his gaze roves over my body, I cross my arms even though I know the hoodie stops him from seeing anything.

89

"I'm not sure I like what you're getting at."

He licks his lips and smirks before reaching out a hand, which I promptly slap away.

"I'll throw it up right now if it means that much to you."

He shakes his head but reaches for me again, this time grabbing my hand and dragging me over to the sofa. "Since I'm on babysitting duty, you can play this with me. I'm bored as fuck. Unless you want to entertain me in other ways?"

"If other ways are anything besides charades or a series of interpretive dances, then I'm going to have to pass."

"Figures. Here." He hands me one of the controllers and points out the buttons and their functions.

"Shoot, jump—"

I tune him out and focus on the screen when his cell starts ringing.

"Practice while I take this." He starts the game and walks away to take his call.

I get in the zone and ignore everything else around me as I run around the base camp, shooting the other team while looking for the flag. I'm so in the zone that I don't realize he's back until I hear him curse.

"What the fuck?"

"What?" I ask distractedly, not looking at him because there is a camping motherfucker on top of the building trying to take me out. I watch him for a second before I take my shot.

"Take that asshole," I mutter, chuckling when the round finishes. I look at the stats, nodding when I see my avatar's name on top, before looking up at Slade, who is looking down at me with shock on his face.

"What?"

"You can play?"

I look at the stats, then down to the controller in my hand, and then back up to him and shrug.

"Most women I know have little interest in video games."

"Yay, one more thing to make you suspicious of me for."

He sighs and sits beside me, picking up a second controller. "Play again?"

"I guess," I say, but secretly I'm doing a happy dance. I was going stir-crazy in that bedroom.

So, that's what we spend the next three hours doing. It isn't until the door opens that we stop. Jagger stands frozen in the doorway, watching us as Slade turns the television off and takes the controller from my hands.

"I was wondering how much longer you were going to be. I've got shit to do too."

I flinch at his tone. I guess our little truce is over now. I stand and walk away, leaving them to argue as I head back to the bedroom. I cross the room and climb on top of the bed, lying down on my side, facing away from the door. Might as well take a nap. Not much else to do. I hear someone enter the room, but I ignore them and close my eyes. I fold in on myself and let my thoughts drift away, distancing myself from these two men who are giving me emotional whiplash.

When I open my eyes, I feel disoriented—the room seems darker, though it's hard to tell with the stupid shutters down all the time. I climb from the bed and bite back a groan when I stretch, my body still feeling the aftereffects of being slammed into the ground by a freight train. I use the bathroom quickly and check out my face. My cheek is turning a lovely shade of deep purple, but the swelling seems to have gone down some. And the cut on my forehead looks pretty good, considering.

I splash some water on my face and gently pat it dry, feeling a headache beginning behind my eyes. It's my fault for playing video games without my glasses on. I know better, but honestly, I didn't think Slade would get them for me. I didn't want to miss out on my only chance of escapism since I got here.

Time to suck it up. I have no idea how long they plan on keeping me, but I can't carry on like this. I need my glasses and some real damn food. I make my way back to the living room, this time finding Jagger leaning against the counter with his cell phone to his ear. I take a quick look around but don't see Slade. I'm not sure if I should feel relieved or disappointed.

When Jagger spots me, he lifts a finger to tell me to hold on.

"Alright, if you're sure, we'll be there in five." He hangs up and slides his cell into his pocket as his eyes move over my body, taking in my borrowed clothes.

"You look cute in my things."

I dip my head when I feel my cheeks heat.

"You want to come to the main house and get something to eat?"

My head snaps up so fast that I almost hurt my neck. "Really?"

He nods. "That was Zig on the phone, telling me to bring you over."

I bite my lip, wondering if I'm about to walk into another interrogation.

"Just food, Astrid," Jagger reassures me, as if reading my thoughts.

"Okay," I say quietly.

I wait for him to say more, but he just holds out his hand for me. After a moment of hesitation, I reach for it. When his hand closes around mine, I let him guide me toward the door, stopping him once we reach it.

"Um…shoes?"

He looks down at my feet, then looks around the room and curses. "I have no idea where Slade put them," he admits before bending down and scooping me up in his arms.

I yelp in surprise but wrap my arms around his neck so that I don't fall as he steps outside and kicks the door closed behind us. I look around and notice that all the construction vehicles are gone. Before I can take in much more, we're already inside the main building.

I hear voices talking and laughing, which all stop when they catch sight of Jagger and me.

Fighting the urge to jump out of Jagger's arms and run, I offer them a small wave. "Hi," I say softly as I take in the faces sitting around the table. Some I recognize, others I don't.

"What the fuck?" Greg—I think his name is—snaps, jumping to his feet as he approaches. I burrow my head against Jagger as he holds me tighter.

"What the fuck happened to her face?" he yells as he gently lays a hand on my arm, startling me more than if he'd hit me.

Dammit, why is kindness always so shocking to me? I turn toward him, his concerned eyes meeting mine.

"She tried to run. I told you that. Slade stopped her," Jagger answers with a sigh before I can say anything.

"Slade did this?" Greg's voice drops into a low growl, which, I'm not going to lie, is incredibly sexy, even though he's far older than me.

"He didn't hurt me on purpose," I whisper, wondering why the hell I'm defending the man. For some reason, I don't like the idea of them thinking he took his fists to me.

"If you put her down, I can—" Salem's words are cut off by Oz's.

"No."

The room goes quiet after that, the atmosphere so tense that I'm about to tell them I'll just go back to my room when Greg slides a finger under my chin and tilts my head back.

"Are you hungry?"

"Starving," I admit, my stomach rumbling loudly in confirmation.

"Well, then, let's get you something to eat. Jagger, you can put her down now."

He seems reluctant to do so, but eventually, he lowers me to my feet. Greg motions for me to follow him when the door behind us opens and slams closed again.

"What's going on?" Slade's voice calls out before he spots me standing just in front of Jagger. "I thought the whole point was to keep her away from Salem."

I flinch at his words and turn away from him.

"I told Jagger to bring her, so you can stop being a dick now," Zig replies.

Greg pulls a chair out for me, and so I lower myself carefully into it, keeping my eyes averted from everyone else's. I've never been a social butterfly. You have to have friends for that. If this is what I've been missing, I think I'll pass.

"At least tell me you're not in any pain," Salem asks, her voice cracking. I look up to see her glaring at Slade.

"Oh, I'm sure she blamed me, but Astrid was the one who ran. I was just doing my job," he snarls, yanking out a chair at the end of the table.

"Actually, Astrid defended you, though God knows why."

When Salem's eyes come to mine, I offer her a small smile.

"I'm fine. It doesn't hurt at all," I lie through my teeth. And everyone knows it, but they don't call me on it.

She swallows and nods before standing and heading to the kitchen. Gregg sits on one side of me, and Jagger takes up the last remaining chair on the other. Oz jumps up to help Salem, along with one of the guys I don't know. He glances over at me but doesn't say anything. He's as attractive as the rest of the guys here, but his look has more of a rocker vibe. Between them, they carry out bowls filled with vegetables and what looks like a pot roast. My stomach lets out a loud rumble, making my cheeks flush.

"The boys not feeding you?" another stranger at the end of the table asks with a grin. His smile seems genuine enough. In fact, out of all of them, this guy seems the most approachable.

I look from him to Slade and bite my tongue. And cue another uncomfortable silence. My skin crawls, and my palms sweat to the point where I know I have to get out of here before I do something stupidly embarrassing like cry.

I stand up and look at Salem. "I'm sorry, I'll just go back—"

She frowns. "No. You need to eat. Ignore these guys. Lord knows, I'm going to."

"Hey now," Oz complains, but she does indeed ignore him.

I keep my eyes on her and slowly lower myself back into my chair. She grabs a plate and starts spooning vegetables onto it before moving on to the pot roast. She pauses before looking at me again. "You're not allergic to anything, are you?"

I bite my thumbnail, glancing around nervously. Her eyes soften as she realizes I don't want to answer and give these clearly hostile men a weapon to use against me.

"Nobody here would ever use it against you."

I'm not sure I believe her, but I admire the faith she has in these guys. "Peanuts. I'm allergic to peanuts," I admit, and Slade stands up abruptly, knocking his chair over, and stares at me for a second before he storms out of the house.

I drop my head and sigh, wondering why I'm the one who feels bad in this scenario.

"What the fuck is his problem now?" Greg hisses.

I don't answer him, and neither does Jagger. I take the plate Salem offers me and thank her quietly as I wait for everyone else to get theirs. They watch me curiously, but I pretend I can't feel their eyes on me.

Slade storms back in a few minutes later with a tray full of things. I look at him, confused until I spot the jar of peanut butter. I watch as he tosses it all in the trash before he leaves the tray on the counter and washes his hands.

He stares at me as he takes his seat, his eyes glistening with something. Oh, he's mad at me, but there is something else there too. Guilt, maybe? Or remorse. I can tell by the way he scowls at me that he doesn't like feeling it one little bit.

"So, Astrid, why don't you tell us about yourself?" Greg asks as they all dig into their food.

I look at him and laugh, but it's not a happy sound. "Why? You guys already know everything, and what you don't know, you'll probably dig up in a day or two." I take a deep breath to calm myself. "I think right now the best thing is for me to eat the meal Salem was kind enough to make and go back to my room. I'll stay out of everyone's way until you guys tell me I can leave, and then you can pretend I was never here."

CHAPTER TWELVE

Jagger

J esus, I've never felt so uncomfortable in my own home
before. But looking at Astrid right now, seeing how miserable she looks... I have to remind myself that we're the
good guys. We're just trying to keep everyone safe.

And if I say it often enough, I might start believing it.

"Well, I'd like to hear about you from you, Astrid. You have
pretty eyes by the way," Greg says with a soft smile, smoothing
the way. If anyone here is gifted, it's him. He has the ability to
defuse any situation, but even he is pissed right now. Not at
Astrid, ironically, but at all of us. Jesus, how did this all get so
fucked up?

"What do you want to know?" she asks him warily, taking a
bite of her food and moaning in appreciation. "This is amazing,
Salem. I wish I could cook like this."

"You don't like to cook?" She grins.

"It's not that I don't like it, it's that I suck at it. I'm one of those people that could burn water. I think my problem is that I'm easily distracted," she admits as I sit and listen to her talk, the melodic tone of her voice soothing me.

"Sounds like Slade," she jokes, but Astrid just continues to eat, pretending not to hear.

"Where do you live?" Creed asks her.

She sighs and finishes her mouthful of food before replying. "Are you telling me you don't know? Or are you trying to see if you can catch me in a lie?"

He doesn't answer, which again makes the room feel tense. Jesus, this was a bad idea.

"You know what? Let me take you back, and we can watch a movie or something," I offer, which has Slade scowling.

"What?"

"Nothing. If you want to get cozy with our—"

"Prisoner," Astrid interjects, making Slade turn to her.

"Prisoner," he agrees with a grin. "Then, by all means."

"Funny, you didn't seem bothered when you were playing video games with her all afternoon."

"It wasn't all afternoon." Slade shakes his head.

"I feel like the red-headed stepchild that nobody wants to play with. Seriously, don't do me any favors. I'm more than happy to go sit in the room with the shutters down and the killer peanut butter and jelly sandwiches. I'm clearly not missing much." Astrid places her fork in the center of the plate and starts to get up, but Greg growls.

"Stay seated and eat your food. Ignore these motherfuckers,

and when you're done, I'll take you for a walk so you can get some fresh air."

"Really?" she whispers to him.

God-fucking-dammit, I am an asshole.

"Really. I don't like being cooped up inside, either. Wait, you're not claustrophobic, are you?"

She shakes her head and touches his wrist lightly with her hand. A red haze drops over my eyes for a second, and I have to fight the urge to snap the motherfucker's arm.

"It's not small spaces, though I'm not a big fan of them. I don't like being confined," she admits, her voice dropping to a whisper. But there is something in her tone that has the hair on my arms standing up.

"Well, who the hell does?" Greg agrees, glossing over her discomfort. "Trust me, the walk will do you the world of good."

She bites her lip and leans closer to him. I grip my fork so hard I'm surprised the thing doesn't bend.

"I don't know what happened to my shoes," she murmurs.

Greg jerks his head around to glare at Slade and me. Slade, of course, can't hear what's being said.

"What?"

"Where are Astrid's shoes?"

Everyone looks from Astrid to Slade.

"In my room. I don't know why you're all looking at me like that. She tried to run. I took care of the problem by taking her shoes," he shrugs, and I know some of the others see his logic, though I can tell both Greg and Salem are pissed. I don't bother to tell them she was barefoot when she ran.

"Reminds me of when I was held prisoner. They took my

shoes too," Salem states as she slams her glass of water down loudly on the table.

"Of course, I had my own clothes. I can only guess from Astrid's outfit that she doesn't even have that."

Astrid rubs her hands over her eyes and sighs. "I appreciate you sticking up for me, Salem, but it's fine. They said I could have everything once it's been searched. What I'm wearing is comfortable enough. Shoes would be good, though," she admits with a wry grin, trying to defuse the situation. It's ironic, given the circumstances.

"If anything, what I'd like are my glasses, my toothbrush, and my EpiPen. You know, just in case." She trails off when she sees the looks turn shocked.

"Or not. I can wait. It can't be too much longer before you let me go, right?"

"Your stuff is ready for you, Astrid, and has been since last night," Evander informs her as he strolls into the kitchen, catching the tail end of the conversation. His jaw ticks as he avoids looking in my and Slade's direction.

"Oh." She folds her arms over her chest and nods. "Thank you. I'm sorry, I'm really not that hungry anymore." She stands, and Greg stands with her.

"Come on, I'll help you find your shoes, and then we can take that walk. Funnily enough, I'm not that hungry either."

Slade stands too, but Zig looks at him. "Stay. Greg's got her."

Wisely, Slade sits as Astrid and Greg make their way outside. I grunt when I watch Greg swing Astrid up into his arms and carry her across the walkway.

"I think we need to go over a few things," Zig announces.

I turn my head to look at him and see Salem staring at me with an odd expression on her face. "What?"

"You like her?"

"And?" I don't deny it.

Hawk laughs. "Well, fuck. You've got your work cut out for you. She's prickly as a porcupine, and after seeing what you two are like with her, I can see why."

"Funny, I didn't hear any of you complaining when she got here. And you were fine with me and Jagger taking care of her, keeping her out of your way while you decided if she could be trusted or not, and I haven't received word to say that's changed. Am I a dick? Yeah, but I'm always a dick. Why are you acting like any of this is new?" Slade argues.

"You're not a dick to me," Salem tells him, and I watch as his eyes soften for the woman we've all come to care about.

"I trust you," he states.

"But once upon a time, I was a stranger, and you still never treated me like that."

"Oz and Zig claimed you. For them to do that, we knew what kind of woman you are," I tell her. She rubs her forehead for a minute, as if trying to make sense of it all.

"So, you being nice to me had nothing to do with me and everything to do with Oz and Zig?"

My brain sends up a red flag. Warning. Danger ahead.

"Is this a trick question, like, *does my ass look fat in these pants?*"

She picks up a roll from the basket in front of her and throws it at my head. I catch it and grin at her before taking a big bite.

She blows out a breath and tries again. "I understand why you're being cautious, and it's sweet, to an extent. But what you're doing to her, not so much. I might not be able to see inside her mind, but I like to think I'm pretty good at reading people. And Astrid Montgomery is about as evil as my big toe."

"I don't think she's evil, Salem. But good people can do bad things for the right reasons, at least in their heads. This connection she has to a man from your past, and another gifted person at that, is suspicious enough. But knowing what this man is capable of—that's what worries me. He took out that clinic without blinking an eye."

"Did he?" She crosses her arms.

"You know he did. She told us so."

"Nooo. Astrid told us he took care of the problem, and you all latched onto that and decided he was the one to blow up the clinic. This isn't you. I don't get it. You guys are trained to do shit I've never even dreamed of, but right now, you're acting like children. And not even nice ones."

"Oh, come on!" Slade protests.

"You kept her clothes, took her shoes, starved her, withheld her glasses and medicine—"

"Okay, when you say it like that, it sounds bad. But we didn't think about her needing her glasses. Hell, we didn't know she needed an EpiPen because we didn't know about her peanut allergy."

"It was in the file I made." Ev points out.

"Which none of us have had time to read yet." Slade sighs. "She didn't tell us, or I would never have given her those sandwiches. Heck, you saw me throw it all away when I found out. I don't want to hurt her, Salem. I just don't want to lose someone else."

Everyone is silent for a minute, but then Zig speaks up. "If you're talking about Cooper, he was a traitor," he growls.

"I know, Zig. I fucking know, okay? But before that, he was my friend. Fuck, he was the only father figure I had for a long time. I trusted him, and he fucked up, and he's dead, and that's where he deserves to be, but that doesn't mean I'm not allowed to grieve for the man he was before his wife got sick."

"And then we lost her too," I say, understanding why Slade's been pissed. He lost a lot being inside, and to be released and then have Copper taken from him too is a lot.

"He was a fucking traitor. I'm not sorry he's dead, but you're right. He wasn't always that man, and although I'm still not convinced having Astrid here is a good idea, you have to sepa-rate the two. Cooper betrayed us. He willingly sacrificed me and Zig and was willing to subject Salem to God knows what horrors in an attempt to save his wife. Part of me gets it. I'm not sure there is anything I wouldn't do to save Salem, but there has to be a line we won't cross to stop us from becoming the very men we fight against." Oz wipes his mouth and pushes his chair back.

"Cooper handed out a death sentence to us. It's not the same with Astrid. If she's lying about who she is, we're all in danger. If she's telling the truth, then Salem is. We're damned either way." Zig sighs.

Salem climbs to her feet and walks around the table to where Slade is sitting. She leans down over him and wraps her arms around his neck. "I'm sorry you lost Cooper, but I think he was gone a long time before he died. I can promise you now that you won't lose me. You won't lose any of us as long as we work together. That's where Cooper fucked up. He pulled away. He stopped being Apex a long time before he heard about me. Astrid is not Cooper. She could quite possibly be holding the only key we have to avoid an attack."

Slade leans into Salem and groans. "Fine, you win. Besides, it's hard to hate someone who can kick my ass on *Call of Duty*."

The others snicker, but I just look at Slade, wondering if he's telling the truth. As if he can feel the weight of my stare, he looks my way once Salem releases him. Somehow, I don't think his answer is going to be as cut and dry as he's saying.

"So, what do you want us to do now?" I question Zig, feeling a little pissed that somehow Slade and I are the bad guys in this.

Zig leans back and shrugs. "Ev hasn't found anything to say that Astrid isn't exactly who she says she is. We should just treat her like anyone else we're getting to know. She's not our enemy."

"At least until she proves otherwise," Oz mutters, making Salem snap at him.

"You know you're acting like a baby. Maybe you'd like to sleep in the spare room so there is enough space for you and your giant stupid head."

There's a beat of silence before we all laugh hysterically.

"She really is adorable when she's trying to be mean." Creed pokes fun at her, making her blush.

"I'm not adorable. I'm a badass. You guys just don't appreciate it."

"Alright, slugger. Don't hurt me." Creed cowers.

"I hope you're all looking forward to cooking your own meals next week," she warns, which shuts us all up.

"I take it back. You're mean."

"I am, and don't you forget it. Look, all I'm asking is for you all to give Astrid a chance. I love you guys, you know that, but it would be nice to have another woman around here whose IQ is larger than her cup size. Yes, Slade, I'm talking to you."

"You're right, Creed. She is mean." Slade looks at her with a frown.

"Alright, now that we've got that out of the way, I'm going to track down—"

"No," Zig interrupts me. "Let Greg spend some time with her. With the exception of Salem, we've all pissed her off. Greg is the only one who wasn't on board with our plan from the start, and he never hid that from her. Right now, she needs a friend, and that's Greg."

I clench my hands into fists. I don't want Greg to be fucking friends with her, and if Slade's expression is anything to go by, he's not too impressed with the idea either.

Oz smirks. "Something wrong?"

"No. Hey, Salem, you want to come play—"

"Finish that sentence and die," Oz snarls.

"What? Video games?" I ask innocently.

Salem giggles, leaning into Oz to kiss his cheek. "He's just messing with you. Besides, he has a thing for violet eyes," she teases.

I shrug. Again, no point denying it. And now that she's been downgraded from enemy to person of interest, I have every intention of getting that woman underneath me. Then maybe I'll be able to fuck her out of my system.

CHAPTER THIRTEEN

Astrid

I take a long, deep breath and blow it out. Being outside instantly soothes my frayed nerves, with the sun warming my skin as the breeze blows across my face. Lately, all I've felt is cold and wary.

"It really is beautiful out here. Thanks for this." I keep my eyes on the view, not wanting to miss a second of it because I know before long, we'll have to head back and face the others.

"You're welcome. Anytime you want to take a walk, come find me."

"Why are you being nice to me when the others hate me?"

"They don't hate you. They have their own shit to deal with, and it's easier to lump everything together than it is to separate and deal with it." He takes a step ahead of me, sliding his hands into the back pockets of his jeans, and looks up at the sky.

"Not long ago, one of our teammates, one of our brothers, died."

"I'm sorry, I didn't know."

"How could you?" He turns his head to look at me before looking back up. "Anyway, it's not just his death we're dealing with. He betrayed us. He sold out Salem and arranged to have Zig and Oz killed. He played us all, and none of us suspected a thing until it was too late."

His voice cracks at the end. I step closer and lend him my support without touching him.

"You were close before?"

"He was my best friend," he answers, turning to look at me again.

"Guess the joke's on me. The man I thought he was didn't exist. It was all nothing more than an illusion."

"At least you weren't alone. I mean, you all believed the lie, right? I'm guessing that's where the anger comes from and why everyone looks at me like I'm going to drive a knife into their backs any second."

"We all trusted him. We were all blindsided."

"But you think because you were best friends, you should have seen it somehow, right?"

He doesn't answer, but he doesn't need to. He's not that hard to read.

"I'm guessing if he had that kind of loyalty from you all, he earned it at some point. I'm not sure what makes a person do the things they do—betray the people they love like that—and I don't think we're supposed to. We're not wired the same way. To understand means to comprehend, and to comprehend means to sympathize, and sympathy means putting yourself in their shoes. But I've found that the only shoes a person should walk in are their own."

He looks at me, taking in my words. I don't know if he's humoring me or if what I'm saying is making sense, so I push on.

"What he did and who he became are on him, not you. Some people are born bad, but most people are just born blank slates. It's their experiences that dictate who they'll become. He wasn't always bad—if he was, you all wouldn't have cared so much. Something happened that led him down a different path than the one he was on when he was your friend. I didn't know him, so I don't know if he made that decision lightly or if he stood at a crossroads when he made his choice, looking over his shoulder every step of the way. Nothing is ever as black and white as we think it is."

"His wife was sick."

"What?"

"His wife. She was sick."

"Was?"

"She died. She had an aggressive form of cancer."

And suddenly, the picture becomes clearer. "She was the fork in the road. What he did was unforgivable. But I don't think the man was evil. And that's why you didn't see it. He loved his wife. That's the be-all and end-all of it. People think love is this wonderful and miraculous thing that we should all strive to find. And I'm sure for some, it's true. But this bullshit about love conquering all is what always gets me. Love can't save you. Most of the time, it's what ruins you."

He shakes his head and frowns, confused.

"Love is more than kisses and someone to share a life with. Most people see the light love brings, but they forget that with light, shadows are cast. And within those shadows lie the other aspects of love. Possession, obsession, jealousy, pain...

"All love has the ability to become toxic. Something that starts out sweet inevitably rots away in the end."

"How did someone so young become so..." he trails off, thinking of the right word.

"Jaded? Cynical? Guarded? It's okay. You can say it. I'm not ashamed. Just like this friend of yours stood at a crossroads, so did I. He walked away from you all, forsaking everything he believed in for the woman he loved. You know, in another life, that would make him the hero of the story. Funny how that works, huh?

"For me, it was all about survival. After being used time and time again, I chose to love me and to stop giving away pieces of myself to people who didn't deserve them. Being jaded, cynical, and guarded might make me hold myself back a little more than I used to, but I don't trust my instincts anymore. I want to love people. I want them to love me back, but I've realized I'm just unlovable. Anyway, one day I woke up and decided I was going to love myself instead. That doesn't mean that I've given up on someone else coming along and finding me worthy. It just means that they'll have to work to prove that they want more from me than what I can offer them. I'll never get back the pieces of myself that I carelessly threw away, but that's okay because they don't hold the power they used to. Now if someone wants a piece of me, they have to earn it."

"And the difference between earning a piece and being given one?"

"It's like getting a medal for winning over getting a sticker for participation."

He throws his head back and roars with laughter, making me grin.

Nudging my arm, his laughter calms to a chuckle. "I like you, Astrid. I suspect, hidden under their asshole exteriors, those boys in there do too. They're jaded, cynical, and guarded, too, though maybe for different reasons. I'm not saying you should take their shit. I'm just asking you to keep that in mind. Even big, scary mercenaries can get hurt. Only we're men, so we don't admit shit like that. We bury it down, rub dirt on it, and walk it off."

I gasp, placing my hand on my chest. "What? Men have feelings," I say sarcastically.

Greg looks from side to side before placing his finger to his lips. "Shhh, don't tell anyone."

I can't help the laugh that escapes me, and Greg smiles.

Once I've calmed down, we sit in comfortable silence, and I tuck my hands into the front pocket of the hoodie I stole.

"When do you think I'll get to go home?"

He doesn't rush to answer, thinking his words over before turning to look at me. "Can I ask you a question first? And I want you to really think about the answer before you reply."

"Okay."

"What do you have to rush home to?"

I open my mouth but snap it shut.

"Would it be so bad to stay here? If what you saw comes to

fruition, you might be the only person who can stop it from happening."

I stare back at the pretty landscape and remind myself of all the reasons I need to get out of this place. Mostly because I'm not a huge fan of assholes, and this place has more than a proctologist's office. The truth is, I don't have anything to rush home to. More importantly, I don't have *anyone* to rush home to. Of course, I don't say that part out loud. I want them to think that someone out there will miss me and note my absence, even if it's not true.

"I wouldn't have come all this way if I didn't want to help. But I'm not going to let people treat me like crap when I've done nothing to deserve it."

"And you shouldn't. But something tells me those boys might just be seeing the error of their ways." He leans closer and slings his arm around my shoulder in a brotherly way.

As wary as I am around most people, nothing Greg does seems to raise any red flags.

"And why's that?"

He tugs me so that I turn with him. When I do, I see Jagger watching us from the deck with his arms crossed over his chest.

"Because they're beginning to realize you don't fit in the box they tried to shove you into."

AN HOUR LATER, I'm mulling over Greg's words as I stand under the spray of the shower. I spend far longer in here than I need to but getting out means facing Jagger and Slade. And I'm not sure I have it in me.

When my skin resembles a prune and the water is tepid at best, I turn the shower off and climb out. I wrap myself in the large towel I find hanging on the back of the door and take a deep breath before tugging the door open.

The bedroom is empty, but on the bed is my suitcase and tote bag. For some ungodly reason, I feel tears pricking my eyes, but I ignore them and make my way over to my bags. I open them, and seeing my things there, all neatly folded despite having people rummaging through them, loosens something inside me. I run my fingers over the top item, which happens to be a pair of heather gray yoga pants.

I'm not a fashionista by any means. Yes, some of my items are expensive, basically because I have the money to afford them. I don't, as a rule, go out anywhere special, so my closet at home is full of mostly casual clothes—jeans, T-shirts, workout clothes, and a handful of little black dresses for when I have to attend a funeral. That might seem odd to some people—having a little section just for funeral attire. But when you *see* death as much as I do, it's always best to be prepared.

As basic as my clothing is, there's something to say about having your own things. I opt for the yoga pants and a white tank top before sifting to the bottom of my suitcase for a pair of white boy shorts and a matching sports bra.

I slip the underwear on with the towel still wrapped around me. Once the important parts are covered, I pull the rest of the clothes on before braiding my hair and putting my glasses on.

Closing the suitcase, I place it on the floor in the corner with my other bag on top of it.

With nothing left to do, I leave the room to find the guys. I'm surprised neither of them has bothered me yet. I ignore the butterflies taking flight in my stomach. There is nothing these guys can do to me that I can't handle. I've handled far worse.

With my mini pep talk out of the way, I walk down the hall and come to a stop when I find them both in the kitchen cooking. Frozen, I'm not sure what to say when they turn their eyes on me. Neither of them tries to hide the fact that they're checking me out. I pretend I'm immune to it all, but I still feel my cheeks flush.

"You didn't eat much before, so we're making burgers. I was going to grill them, but it's just started to rain." Slade shrugs before returning to slicing the hamburger buns.

"You want a drink? We've got wine or beer," Jagger offers.

"Just water is fine, thanks. I don't drink."

Slade lifts his head at that, his eyes on me despite the sharp knife in his hand. "You don't like it or…"

"Or do I have another issue you can hold over my head?" I ask defensively.

He holds his hands up in surrender, which would have been far more effective without the knife.

"Just curious, Astrid. That's all."

"Stupid," I mutter to myself, knowing I'm being a bigger bitch than usual. They sure do seem to bring it out in me.

"I don't drink because I don't like to have my senses impaired," I admit, which is the truth without giving too much away.

"I understand that," he states quietly.

Jagger hands me a bottle of water and then ushers me over to the island to sit on one of the bar stools. I sit down cautiously, unsure how to manage the new and nicer versions of these two. When they were being dicks, I knew where I stood. Now, not so much.

"Relax, Astrid," Jagger reassures me.

"Sure, why didn't I think of that?" I mumble, taking a big swing of water as Slade laughs.

"Alright, we were assholes. I was a dick, and I'd like to say we're not usually like that. But, well, that's not true. At least when it comes to me. I can say it's nothing personal. We'd have been this way with anyone coming to us like you did."

I raise my eyebrows at that. "So, if an old man stumbled in here, claiming he saw what I did, you'd have slept with him too?"

They both pause at that and look at each other before their warm gazes return to me.

"That was different," Jagger admits.

"How? We would have come with the same warning."

"We're not attracted to men. It's you we want to fuck." Slade shrugs, like dropping that clears up everything. I gape at him like a fish out of water.

"Too much? I'm trying to be more open, but I'm not sure how that's working out for me." Slade seems genuinely confused, while Jagger tries to hide a smile behind his hand.

"Is he being serious right now?"

"About fucking you? Oh yeah," Jagger answers, taking a bite out of a pickle.

"So, you were mean to me because you like me? What are we, in kindergarten?"

"I didn't say I liked you. I said I want to fuck you," Slade replies, looking at me with a frown when I scowl. "What? I didn't say I didn't like you. I don't know you. I'd like to, though. Get to know you, that is."

"Because if you like me, you can fuck me?" I ask, trying to understand his thought process, but I'm so lost.

"I don't need to like you to fuck you. There is a lot to be said about hate fucking."

I swallow hard, and the words slip out before I can pull them back. "Not if it's all you've ever known."

The knife in Slade's hand drops to the counter as his angry gaze jumps to mine. Jagger rounds the corner and stands beside me, tipping my head back so he can look into my eyes. Boy, if I thought Slade was pissed, then Jagger looks like he's about to go nuclear.

"Someone hurt you?" he snarls.

"Not in the way you're thinking. And maybe hate sex is the wrong term. Pity fucking is probably more apt and I have nobody to blame but myself. I slept with boys who said all the right things, but I was nothing to them."

"You are not nothing." he dips his head and murmurs against my lips.

"In the dark of night, I thought they loved me but when the sun came up, the girl they worshiped so reverently became nothing more than a dirty little secret."

"How old were you?"

"Young–*too young*. I was looking for love in all the wrong places."

"So, you were young and naïve. That's normal."

I push him away and spin in my chair. "I'm a freak, Jagger. I'm the girl you fuck, not the girl you marry."

A hand in my hair yanks me backward until I'm arched over the island. and Slade's angry face appears over mine. "I don't like you calling yourself names."

"Why? Everyone else does," I argue, not sure where my defiance is coming from.

"Nobody else matters." His eyes drop to my lips, then he shocks the shit out of me by slamming his mouth down over mine.

A sound of surprise escapes me, but he swallows it down as his mouth plunders mine in the most delicious way. It should be awkward as fuck in this position, but it's not. It just adds to the spontaneity of it all. I jolt when I feel Jagger's hands on my hips, holding me up as my legs shake, my toes barely touching the floor. His thigh pushes between my legs and rubs against me.

Abruptly, Slade pulls away, his eyes glistening as he stares at me. This time it isn't anger driving him, but white-hot lust. Jagger pulls me up and eases me back onto the stool as I struggle to swim out of the foggy haze Slade's kiss left me in.

"You need to eat first," Slade tells me, his voice firm and brooking no argument.

I look at Jagger, and he winks at me.

"Let the man look after you. It will help balance out all the times he'll piss you off."

118

I nod absently and watch as they both finish making the food. I should offer to help or something, but I'm still processing the kiss. What did it mean? Does it mean anything? Or was it a way to shut me up?

"Here. Eat." Slade slides a plate in front of me with a cheeseburger and fries on the side. My stomach rumbles in approval.

"Thank you," I choke out. I take a bite of the burger and groan, my eyes slipping closed. Damn, this is a good burger.

When I realize how quiet it's gone, I open my eyes and find them both watching me again. "What?"

"Nothing. Good?" Slade asks, sitting on my left with his plate, as Jagger moves to the chair on my right.

"Amazing."

We eat the rest of the meal in silence. They seem content, whereas I'm just too chicken to talk about what just happened. Fuck, I don't even know if I like them.

I'm so full by the time I've finished that I have a little food baby poking out, making me grateful I opted for yoga pants.

"Do you want to watch a movie?" Jagger asks, breaking the silence as he takes my plate from me.

If the alternative is going back to the bedroom and staring at the four walls, heck yes. "Sure."

"Okay, why don't you and Slade go pick something while I clean up?"

"I can help."

He shakes his head. "I've got it."

I look at Slade, who, as usual, says nothing. I'm hoping that means he's okay with this. This is Slade we're talking about. He'd tell me to fuck off if he wanted me to go, right?

I climb off the chair as Slade moves into me and takes my hand. I look down at our joined hands in surprise and let him lead me to the sofa.

"What do you want to watch?"

"Um… I don't know."

"Here." He sits on the sofa and tosses me the remote before tugging me down beside him.

I swallow and hope he doesn't see my shaking hands as I scroll through Netflix and select the first thing I can find.

"Nice," he comments, his eyes on the screen as he takes the remote from me and cues it up.

That's when I realize I chose the movie *It*. I'm usually good as far as horror movies go, with one teeny tiny exception. I hate clowns. I bite my lip and consider telling him I've changed my mind, but then he pulls the throw off the back of the sofa and covers me with it, distracting me from the thought of clown carnage.

"Are you sick?"

"No, the blanket's for you." He looks over at me, confused.

"Nice Slade is freaking me out," I admit.

He smirks. "You want me to be a dick again?"

I open my mouth, but before I can answer, his lips are on mine, and everything else fades away.

CHAPTER FOURTEEN

Slade

It has to be said, kissing Astrid is right up there with my favorite things to do. If her lips have this much power over me, I can only imagine what her pussy can do.

"Do I need to throw a bucket of water over you?" Jagger huffs.

I pull away with a grin on my face that screams *fuck you*. He looks at me and rolls his eyes before taking the seat on the other side of Astrid. Her eyes flutter open as she becomes aware of her surroundings once more. She bites her lip and looks up at me, all wide-eyed and innocent. Fuck me, it makes me want to strip her bare and bend her over the sofa.

I wink at her and hit play on the movie as we all settle in. Jagger dims the lights and leans in closer to Astrid so she's pinned in between us. It doesn't take long for Astrid to lose herself in the movie. But for me, I'm more distracted by the woman herself than what's playing on the screen.

I look over at Jagger and see him looking down at Astrid, too, with a soft expression on his face. Feeling my eyes on him, he looks up at me. He doesn't need to speak for me to see the question in his eyes. *Are we really doing this?*

I nod once, giving him the green light. It's like it's all the permission he's been waiting for, and he slides his hand behind her on the back of the sofa, taking a strand of her hair and twirling it around his fingers. Astrid jumps and squeals, hiding her eyes in the blanket, making me chuckle as I look at the screen to see what scared her.

"Don't worry. I've got you." Jagger grins like he finds the whole thing adorable, tugging her into his side.

"I'm not usually a jumpy person, I swear."

"Of course you're not."

She looks at me and frowns. "It's true. Scary movies are my jam."

"Your jam?" I grin. I can't help it. Jagger's right, she is adorable. Especially when her guard is down and she forgets that she hates us. Of course, I'm rather fond of prickly Astrid too. There is something incredibly sexy about the woman when she is pissed off and ready to take on the world.

"Yes," she huffs, throwing me a death glare before letting it go and turning back to the movie. We fall back into silence until the children on-screen find themselves trapped in an old house with the serial killer clown.

"Oh, my fucking God!" Astrid gasps, practically crawling into Jagger's lap. The lucky bastard.

"Not a fan of clowns, huh?" I laugh, realizing what the issue is.

She looks at me. "Clowns are Satan's minions sent to distract us with their balloon animals and big feet while they suck out our souls," she says, completely serious.

I can't help it. I laugh in her face. Jagger is fighting back a laugh of his own, but he's much better at it than me, which is why I'm the one she's looking at, like she's plotting my murder.

"Just you wait. One day, when the world is overrun by zombies—"

"Wait, zombies? I thought you had an issue with clowns?"

"And who do you think will be controlling the armies of the undead?"

"Right, of course, clowns. I should have thought of that." Said nobody ever.

"Exactly. People are taken in by their painted faces and fake smiles. But all that makeup does is hide the killers beneath."

"Maybe the makeup is just a deterrent so the zombies won't eat them," Jagger jokes. But Astrid tilts her head as if considering his words.

"That makes sense. You see it with creatures in nature all the time—chameleons, frogs, even some species of spider. The colors act as a warning. Danger, do not eat me."

I nod, knowing in this moment that it would be so damn easy to fall in love with this woman.

"I can see that. If there was a line of clowns and you were standing with them, I'd choose to eat you every time too."

This time, Jagger does laugh. But Astrid doesn't pay him any attention as she points her finger at me. "If you ever find me in a line-up with a bunch of clowns, it means I've been kidnapped. Again."

"Then I'll be sure to rescue you and eat you afterward."

Her eyes widen as she finally realizes what I'm talking about. "I… You… Dammit, Slade," she curses before turning back to the movie. I reach for the remote and pause it.

"Come on, I'm only teasing." I reach for her when I realize she's genuinely angry.

"You're sending me mixed signals. It feels like some kind of test I'm gonna fail because I didn't know I needed to study for it. Hell, I don't even know what the test is for. Are you deciding my worth? Is there a punishment if I don't meet your expectations?"

"Hey." I pick her up and sit her on my lap, facing me, with her straddling my legs, hating that she seems genuinely upset. "I'm sorry. I didn't mean to upset you."

"You didn't. It's the stupid clowns," she grumbles with a pout, refusing to admit anything.

"Clowns make you sad now?"

"Clowns should make everyone sad. Like, were clowns always evil, or did something tragic happen to make them that way? And what happens to clown babies? Can they—"

"God, you're adorable."

Her mouth slams closed, and her eyes widen, making her look like an anime character.

"I know I'm confusing the fuck out of you right now. I'm confusing myself. You stumbled in here looking like something out of a fairy tale, and I wanted you so fucking bad. When I realized you could be a potential threat, I was pissed. Pissed at myself for wanting you. Pissed at you for tempting me. I know it's not fair, but it's been a long fucking time since I've craved anything as much as I crave you. I'll admit, I haven't handled it well."

She cocks an eyebrow at that.

"How about a do-over? Hi, I'm Slade. I think you're so fucking beautiful it hurts to breathe, but I have a fucked up past and lash out when I'm angry."

I hold my hand out to her and wait to see if she'll respond. She looks from my hand to my face, her eyes boring into mine, looking for the lie. She won't find one, at least not about this.

Eventually, she slips her hand into mine and shakes it. "Hi, my name is Astrid. I think you're really handsome, even with the perma-frown you've got going on. I can see the future, but because all I see is death, it messed me up, and I turn into a raving bitch as a defense mechanism to protect my soft spots."

"I promise to be careful of your soft spots in the future," I murmur, sliding a strand of hair behind her ear.

"I have never felt more like a third wheel than I do right now," Jagger mutters, making Astrid giggle.

"You're not a third wheel. A cockblock for sure, but never a third wheel," I answer.

"He's not a cockblock. I'm not having sex with you." Astrid shoves my chest, but my hands slide to her hips and hold her in place.

"Ever? Or just right now?"

"Right now. Though, I make no promises. You might be pretty to look at, but half the time, I want to set you on fire."

"You hear that, Jagger? She thinks I'm pretty."

"Ah, selective hearing at its finest." Jagger snorts before sliding closer, taking the spot Astrid previously occupied.

I watch as his large, scarred hand reaches up and cups her jaw. "I don't want to start over because, right or wrong, getting to know you has been the highlight of my year. I don't want a redo. I just want to make amends." He leans in closer and presses a barely-there kiss against the corner of her mouth.

Her eyes flutter closed for a second before they snap open. "Wait. Let me get this straight because I'm not sure I'm reading you right.

"You want me?" she asks me, looking unsure.

With my hands still on her hips, I yank her closer so she can feel how hard my dick is. "Fuck yes, I want you."

She gasps at the contact before swallowing and turning back to look at Jagger. "And you want me?"

He reaches for her hand and slides it over his jean-covered dick, leaving no room for arguments.

Her mouth drops open, like she's simply run out of words, before she shakes her head and pulls herself together. "Do I have to choose between you?"

"You don't have to do anything you don't want to. But if we had a choice, it would be to see you squirming between us. Like most of the guys here, we like to share." Jagger tells her straight out.

She looks at us both with curiosity. There is a hint of fear in her expression, but I can see the lust in her eyes too.

"It's twice the fun." I lean forward and press a kiss to her jaw.

"And twice the heartbreak," she whispers.

"Princess, I'm not planning on breaking anything but the bed."

She laughs in surprise at that before sighing. "I don't get it."

"Get what, princess?"

"Look, you guys are—" She waves a hand over both of us as if that's the answer.

"We're…"

She huffs. "Women would trip over themselves to jump on a ride either of you offer. I guess I'm asking, why me?"

"No, you want to know if we want you because it's convenient. Not looking for a sex slave, Astrid," Jagger tells her.

"Speak for yourself," I grumble.

She pokes me in the ribs, making me smirk.

"I'm not going to apologize for having very wicked thoughts about you."

She shakes her head.

"Well?"

She releases a sigh before her shoulders slump. "I'm not saying no. But you should know I'm pretty boring. I keep to myself, and I like it that way. Coming here has been terrifying, but…"

"But?" Jagger pushes.

"But it's made me feel alive. I've been going through the motions for so long that I don't think I even realized I was doing it until I came here. In trying to keep myself safe, I stopped putting myself out there. Taking risks wasn't worth the inevitable heartache."

"And now?" I ask softly, needing her to take this risk. But it has to be her that takes the first step.

127

"And now I'm questioning everything. You said it yourself, I'm like a fairy tale character. Only I'm the one who locked herself away in a tower."

She bites that damn lip of hers before she nods, coming to a decision.

"I'd like to get to know you both a little better before this goes any further. I told you a little about my past with men. Well, I made a lot of mistakes when I was younger. The worst was punishing myself for things that weren't my fault, no matter what other people said. I drank, I smoked, I even dabbled in drugs. And when I was high or drunk, I believed every pretty boy who promised me the world. When the haze would lift, all I'd be left with was a handful of broken promises."

It hurts her to admit it—I can tell by every rigid line of her body. I'm surprised she said anything at all.

"They were never worth your time. But if you think you're the only person who did a lot of fucked up shit when they were younger, you're wrong," Jagger tells her.

I tense at his words, waiting for him to reveal shit about me that I'm not sure I'm ready for her to know, but he doesn't.

"But if you need time to get to know us, then take it. We're not going anywhere, Astrid," he tells her before leaning closer.

"Okay," she whispers.

"Okay?" he confirms.

When she nods, he closes the gap between them and kisses her. His hands slide into her hair and hold her in place as he seals the deal. It might not be as slow as she wanted, but then she should have been more specific.

When he pulls free, I swoop in, not wanting to give her a

second to think. I yank her hips down and move her against my hard cock as I fuck her mouth with my tongue. She doesn't fight it, despite her initial hesitation. When her hands move to my shoulders, and she grabs hold of me instead of pushing me away, I growl in appreciation.

Yeah, it would be really easy to fall for a woman like this. And that scares the shit out of me.

CHAPTER FIFTEEN

Astrid

I stir when I feel myself being moved. Opening my eyes, I see
Jagger looking down at me as he lifts me into his arms.

"I fell asleep?"

"I think your brain hit its clown limit," he teases. I shudder
when I picture Pennywise's sneering face.

"I just don't understand how other people don't sense the
evil in them," I mutter, snuggling into him.

I vaguely remember telling them I wanted to take this slow
and get to know them better, but I'm too comfortable to
protest. I'll take the diet approach and start tomorrow.

Jagger carries me to the bedroom and sits me on the side of
the bed as Slade calls out that he's going to lock the house up.

"You need help getting changed?"

I shake my head. "I'm okay. Can you pass me my suitcase so

I can find something to sleep in?" I ask, taking off my glasses and placing them on the nightstand.

He doesn't pass me my suitcase, though. Instead, he pulls his T-shirt off over his head and hands it to me.

Slow Astrid. Slow, slow, slow. I can repeat the mantra as many times as I like, but seeing all that bronze skin in front of me and that freaking V that leads down to the Holy Grail... Yeah, no. I'm going to fail this diet like I've failed so many before.

"Are you sure you don't need help?" His voice sounds like liquid sex.

"I need help not breaking this diet," I mutter as I reach for the T-shirt and slip it over my head. It smells like him, which, of course, makes me want to curl up and purr like a contented cat. I'd be pretty disgusted with myself if I wasn't busy fighting the urge to rub myself all over him.

"You're on a diet?" He sounds pretty angry about that, which makes me snicker. *You and me both, Jagger.*

I stand up and pull my arms back into the T-shirt and slide the straps of the tank and bra down my arms before pushing them back through the sleeves. Then I reach under the T-shirt and shimmy the material down my body before letting gravity take over. Stepping out of them, I shove my pants down my legs as I answer him without looking. "I'm on a dick diet." I kick my pants off and pick up my discarded clothes, freezing when I realize how close my head is to Jagger's cock.

"How do we keep ending up like this?" he asks. When I look up at him, he groans and fists his hands at his sides, like he's trying to restrain himself from reaching out and grabbing me.

"I blame you," I complain, standing up so quickly I lose my balance.

I don't fall, though, because Jagger and his ninja reflexes catch me, his hand going around my back, which pulls my body flush with his.

"I was going to ask how it was my fault, but I think this is exactly what you're referring to."

"Huh-uh," I murmur in agreement as my breathing picks up.

He takes a deep breath and lets me go once he knows I'm steady, then takes a step back. "You make it hard to remember I'm a good guy," he tells me, his eyes drifting down to my chest. He swallows as if he can see right through the cotton T-shirt.

"They're just boobs, Jagger."

"It's not just your boobs," he answers without skipping a beat, his eyes dropping to my now bare legs. "It's your legs I picture wrapped around me as I'm moving inside you, your hair I imagine spread out over my pillow, and your eyes staring at me as you feel me coming inside you."

I blink, not expecting that. I should protest, remind him of how we said we'd go slow, and ignore my now-soaked under-wear. But when he looks at me like that, it's hard to remember all the reasons I wanted to go slow in the first place.

Slade walks in behind Jagger, breaking the tense moment between us. He looks from Jagger to me and frowns. "What did I miss?"

"Astrid was just telling me she's on a dick diet," Jagger answers with a grin.

"Meaning you can eat as much dick as you like? Allow me to

volunteer my services," Slade offers graciously, stripping out of his T-shirt and tossing it aside.

I whimper before I can stop myself and cross my legs, unconsciously rubbing them together to ease the ache. "I'm giving up dick," I blow out, trying to regain my composure.

"Like for Lent?" Slade cocks his head.

"No, because it's bad for me."

"Oh, baby girl, you just haven't had the right dick, that's all." He adjusts his cock as he takes a step closer to me, as does Jagger, until all I can see is them. "Don't worry, we'll go slow."

"I don't think slow means what you think it does," I whisper.

Jagger sticks his arm out in front of Slade to stop him from pushing any further. "You want us to back off?"

"I don't want you to, but I need you to." Everything is starting to overwhelm me.

"Then we'll back off," he states, as simple as that.

Slade grumbles under his breath, but he takes a step back, putting some much-needed distance between us. He turns to Jagger. "I'll take the bed, you take the sofa, and tomorrow we'll switch."

Jagger shrugs. "Works for me."

"Wait? What? Oh, crap, I forgot about there being only one other bed. You can stay here with me, it's fine," I tell Jagger, watching Slade's shoulders slump, but he doesn't say anything.

"You sure? There's no pressure," Jagger reiterates.

"No, it's good, actually. It'll be nice to have someone between me and the door. That way, when the clowns come, they'll eat you first."

"I'll happily take one for the team."

Slade nods and turns to leave, but when he gets to the door, I call his name. It doesn't feel right to let him leave. He looks over his shoulder at me.

"What if they come through the window?" I say, playing with the hem of my T-shirt.

He looks at the window, then back at me like I've lost my mind because the damn shutter is down, so how could anything get through it? Then I see the light dawn in his eyes. He closes the door and walks over to the bed, nudging me out of the way as he pulls the comforter back before crawling in and moving to the far side. He holds the blanket up, waiting for me to join him.

"I won't let anything hurt you," he states. Somehow, I don't think he's talking about clowns anymore.

I take a chance, hoping I don't regret it, and crawl onto the bed beside Slade. He keeps holding the covers up until Jagger climbs in behind me after turning the light off, plunging us into darkness. The sound of our breathing mingles as we settle in. Nobody speaks, and none of us are touching. Yet there is something oddly intimate about this moment.

Eventually, the tension leaks from my body, and I relax, even when both of them move closer. But it's when Jagger's leg slides over mine and Slade's hand moves to rest on my hip that a feeling of rightness washes over me.

I'm alone in the dark and vulnerable with two men who have spent more time being hostile toward me than kind, and yet I'm not afraid. Even when I thought they hated me, they didn't hurt me. Well, not counting the football tackle, of course.

I've always been afraid of what goes bump in the night. But more than that, I was well aware of all the monsters that roamed freely in the light. I've never truly felt safe before.

Until now.

I'M warm when I wake up. Too warm. I try to kick the cover off but find myself unable to move. It takes my brain a second longer to process the reason why.

I must have rolled during the night because my head is resting on Jagger's chest, and my ass is pushed back into Slade, who has curled around me. I lift my hand to make sure I haven't drooled when I realize there is an arm blocking my way. An arm attached to a hand that is currently cupping my breast.

Holding my breath, I try to figure out a way to escape without disturbing either of them. Slade moans in his sleep and moves closer, his morning wood pressing against my ass as his hand spasms around my boob. I suck in my breath and nearly choke on it when he starts grinding against me in his sleep. I don't know what he's dreaming about, but when he lightly pinches my nipple, I'm not sure I care.

I squirm at his touch, feeling hot and needy.

Any minute now, I'll pull away.

Any minute.

Slade pulls away before I can make my move, and instead of being relieved, I'm disappointed. At least until his rough hand lifts my already bent leg and pushes it higher until I'm virtually sprawled across Jagger. When he has me where he wants me, his hand slides from my thigh to my now-exposed pussy. He palms me over my panties. If he were awake, he'd feel just how wet they are.

A sharp intake of breath has my eyes snapping open. That sound didn't come from Slade, it came from Jagger. I tip my head up, and his eyes clash with mine. I know he can't see what Slade is doing, but it doesn't take a genius to figure it out.

"Want me to wake him up?" he whispers, his hand lifting to my face. He palms my cheek and rubs his thumb across my bottom lip.

I open my mouth to tell him yes, but when his thumb slips inside and I taste the tip of it on my tongue, I lose my train of thought. I close my lips around his thumb and suck, making him groan. I feel it rumble through his chest and let it embolden me, swirling my tongue and sucking harder.

When I feel Slade's fingers hook the crotch of my underwear and pull it aside, I don't protest. Nor do I stop him when I feel his finger at my slick entrance. I vow to start my dick diet tomorrow. Wait, does this even technically count if we aren't awake yet?

Jagger pulls his thumb from my mouth before dipping his head and kissing me. His tongue pushes inside my mouth just before Slade thrusts two fingers inside me. Jagger swallows down my gasps, cupping my head and holding me in place as he turns into me a little more. My leg slides farther over his hip as he turns. Now I can feel his erection pressing against my stomach.

Jesus fuck, I suck at dieting. I promised myself I'd be good, and now all I can think about is being the filling in a double-dick burger.

I wrap my hand around Jagger's arm, anchoring myself to him as Slade pumps his fingers in and out of me, curling them in just the right way to make me see stars. I'm so close to coming that I find myself thrusting back into his hand. But when he pulls his fingers free, I tear my mouth away from Jagger's and look over my shoulder, wondering if my movements have woken him.

"He's still asleep. He does random things like this, though usually he eats or plays video games while he's asleep," Jagger tells me quietly.

"Will he be mad when he wakes up?" I turn back to Jagger as Slade moves closer behind me.

"No. That man wants you any way he can get you. But if you want him to stop, now would be the time to do it. I don't know how far he'll go."

As I feel the blunt head of Slade's cock probing me, I'm pretty sure I know the answer.

"Astrid," Jagger warns me, but anything I might have said dies on my lips as Slade thrusts into me.

I come around him as he bottoms out inside me, arching my back and yelling his name. His movements falter for a second, and I know this time he's awake as his hand grips my hip hard enough to leave bruises.

Jagger must realize something is wrong because his eyes move from mine to Slade's. "Fuck her, Slade. She wants it. Tell him, Astrid. Tell him how badly you want him."

The urgency in Jagger's tone makes me pick up quickly that

Slade is panicking. I push back into Slade, who seems frozen, and wrap my hand over his on my hip.

"Don't stop Slade, please. I need you," I whimper, not caring that they both hear the begging tone in my voice.

I feel Slade's whole body shudder—with relief or arousal, I don't know. But when he starts hammering into me, I figure it's a little of both. Jagger tips my head back up so I'm staring at him, his eyes glazed as he watches his best friend fuck me. He slides his hand down between us and starts stroking my clit, and my eyes roll back as Slade sets a punishing pace. Despite already coming once, I can feel another orgasm building.

"You like that, Astrid? You like feeling Slade inside you?"

I moan and nod, not sure I can remember how to form actual words. But that's not good enough for Jagger. He swipes his tongue across my lip before biting down on it.

"Words, Astrid. I need you to tell me everything."

"It feels good. So good!" I gasp as Slade hits a spot that's both pleasurable and painful.

"He feels so big, it's almost too much."

"You like the stretch, though, don't you? Imagine what it would feel like to have us both in there."

His words set off a series of images in my head, each one more pornographic than the last. I come with a scream, clamping down around Slade's cock, which triggers his release.

My heart is thundering in my chest as I try to catch my breath. Slade presses a kiss to the back of my shoulder, and I squeeze his hand.

"You're okay? You are sure? I didn't mean for that to happen. Not that I'm sorry because fuck me, that was hot, but still…" he trails off when I still don't say anything, his body becoming tense again as if waiting for me to shout or cry.

"Fuck, Astrid, say something," his voice croaks.

I turn my head and look over my shoulder at him, saying the only thing that comes to mind.

"Fuck the diet."

CHAPTER SIXTEEN

Jagger

"You seem in a good mood this morning."

I turn at the sound of Salem's voice and shrug. "The weather is beautiful. The refurb is almost done. What's not to be happy about?" I smile as I grab the mail and sift through it.

"My imminent death?"

I freeze at her words, feeling like an utter dick.

She snickers. "Relax, I'm kidding. If there is one thing I know, it's that none of you will ever let something happen to me. This place is probably the safest place on earth right now."

"Fuck, I'm still sorry."

"Oh, stop it. You're allowed to be happy. I want that for all of you. There is no right time to find it. There are always going to be rain clouds on the horizon. It's far better to weather the storm with someone who'll shield you from the rain than stand alone in its downpour."

"I'm not sure I understood all of that, but I think I get the gist."

She smacks me in the chest with the dish towel. "My point is, shit happens. And it's better to have someone by your side when it does."

"Okay, I get it. I get it." I wrap my arm around her and kiss her temple.

"Do you nag your men as much as you do the rest of us?"

"Of course not. My guys are super smart. They claimed me, didn't they?"

"Good point." I laugh.

"So, how is Astrid this morning? Where is she, by the way? I thought she might come over for breakfast now that she's considered a guest and not a prisoner." She rolls her eyes at me.

"She's good. Really good. Slade is finishing up the tour Greg started yesterday."

"You didn't want to go with them?"

"I wanted to give them a little time alone together."

She frowns.

"Don't read too much into it. Everything is fine."

I like Astrid. I do. But Slade needs her more than me right now. He thinks I haven't noticed him struggling lately, but I know that man better than he knows himself.

"I'm not reading into anything. I was just asking a question."

"Salem," I sigh. "Look, I don't know what's happening, it's too soon to tell. We have a lot of things to work out. We weren't exactly welcoming when she got here."

"Funny, that look on your face when I walked in says you've been a whole lot more welcoming since then."

"What are you two talking about?" Oz's voice pulls our attention to the door.

"Your woman has no boundaries."

"Oh, I know. How do you think I managed to get her to agree to—"

Salem is across the room with her hand over his mouth before he can finish his sentence. I have no idea what he was going to say, but the red tinging Salem's cheeks makes me curious.

"Finish that sentence, Oz Cartwright, and you'll regret it."

He tugs her hand free from his mouth and wraps his arms around her with a laugh. He dips her low and kisses her as if we're standing on the set of a movie or something. Usually this would be my cue to leave, but watching them together stirs something inside me now that Astrid is here. Before, I was happy for my brothers, but it was with the knowledge that they were the lucky ones. Shit like that doesn't happen to everyone.

Now I'm left wondering if that's all a bunch of bullshit. What if it does happen to everyone? What if it's just that some of us aren't as open to the idea as others? The right person could have been standing in front of you all along, but if you have your eyes closed, you'll never know.

I go back to flipping through the mail in my hand, separating the ones for me and Slade from the others, which I place on the table before moving to the coffee pot to pour myself a large mug.

Oz and Salem finally manage to pull themselves away from each other.

"Is it me, or is it fucking quiet this morning?" Oz asks, grabbing a mug.

"Shhh! Don't jinx it," Salem hisses, her eyes wide as she stares at Oz before she turns and starts dragging bowls and utensils out of the cupboards. And I can't help but chuckle at the look on Oz's face.

"What are you making?" I ask because that seems like the most important question right now. And I'll need to know when to come back so I can get myself something before the rest of the vultures descend and steal it all.

"Cookies, brownies, and a cheddar and sun-dried tomato bread."

"I love it when you talk dirty to me," I groan, earning a laugh from Salem and a punch in the arm from Oz, which has my coffee spilling over my hand.

"Asshole," I curse, sliding the mug and letters onto the counter while I clean myself up.

"Hey," Creed greets as he walks in and heads to the coffee maker.

I haven't seen much of Creed since Astrid showed up, but the man looks dead on his feet.

"You, okay?"

He yawns and nods. "Nothing a vacation in the Bahamas wouldn't fix. We completed the protection detail yesterday for Judge Jones's ex-wife and kid. And then the construction crew woke me up at the ass crack of dawn."

"How'd it go with Jones?" Oz asks him.

Creed leans back against the counter and takes a drink of his coffee. "Hawk is debriefing Zig right now, so I'll just give you the highlights. Getting the case extradited was the right move. The judge presiding over the divorce was not a happy bunny with what was presented to her, and she sure as shit isn't part of the old boys' club Jones controls. She granted the wife everything she asked for, including full custody of the kid."

"No shit? I didn't see that coming. I guess we won't need E to get them both a new identity then."

"No, she still wants that, and I'm inclined to agree. Jones was pissed. I can't see him giving up, not now that she's humiliated him."

"Men like that need a bullet between the eyes," I snap, thinking about everything that asshole put his ex-wife and kid through.

"It's not just him that's the problem, though. It's all the assholes that support him, offering him protection when they know exactly what kind of monster he is."

"You'll get no arguments with me. What really pisses me off is that Jones will get away with all this. Yeah, he's losing his wife and kid. But let's be honest, he didn't give a fuck about them anyway. They were just accessories he pulled out when he needed to make himself look good. He won't see a minute behind bars or even lose his job unless some brave soul steps up to fight the system," Creed complains as he takes a seat at the table.

"What worries me is what happens to the next woman that comes along? If all this is swept under the rug, she'll have no idea of the danger she'll be walking into. I mean, on paper, he's the kind of man mothers dream their daughters will bring home. Ivy League educated, no criminal record, important, well-paying job... I miss the days when it was fucking easier to tell just who the bad guy was," Oz grunts out, taking a seat next to Creed.

Zig walks in and takes us all in before strolling over to Salem and placing a kiss on her temple.

"I take it Creed has filled you in."

"Yeah. It's a great result, but I can't help but think this is far from over. Think he'll cause issues for us?"

Zig shakes his head. "As far as he is concerned, we were hired for protection. Nothing more, nothing less. He has no idea who we are or what kind of connections we have, and I'm happy to keep it that way. We'll keep an eye on him just in case, but I'm not overly concerned."

"Must be nice to know you're untouchable." Oz sighs, leaning back in his chair.

"Don't count E out yet. The man has been digging for dirt like a motherfucker, and last night he found something." He holds his hand up before we can all start bombarding him with questions.

"I don't know any more than that. You know what E is like when he catches a thread. He stays working on it until the whole thing unravels. When he's ready to share with us, he will."

"I take it he's holed up in his office. Should I take him something to eat?" Salem asks softly.

"He's gone out, little one. He's tracking down some information."

I frown at that. When Ev started, it was with the understanding that he'd take control of the bulk of the IT shit because the man is a wizard with a computer. But lately, especially now that Cooper is no longer here, he's been venturing out into the field.

"If E is going to be doing fieldwork, he needs a second," I point out.

"I know. Me and Oz have been talking about it. Greg is the obvious choice with Cooper gone, but I don't know if it's the right fit." Zig shrugs.

I get what he means. Partnering means more here than it does elsewhere. After a drunken, whiskey-fueled talk with Ev not long after he joined us, he admitted he liked the idea of sharing a woman, but one of his choosing. He didn't want to end up with a partner and woman by default. He brushed it off, calling it something like middle-child syndrome. But even then, in my drunken state, I knew it was more than that.

Greg is the odd man out. It's why his teammate was Cooper. Both men were not interested in sharing. Cooper because he met and married his high school sweetheart, and Greg because he wanted someone who was solely his. Again, his vague answers about the situation made me think there was more to it, but I know when to push and when to not.

"Yeah, I don't think they're the right fit either, but as a temporary measure, it can't hurt. We've seen too much shit to take risks with our safety."

"Where is Greg, anyway?" Zig frowns.

Creed looks uncomfortable when he answers. "He's at the cemetery."

The room goes silent after that. There is only one person buried at the cemetery that he could be visiting, and that's Jan, Cooper's wife. Yeah, there is more to Greg's story than he's told.

Zig changes the subject. "Wilder and Crew are leaving tonight. They're wrapping up the Frendfell project. They'll be home in a few weeks."

"That asshole better pay up first. Wilder owes me a hundred bucks." Oz rubs his hands together with glee.

"Do I even want to know why?"

"Let's just say he scored with a woman last night who was packing more than just an Adam's apple." Oz grins, making me choke on my coffee.

The backdoor opens, and I turn to see Slade and Astrid walk in hand-in-hand, making all eyes turn their way. Astrid flushes and looks down, not a big fan of the attention she receives, which is ironic because, looking the way she does, she must get her fair share of it.

"Hey, Astrid!" Salem greets her with a huge grin and a friendly wave.

"Hi." Astrid waves back, coughing when her voice cracks.

"Take a seat." Zig points to the chair at the far end of the table. "You want coffee?"

Astrid looks startled for a second before nodding. "That would be great. Thank you."

I walk to the table and pull the chair out for her. Her eyes light up when she sees me, and shit, it makes my chest pull tight. I resist the urge to rub it. Instead, I run my finger over the bridge of her nose.

"Everything good?" I ask her quietly.

"Yeah, Slade's been taking good care of me," she replies quietly.

"I bet he has."

She elbows me as Slade laughs and pulls out the chair beside her. "No, don't worry, Jagger. I'll get my own chair."

I flip him off and take the seat on the other side of Astrid.

"Do you want something to eat, Astrid? I can whip something up for you if you like," Salem offers.

"No, I'm good, thanks. We ate already. Though I won't say no to whatever it is you're making over there."

Salem beams at her. "Sweet tooth, huh? You'll fit right in with this bunch, then. I don't know how they eat the crap they do and still look like they've stepped out of the pages of a magazine."

"Men suck," Astrid agrees as I lean over and press my lips against her ear.

"I do, actually. Suck, that is. I also bite, lick—"

Her hand covers my mouth, muffling the last of my words.

"Are you okay, Astrid? You look a little flushed," Oz asks, feigning innocence. But even I can hear the mocking tone in it.

Astrid pulls her hand from my mouth as she glares at the man, clearly not intimidated by his size. "I'm fine, and thank you for helping me."

Oz frowns. "What did I do?"

She smiles at Zig, who places a mug of coffee in front of her before turning her gaze back to Oz. "Thanks for helping me figure out which twin you are."

"Let me guess, you think I'm the evil one?" He rolls his eyes as if Astrid bores him. Brother or not, I'm going to punch the dick if he keeps antagonizing her.

"No, the dumb one, actually."

"What the fuck? I'm not dumb. Everyone knows I'm the best twin."

"What are you, five? I'm starting to wonder if you're twins at all. Maybe Zig got all the good genes and you're just the afterbirth."

Choked laughter bursts out of Zig, and Slade full-out laughs.

"That's rich. Have you looked in a mirror lately? You look like the offspring of a Disney villain."

"Please, my parents created perfection, and they knew it, which is why they stopped at just one. Yours took one look at you and started working on your sister."

"Because I'm amazing, and they wanted another baby just like me."

"Like Zig, maybe. He was the orgasm. You were the dribble that came after."

Oz gasps and holds his hand to his chest as the rest of us die around them.

"Your mother didn't have any more because she sensed evil in you and was worried you'd eat them."

"Well, you would know since every time your mother looked at you, she was reminded that she should have swallowed instead."

Oz cracks up at that one before picking up his coffee.

"I think I might steal your girl," Creed teases with a wink at Astrid, who blushes even after the nasty shit she just spit out. The woman is a hilarious contradiction.

"Fuck off and get your own," Slade snaps at him, then winces when he realizes what he said. He looks at Creed apologetically, but Creed just waves him off.

Sometimes it's easy to forget that Creed was married. Both he and Hawk shared a wife before she up and left them without a word. It's been three years now, and neither of them has heard from her. Some people would assume they were over her by now, but I know better. For a start, there hasn't been a single woman for either of them since Avery left. I don't know if that's because they are still reeling from their loss or if they are hoping she'll come back. At some point, they're going to have to make peace with the situation and move on.

"At the risk of making everyone hate me again, what are the odds of me getting my laptop back?" Astrid asks as she fiddles with the cuff of her sleeve.

Zig tilts his head, considering. "Do you need it for something specific? Not being a dick here, we'd just need to make sure it can't be tracked."

"That's fine. I just thought I might do some work."

Slade zeroes in on that. "I didn't realize you had a job."

I wince, realizing how that came out.

"How else am I going to book clients? It really is the safest way for a sex worker to make contact these days." She takes a sip of her coffee as Slade's eyebrows reach his hairline before his eyes narrow.

"You're fucking with me."

She grins behind her mug. "Am I?"

"Alright, fine. I shouldn't have assumed. But in my defense, E didn't mention anything about you having a job. And given what we did find, it's not like you needed to work, so..." he trails off, looking over at me for help. I keep my mouth shut and watch him struggle.

Luckily, Astrid doesn't seem offended. "I use an alias. I like to keep my work life and private life separate."

"We get that, trust me," Oz agrees.

"So, what do you do?" Slade asks, too curious to shut up.

"You mean other than you?" She smiles widely, making Salem laugh.

"I knew it."

"You know I have a remedy for smart-mouthed little vixens," Slade warns her.

"Oh really? Do tell." Astrid winks at him.

"Well, it involves handcuffs and a bed."

And just like that, Astrid shuts down. It's as if a wall slides over her eyes, and I watch as she retreats behind it. I reach out and take her hand—throwing her a lifeline—while making a mental note to revisit the subject later. I have no doubt the others saw it too, but I keep all my focus on Astrid.

"So, tell me about this job that requires a super-secret alias. Oh, I know, I bet you're a writer."

I feel Oz tense beside me, but he says nothing.

Astrid shakes her head. "No. Not a writer. I have a vivid imagination but the concentration span of a fish when it comes to putting anything down on paper."

Oz relaxes making me wonder what he was thinking.

She blows out a breath and looks around. When she sees that she's still the center of attention, she looks down.

"I design video games."

"That's why you were so good before," Slade exclaims, and Astrid looks up at him.

"Yes, because it couldn't just be something as simple as I'm better than you."

"No, exactly," Slade agrees, making me laugh.

"And this, ladies and gentlemen, is why Slade is single," Astrid deadpans. But as I look between Slade and Astrid, I have to wonder if that's true anymore.

CHAPTER SEVENTEEN

Astrid

Things have settled down. I don't feel like such an intruder anymore, and surprisingly, I like it here. What a difference a few days can make! Sure, these guys are busy and have other things on their minds besides me. But if they still thought I was the bad guy, they'd have made it known. Even Oz seems to have softened.

Getting my laptop back has meant that I've been able to put the finishing touches on my project. Taking a deep breath, I press send. Now all I have to do is wait and see what they think. It's tricky doing it remotely. My setup at home was worth every penny I poured into it, but when I started, I did it with the basics. It's been kind of cool to strip everything back to that again.

I sign off and shut everything down, rubbing the bridge of

my nose where my glasses have been resting before standing up and working out the kinks in my back. Making my way to the kitchen, I pull open the fridge, looking for something yummy to jump out at me. Unfortunately, all I find are ingredients. I blow out a breath and wonder if it would be okay to order a pizza. Security is pretty crazy here, so—

I pause at that thought. If security is so crazy, why was I able to get as far as the front door? Yes, they might have been aware I was there the second I took the turn, but they had no idea if I was armed. Hell, I could have had a bomb, for goodness' sake.

A knock on the door makes me jump. Shit, did they hear my thoughts? In any other place in the world, the answer would be, of course, no, that's impossible. But I learned a long time ago that nothing is impossible. The fact that I'm here—a person who sees the future, staying with a woman who can heal—speaks for itself.

I creep toward the door, knowing neither Slade nor Jagger would knock. I wish they had thought to add a peephole to the freakin' door. Again, I'm questioning their ideas about security. I crack open the door and peek out, breathing a sigh of relief when I see it's Evander. I don't know the man very well. Heck, I've seen him less than the others combined, but he's never been mean to me.

"Um... Hi. Is everything okay?"

"I've been monitoring your outgoing email," he blurts out. Though I'm not happy about being spied on, I'm not surprised. I expected them to do it. Maybe I should email my gynecologist tomorrow just in spite.

"I figured you would," I say quietly, unsure where he's going with this.

"You're Miss Evo." His eyes are wide when he says it, making me blink.

"Yeah. Are you okay?"

His face pales as he holds the door frame for support. "You created *Abstract Seven*. The best immersive open-world action role-playing game in the fucking world."

I blink before a smile spreads across my face. "You're a fan?"

He looks at me as if to say, duh. "Understatement. If I didn't think you'd freak out, I'd propose to you."

I pretend to consider his words as Jagger walks around the corner, frowning when he sees Evander talking to me.

"Would you get down on one knee for this proposal?"

He drops to his knee before I can say anything else.

"What the fuck?" Jagger asks, but I wave him off.

"Shhh. We're just getting to the good part. Evander is proposing to me."

"He's what?" Jagger yells, storming over.

"You don't understand. I love her!" Evander yells back, wrapping his large hand around my calf when Jagger tries to drag him to his feet.

I can't help the laughter that pours from me.

"You are not marrying my girl."

"I saw her first," Evander snaps at him.

Jagger narrows his eyes as Evander stands up and faces off with him. I'm laughing so hard at this point that I have tears streaming down my face, and I'm having trouble catching my breath.

"Oh, hey, Slade," Jagger calls out. Evander whirls around, which is exactly what Jagger was after. Jagger picks me up and tosses me over his shoulder and carries me back inside, slamming and locking the door behind him.

Evander thumps on the door. "Come on, I just want to lick her brain."

I stop laughing and look at Jagger, who looks grossed out.

Evander sighs heavily through the door. "I made it weird, didn't I?"

"Just keep your tongue and dick away from my girl, and we'll be fine."

"What about my fingers?" Evander calls back, making me snort again.

"Oh, you think this is funny, huh?" Jagger puts me down and glares at me.

I can't even pretend otherwise when I can't stop giggling. "You have to admit, it's kind of funny to see big bad Evander go all fanboy on me."

"She thinks I'm big and bad. In your face, Jagger," Evander calls out, threatening to set me off again.

"I can see neither of you are listening, so instead of telling, how about a little show?"

Before I can ask him what he means, he has my T-shirt up and over my head. I suck in a breath before I'm spun around and bent over the side of the sofa. His hands move to the waist of my shorts, yanking them down over my ass with my panties.

"Jagger..."

He stills his hand as he leans down over me. "You tell me to stop, and I'll stop."

I hesitate, questioning what I want. I can feel how wet his actions have made me, and the second he touches me, he'll know too. "No, don't stop."

"Good girl. Now hold on while I remind you who you belong to."

He doesn't ease me into it. He simply lines himself up with my wet pussy and surges inside. I curse loudly as he grips my hips tightly.

"Who's fucking you?"

"You are."

"Say my name, Astrid. Tell the world whose dick is inside you."

"Mmnh," I moan as he thrusts into me even harder, punctuating every word.

"Say. My. Name."

"Jagger, Jagger, Jagger, oh God," I sob as I hold on for dear life. He's so deep, I swear I can taste him on my lips in this position.

"That's right, Astrid. That's my cock you're gonna come all over. Now tell Ev why he can't have you."

I startle at that, having forgotten all about Evander. I try to lift myself up, but Jagger's hand pushes me back down and pins me in place.

"Oh yeah, he can hear you, with all your sexy little moans and groans. He's picturing your wet pussy wrapped around my cock like a glove. And later, when he fucks his hand, he'll think of this moment."

I feel my pussy pulse around his cock, making him growl.

"Oh yeah. You like the thought of that now, don't you, dirty girl? You like the thought of him coming in his hand, thinking about your hot, sweet pussy?"

I hear Evander groan and the sound of banging. Somehow, I just know he's banging his head against the door.

"Tell Ev why it will never be his cock inside you. Tell him," he orders when I don't answer fast enough.

"Because I'm not yours," I whisper to Evander, even though there's no way he can hear me.

"And why's that? Who do you belong to?"

"You. I belong to you, Jagger," I scream as I come hard.

My arms crumple beneath me, and my face ends up buried in the cushions as Jagger thrusts into me over and over until he comes with a roar, pulling out at the last second and coming all over my ass and lower back.

My orgasm sucked all the energy from my body. I don't think I can even move to stand up.

"Shall I let E in so he can see my cum all over you?"

Never mind, I can move.

I push myself to stand and scramble to pull my shorts up. "Asshole."

"Maybe next time, baby. We'll get Slade inside your pussy first while I take you. Having us both inside you... Trust me, it will rock your fucking world."

"I hate you." Evander's voice sounds through the door, making me squeak as I run to the bathroom, ignoring Jagger's laughter.

I take a quick shower to clean myself up, thankful that we'd managed to squeeze in a talk about our sexual history. It's just as well, given how I keep ending up in these compromising positions. They had the paperwork to show me a clean bill of health. Though I didn't have the same to offer—beyond showing them my birth control—they took me at my word. Heck, it has been years since I was last tested. But it's been years since I last slept with someone, too. I'm just glad everything still works like it's supposed to.

Figuring I've given Jagger enough time to get rid of Evander, I slip on a pair of army-green cargo pants and a white tank top. I pile my hair up into a messy bun and pull a few tendrils free to frame my face before putting my glasses back on. Taking a quick look in the mirror, I see that the shower has done nothing to erase the freshly fucked look on my face. Surprisingly, I don't care. For a while, whenever I looked at my reflection, all I saw in my eyes was a hollow void I couldn't seem to fill. Since coming here, I've done nothing but run a gamut of emotions. What I haven't felt since the second I knocked on that door is empty.

As I head back out to the living room, I hear voices. Jagger is probably filling Slade in on our sexcapade. I just hope he's okay with it. I know they said they both wanted me, but the reality of fucking the same girl is different from the fantasy. I don't know how they stop themselves from getting jealous of each other. What we have is still in its infancy, but the thought of sharing either of them with another woman makes me feel like hulking out and throwing things, so I don't take their feelings lightly.

When I walk into the kitchen, I grab a bottle of water from the fridge and move over to the table, but I freeze because it's not Slade sitting with Jagger—it's Evander. This time I don't feel my face going red—I feel it catch fire. I turn on my heel to leave.

Jagger catches me and spins me into his chest, tipping my head back to look at him. "Nothing to be embarrassed about, Astrid, I swear. It was fucking hot."

I squeeze my eyes shut, hoping that when I open them again, Evander will have disappeared.

"He's right. That was spank-bank material, for sure. Later, when I think back on it, I'll switch out you shouting Jagger's name for mine, but—ouch! Motherfucker, that hurt!"

Evander complains when Jagger reaches over and slaps him on the back of his head.

I look over at Evander, and his eyes find mine. He stands up and shuffles closer. I grip Jagger's T-shirt tightly.

"Seriously, please don't be embarrassed. It was hot, but I'm not planning on trying to get in your pants. Hell, in my fantasies, you don't even wear pants—hey! Alright, stop fucking hitting me."

"Stop hitting on my girl."

"Our girl," Slade calls out as he swings the front door open and catches the tail end of the conversation.

Evander's face pales as he turns back to me. "Okay, here it is. I think you're awesome, Astrid, but really, I just want to talk to Miss Evo."

I can't help but grin at his puppy dog face as Slade walks over and tugs me from Jagger's arms so he can kiss me.

"Who's Miss Evo?"

"I am. It's my alias."

"Wait, why does that sound familiar? You're not a porn star. I'd remember you."

I roll my eyes. Men. Seriously.

"Of course she's not a porn star—not that there's anything wrong with that—but gamer girls are so much sexier," Evander says.

Slade glares at him.

"I meant cooler." He holds his hands up and backs away.

"Relax, guys. It's fine." I blow out a breath and take a seat at the table as Evander takes the chair opposite me.

My eyes drift to the sofa for a second. But when I feel my skin heat again, I focus back on Evander. "So, what do you want to know?"

It's as if my words open the floodgates. For the next half hour, Evander fires off question after question in rapid succession, barely giving me time to answer before he's onto the next one.

"Jesus, breathe, E, before you pass out. Who knew our resident hacker was such a geek?" Slade teases.

"Hey! There's nothing wrong with being a geek. I'm a geek."

"And you can talk nerdy to me any time you like, baby," Slade throws in, making me grin. The man is just too smooth.

"I tell you what. I've just sent the latest addition to the *Abstract Seven* series. It's only in the beta stage right now, but if you want to take a look at it... You might see something I haven't. I'm open to suggestions."

Evander's mouth drops open, but no sound comes out.

"Um... Evander?"

"Ah shit, she broke him. E man, snap out of it." Jagger slaps him across the face.

"Ow! What the hell, why is violence always the answer with you two?" Evander snaps as he stands up.

When he looks at me, he smiles like I just gave him an acceptance letter to Hogwarts. "Seriously?! Send it to me. The guys have my email. Oh, and call me E. But are you sure you don't mind me taking a look? I know these things are usually kept top secret for a reason."

"I trust you, E. Besides, it's not often I meet someone who loves the world I created as much as I do. Be prepared for random late-night calls and texts to bounce ideas off you."

He swallows and nods. "This is the best day of my life." He turns and leaves.

"Did that just happen?" I look up at Jagger, who is watching E's retreating figure with a smile on his face.

"Apparently so."

CHAPTER EIGHTEEN

Slade

"I need to head into town. Do you need anything?" Jagger asks as he strolls into the kitchen, dripping with sweat from his morning run.

I swallow my mouthful of cereal before taking my empty bowl over to the dishwasher and placing it inside. "I'll come with you. We can take Astrid with us. She's been working nonstop, so the woman could use a break."

I still feel like a dick when I think about how badly I wrote her off as a spoiled rich kid who lived off her parents. She sure as hell could have been. From what I've been told, Astrid never needs to work another day in her life, and yet she works harder than most people I know.

"Sounds good. Where is she anyway?"

"She went over to the main house to see E about three hours ago."

"Should we be worried about him?"

I shake my head. "I know he jokes around, but I don't get that vibe from him. It's more of a brother-sister thing than anything else. And since Astrid doesn't have any siblings, and Ev misses his, it must be a novelty for them both."

"Hell, if they want siblings, they can have mine," Jagger offers with a grin.

He adores his sisters, but they do drive him insane.

"I'll be sure to tell your sisters that."

"They'll never believe you. They think I'm a god."

I shake my head and make my way to the door. His sisters love him, that much is true. But they pander to the man's ego because it's easier to keep him wrapped around their fingers. A brief flash of my sister's face pops into my head, but I shake it off. Dawn made it clear where her loyalties lie when she disowned me the day I got arrested.

"I'll head over to find Astrid. We'll meet you over there."

"Alright. I just need to take a quick shower. I won't be long."

I nod and walk out into the sunshine. I glance around, but I don't see anyone else. Now that all the construction is done, it's back to being peaceful here. Just the way I like it.

It was an adjustment at first—after getting out of prison, that is. That place was always noisy. Even in the dead of night, you could hear people snoring, talking, praying, or crying. There was no peace, not even a second of it. I'd dream of a place like this when I was there. But when I was released, it took me months to adjust to the quiet.

When I walk into the main house and look around, I spot Salem on the sofa in the den. I head over to ask her if she knows where Astrid and E are when I notice she's asleep. I tug the throw off the back and lay it gently over her before turning and almost plowing into Zig.

You wouldn't think a man his size could move so quietly, but he's like a ghost when he wants to be. He motions for me to follow him, so I do. He walks us into the kitchen, and he offers me a coffee, but I decline.

"Everything okay?"

Zig swallows. For a second, I don't think he's going to answer, but then he nods. "Salem's pregnant."

"What? Holy fuck, that's awesome. Congrats, man."

He smiles, but it's weak, which makes me frown.

"Something wrong with the baby?"

"It's not that. It's Salem. She's freaked out."

"What? Why? Did she not want kids?" I find that hard to believe. I've seen her with Luna's kids. She has this whole nurturing thing going on, and it draws everyone to her. Nobody could take better care of us than she does.

"She's scared it could be a girl. Not because she doesn't want a daughter, but because of what it could mean for our little girl."

"Oh, shit." I forgot about Salem's gift. It presents in the females in her family. They don't know why, and they have no idea how strong the gift will be until she uses it. After everything Salem has been through, I can understand her fear.

"We'll keep her safe—both of them safe."

"She knows that. She also knows that a little girl won't get to live a normal life, one that all parents dream of for their children. It'll be hard for her because she'll always be different."

"She'll be exceptional, just like her mama. I'm not saying it will be easy, but with you and Oz as fathers and with all of us as uncles, the girl won't know a second of being unloved or unwanted. She won't go through what Salem did because we'll be here to shield her from anything and everything that might hurt her."

A sniff has us turning to the doorway, where Astrid is standing, hugging her laptop to her chest. She has tears running down her face, and her hands are gripping her laptop so tightly that her knuckles are white.

"What's wrong?" I hurry over to her and pull her into my arms.

"Did something happen to you?" Zig asks her quietly.

She blows out a shaky breath before pulling back and looking up at us. "I'm sorry. I'm fine, I promise. I just walked in and caught the end of your conversation."

Zig tenses, but Astrid reaches out and touches his arm lightly. "Hearing you speak… Slade is right. This baby will be so loved and protected, and I'm sure Salem knows that in her heart. But in her head…" Astrid blows out a breath.

"Salem is scared because she can only draw on her own experiences. It's the same for me. But what you have here is different, and the moment she holds that tiny bundle in her arms, she won't give a flying fuck if her daughter is gifted, as long as she's healthy and happy."

Zig tugs her from my arms and presses a kiss on Astrid's

forehead. She looks at me with shocked eyes before smiling softly.

"Thank you. We weren't trying, so the whole thing came as a shock. A happy one. But then Salem got freaked, and..."

"And you didn't know how you were supposed to act. How can you be happy when the woman you love is so scared? You're allowed to be excited, Zig. This is your baby, too. You just have to be there for each other. You're a team in all of this. And I think that's what parenting is. Teamwork. It's also love, hope, fear, worry, and a thousand other emotions that will press down on your shoulders. But when that baby is cradled in your arms, they won't feel the burden you carry. They'll only feel the love you blanket them with."

"Can we keep you?" Salem's choked-up voice calls out from the sofa.

Zig curses as he lets Astrid go and heads over to Salem, scooping her up into his arms and carrying her over to us.

"I can walk, you know." She sighs, but she snuggles into him anyway.

Astrid steps closer to me and slips her hand into mine.

"I know," Zig replies, but he makes no move to put her down.

Salem looks at Astrid with tears in her eyes. "Thank you, both of you," she says, looking at me before reaching out and squeezing my hand.

"Astrid is right. I was freaking out because all I could think about was what my life was like. How lonely and scared I was. And I never wanted that for my child. But then, I never had people like you in my life. I never had a father who would fight for me, uncles who would shield me, and friends who would comfort me." She smiles at Astrid again, who is the only person here who has any real idea what life was like growing up gifted. Even if their lives were as different as night and day.

"You also never had a mother like you," I remind her. She jolts at that, but I squeeze her hand. "I don't doubt she loved you, because how could anyone not love you? But she had no idea how to be a mother to someone as special as you. You, however, won't have that same issue with your baby."

Salem starts crying harder now, so Zig carries her away. Turning to Astrid and me, he mouths a *thank you* before he heads out to their house.

I look down at Astrid and see that her eyes are wet too.

"She'll be okay."

"I know. I'm not crying because I'm worried or scared. I'm crying because I'm happy. I feel like I've just witnessed something monumental. It sounds stupid, I know, but—"

I kiss her, my hand sliding into her hair as I slowly take her mouth with mine.

"Not stupid," I murmur against her lips before pulling back and resting my forehead against hers. "You want to come into town with Jagger and me?"

Her eyes widen in shock at the random change of subject, but she gets over it quickly. She nods rapidly as excitement lights up her whole face.

"Yes, please. I love it here, but I feel like I need a change of scenery."

"Good. Do you need anything before we leave?"

She bites her lip. "Sunscreen and a hat?" She says it like a question. "Sorry, I know it's a pain, but…" She leaves it hanging as I frown at her.

"Why is it a pain? You need sunscreen and a hat because your condition makes you more vulnerable to the sun, right?"

She nods.

"Having a medical condition is nothing to be embarrassed about. You do what you have to do to keep yourself safe."

"Okay." She grins, relieved.

"Want me to run back for them?"

"If you don't mind. My hat is on the dresser in the bedroom, and the sunscreen is in the bathroom. Oh, and could you bring my sunglasses too, please? They're on the coffee table, I think."

"I'm on it. Do you want me to take your laptop back with me?"

"Sure." She slides her laptop into her messenger bag and gives it to me, which I slide over my shoulder with a smirk.

"Think pink is my color?"

"Most definitely," she states with a smile before I give her a quick peck on the lips and jog back to the house.

When I first met Astrid, I thought the initial attraction I felt for her would lessen. But now that our relationship has changed, there is something about the woman that soothes the beast inside. I'm not sure if I'm happy or horrified by the notion that she has such a hold over me.

Jagger is in the kitchen when I walk in. He looks at me and frowns, taking in Astrid's laptop bag.

"She doesn't want to come?"

"No, she does. I'm just grabbing a few things for her. She's waiting up at the main house," I tell him, heading to the bedroom as he laces up his boots.

When I come back out with the sunscreen and hat, he reaches for the sunglasses on the table before hooking them over the top of his T-shirt.

"Does she need anything else?"

"No, this was it."

I wait with him as he locks up, then we walk back together.

"You okay? You're awfully quiet."

"And when have you known me to ever be a big talker?" I drawl, making him chuckle.

"Good point."

He doesn't say anything else, but I can see he wants to.

When we walk in, Astrid is talking to Creed, her arms waving animatedly as she speaks.

"Hey, Creed, didn't know you were back."

"Yeah, about ten minutes ago. Hawk detoured to visit his mom, but I came straight back."

I grimace at the mention of Hawk's mom. She loves him. I don't doubt it. But there is the kind of love that boosts you, and then there is the kind of love that smothers you. And ever since Hawk's father died... She's the definition of a helicopter mother. She's always hovering and tries to be involved in every aspect of his life. So, let's just say she's not a huge fan of us since, apparently, we take too much of her baby's time away from her.

"What were you two talking about anyway? All I could see was her arms flinging around all over the place."

"Paintballing. Oz is setting up a course. Thought we could

all use a way to blow off a little steam. I was trying to convince your girl to join us, but she's having none of it."

"What's the matter, Astrid? You don't want to play with us?" Jagger pouts, making me grin.

As usual, Astrid's face flushes from the double entendre. I've never thought about blushing as being sexy. I've fucked my fair share of women, but I can't say I've ever really been with a blusher. There is something about it that makes me hard as fuck. Maybe it's the whole innocent thing. It makes me want to do very naughty things to her.

"Behave." She points a finger at him.

"You should join us, though. It will be fun."

A shuttered look comes over her face before she smiles, but it doesn't reach her eyes. "I'll think about it."

She's lying. I know I shouldn't push, but I can't help it.

"Liar. If you don't want to hang out with us, that's fine." I shrug, not acting bothered.

"That's not what I said, and you know it. Stop twisting my words."

"Is it so wrong to want to spend time with you?" I'm being an ass, and I know it, but I can't help it. I want to know why she doesn't want to play.

"Oh, leave her alone. Not everyone is into running around and getting dirty." Creed offers her an out, throwing me a look.

I ignore him and focus on Astrid. "Can't be that. Our girl likes getting a little dirty." I grin, but she doesn't bite.

She looks up before answering in a small voice, "I don't like guns." She turns and heads toward the garage, leaving us all to look at each other, confused.

"Besides being pissed off, she didn't seem scared when we held her at gunpoint, so I don't think that's true," Jagger points out.

"Agreed. Don't worry, though. I'll get it out of her."

"Just tread with caution," Creed says, looking in the direction Astrid went.

"Are you telling me how to take care of my woman, Creed?"

He scowls at me and flips me off. "I'm saying this might be a game to you, pushing her to see how far you can go, but people have boundaries for a reason."

"It's just a game of paintball." Jagger sighs, but Creed shakes his head.

"To you and me, yeah. But to Astrid, it's something else entirely."

CHAPTER NINETEEN

Astrid

I get lost on my way to the garage, so I make my way outside. It's easier to remember where everything is from out here because that's where the bulk of my tour took place, especially with so many twists and turns in the building. It's a nightmare to navigate for someone as directionally challenged as me.

By the time I find the flipping place, Slade and Jagger are already waiting for me. My stomach cramps when I see them, waiting for them to pepper me with a million questions. Thankfully, they don't—at least not yet. I know they won't stay quiet forever, but I'll take the reprieve.

The garage is huge. When I look around, I can't help but feel like I'm in a car showroom or something. I know there are a few people that live here, but the ratio of cars to people seems excessive. Still, I can't deny how pretty some of them are.

I spot my baby and hurry over to it. "Hi, Lulu. I missed you." I lean my head against the door and sigh when I hear footsteps approach.

"You want to take your car?" Slade questions

"Really?" I ask, looking up at him.

"Sure. As long as I can drive."

"But she's my baby."

"And she'll still be your baby when you're sitting in the passenger seat."

I narrow my eyes at him. "Is this a penis thing?"

I ignore Jagger as he laughs behind me. Slade shrugs, looking unapologetic, as he pulls the keys from his pocket.

"I don't use my dick to drive, if that's what you're asking. Though it sure is long enough to reach the pedals," he jokes.

I shove him in the stomach and head around to the passenger side, knowing I won't win this battle. The last thing I want is for them to change their minds about letting me come.

I hesitate and look at Jagger. "You can sit in the front. There's more legroom."

"You sure?"

I nod and hold the door open for him. He smirks before opening the rear passenger door and motioning for me to climb in. I roll my eyes. Definitely a dick thing. I don't know what it is with opening doors and driving, but they act like they'll get their man cards removed if they don't abide by a certain set of rules. I climb inside and wait for him to close the door before he climbs into the passenger seat.

Slade gets in, well, sorta. "Jesus fuck, Astrid," he curses as he tries to squeeze himself in behind the steering wheel.

I giggle as he adjusts the seat before he turns to look at me. I can't help but smile at the scowl on his face. "What? You wanted to drive," I tell him sweetly, and Jagger chuckles as Slade shakes his head.

With a sigh, he makes sure I'm strapped in before he starts my car.

"You ready?"

"Yep." I nod before turning my attention out the window.

It feels weird leaving this place. I'm an odd mix of excited and anxious. I don't bother to make small talk. I just take in all the lush scenery. Some I recognize from when I got lost finding the place, but most of it looks like something out of a Hallmark movie.

After moving around a lot as a kid, mostly sticking to fancy places in big cities, this town looks like a place that time forgot. It's impossible not to feel nostalgic, even though it's reminiscent of an era way before my time.

I'm so lost in thought that I don't realize we've stopped until Jagger is pulling my door open and holding his hand out to me.

"Thanks. This town is so pretty. I didn't think places like this still existed outside of movies."

"I thought the same thing when I moved here."

"Where are you originally from?"

"All over, actually. My dad was in the army, so we moved around a lot. I've lived in more countries than most people twice my age. Then, when I was old enough, I enlisted myself."

"So, it's in your blood?"

"Yeah, I guess it was."

The moment feels less light-hearted than it did before, making me feel like I've done something wrong, but I don't know him well enough to know what to avoid.

"Something happened. Shit, I'm sorry. That was really insensitive of me. Please don't answer that."

He waves me off. "It's fine. I was a different man back then than I am now. I loved being a soldier. It was all I dreamed of. After my dad died, it became a way of staying connected to him. But I guess in a way, it was like meeting one of your idols and realizing they didn't quite live up to the hype."

I turn my attention from him to Slade, who rounds the back of the car to join us. Trying to give Jagger a break, I smile at Slade and question him instead, not realizing my question is like throwing a live grenade at him.

"What about you, Slade? Were you in the army too?"

His body goes rock solid. This is why I don't interact with people. I suck at it. I don't know what I've said, but I clearly should have kept my mouth shut.

"I was," he answers, but doesn't say anything else, so I drop it. Suddenly, a day out doesn't seem nearly as exciting as it once did.

"I'll be back. I need to grab something." Slade heads off without another word and doesn't look back. As the distance stretches between us, I can't help but remind myself that for all the ways we've gotten to know each other over the last few weeks, there is still an ocean full of secrets between us all. I'm not in a position to pass judgment.

Jagger breaks the silence. "Do you want to get something to eat?"

I feel like I have rocks in my stomach, so the last thing I want is food. But I nod anyway and let him take my hand so he can lead me to wherever it is he wants to take me. I feel on edge, the shine of the town not working its magic any longer. I wish we were back at the ranch, either in the bedroom away from prying eyes or lost in one of my games.

"He's not mad at you."

Jagger's voice jolts me out of my thoughts as he holds the door open to a mom-and-pop diner.

"I know," I tell him softly. He might be pissed that I asked, but Slade has to know I would never ask him something to hurt him on purpose.

"I figured his time in the army wasn't a good one. I should have kept my mouth shut. I'm sorry."

He nudges me into a booth near the window before sliding in beside me.

"It's not your fault. You didn't know it was a hot topic. We don't know each other well enough yet to know what to avoid." He sighs, echoing my thoughts.

"Is he going to be okay?"

"Yeah, he'll walk it off, and when he comes back, he'll be fine. It's been a rough few years for him. I... Fuck. It's not my story to tell, Astrid. I'm sorry. I know that's not what you want to hear."

I slide my hand over one of his and shake my head. "No, I understand. If or when he wants to tell me, I'll be here. He doesn't owe me an explanation, though. Neither of you do. I just feel bad for upsetting him."

"A bit like what we did earlier when we pushed about the paintballing?"

I lean back and look at him as a waitress approaches. We order coffee and pancakes—banana ones for Jagger and blueberry ones for me.

"I don't like guns. I can be around them. It's not the gun itself that's an issue, but the noise it makes when it's being fired."

He opens his mouth to ask more, but I shake my head.

"I'm not ready. If or when I am, I'll tell you, but trust is hard for me. These last few weeks, I've felt closer to both of you than I have to anyone else in a long, long time. If you knew me at all, you'd understand just how big a deal that is."

He flips his hand over and slides his fingers between mine. "Patience is not one of my virtues."

"Sucks to be you, then."

He chuckles and nudges my arm, the moment lightening as the waitress returns with our food.

Once she leaves, I drown my pancakes in syrup and take a bite. I might not have been hungry when I ordered, but as soon as the sweetness hits my tongue, I groan.

He grins. "That good, huh?"

"Oh, yeah." I nod and watch as he takes a bite of his food.

"I think I've ordered everything off this menu, and it's all good, but the pancakes are one of my favorites."

"I can see why. So, where do you need to go?"

"Post office. I've got a few packages to pick up, and I need to go to the hardware store. What about you? Is there anything you need while we're here?"

"Well, considering I don't even know what's here, I have no idea."

"Fair enough." He chuckles and leans back, pointing out the window. "You can see down most of Main Street from here, and honestly, what you see is about it. There's a drugstore, feed store, and hardware store at the far end. Opposite that is the post office, a hair salon, and a bookstore. Down the other way, there's a florist, grocery store, and gym. And on the very far side is a bar that has been there for six generations. There are some other shops in between, but I can't say I've paid much attention to them."

"I don't know, I think you did pretty well. Most men don't remember nearly that much, and especially not places like florists or bookstores. Actually, that's pretty fucking sexist now that I think about it. That's like saying a woman wouldn't remember the hardware store."

He laughs and finishes his pancakes in half the time it takes me to finish mine. He signals for the waitress just as the door opens and Slade walks in. He spots us and heads over, slipping into the seat opposite me. His eyes fix on mine, and the intensity in them makes it impossible to look away.

"I'm sorry."

He shakes his head. "Nope. It's not your fault. It's my issue, not yours. I'll work on my reaction."

I'm saved from replying by the arrival of the waitress. "Do you want to order anything?" she asks Slade.

"No, I'm good."

"Just the check, please," Jagger tells her. She nods and walks over to the counter.

"Are you sure you don't want anything?"

"I'm fine."

He's not, but again, I let it go. This biting-my-tongue thing is annoying as fuck. For as antisocial as I am, I still like to be in the know. But if I force the issue, they'll feel like they have the right to push the issue with me, and I just don't have the strength to dig through my baggage just yet.

"Well, I'm ready when you guys are. I just need to use the restroom."

Jagger slides out of the booth so I can get out, then stands to the side so I can move past him.

I ask at the counter where the restroom is, and the woman refilling the salt shakers points me in the right direction. I'm not a big fan of public restrooms, but this one is clean, and that's always a bonus. Still, I don't dawdle. I take care of business and wash my hands before pulling the door open.

Someone must really need to go because, as I walk out, I'm shouldered out of the way, catching only a glimpse of long sandy blonde hair before the door is slammed closed and locked behind me. She might be gone, but my skin still tingles where it came into contact with hers. Sometimes that's all it takes. Like a watercolor painting in all its hazy glory, a vision flickers behind my eyes as I hold the wall for support.

It's barely more than a snippet, as images flicker. No, not flicker. Flash. One, two, three. There's no sound, which is a blessing because it only takes me a second to realize the flashes are from a gun being fired in a dark room.

As suddenly as it started, it's gone.

And the world around me materializes—the lights of the diner, the noise of the kitchen staff clattering pots and pans, and the cook yelling out which orders are up. I can hear a child crying in the distance. Everything is so overwhelming that I'm tempted to curl up into a ball right here. But I don't. I take a deep breath and blow it out, then take another and another.

Once my heart has stopped racing, I straighten up, wipe my sweaty palms against the legs of my pants, and walk away. A sour sense of guilt threatens to make my stomach revolt, but I keep walking, putting one foot in front of the other, until I spot Slade and Jagger waiting for me next to the door.

"Are you okay? You look pale," Slade asks when I get closer, sliding his arm around my shoulder.

"I'm always pale," I remind him as I lean closer and breathe him in, using his scent to help ground me. The farther we get from the diner, the easier it is to breathe.

I don't look back. I don't think about the woman in the restroom because thinking about it makes me feel like a coward.

The thing is, I'm not. A coward, that is. I'm a realist. A vision is only good if I can get something from it. And in this instance, all I saw were three gunshots. I saw nothing else. I don't know a date or a time. It could happen in five days or five years. I can't change her fate, and with so little to go on, neither could she. That's if she believed me in the first place.

I've tried before—warning people. Sometimes I get full, detailed visions, and sometimes I get murkier ones that are hard to interpret, yet there is usually enough for me to get the gist. Sometimes, all I get is a snapshot like the one I just had. No sound, no color—just a single event that will have devastating consequences.

Warning that woman wouldn't help this time, though—not that it usually does—if there is one thing I know, something that is somehow worse than finding out you're going to be the victim of something horrific is to find out you're going to be the killer.

And that's what I took from that sliver of the future. It wasn't so much what I saw as what I could feel. One day, that woman is going to pull the trigger not once, not twice, but three times.

And her aim will be true.

By THE TIME we head back, I'm dead on my feet. I'm starting to realize how unfit I am. I mean, I've always been a curvy girl. I'm built for comfort, not speed, and given how inactive my job can be, I don't get nearly as much exercise as I should. However, at home, I do make more of an effort to walk along the beach and swim in the pool. Here, I've just been wallowing. And if I keep doing that, I'm going to end up looking like a beached whale.

"You with us?" Jagger asks me as we pull into the garage.

"Yeah, I was just thinking about how unfit I am," I admit with a sigh as I unclip my belt.

Jagger climbs out and grabs my door for me as Slade turns back to look at me.

"We have a gym here. You're more than welcome to use it."

I groan. "Whoa, horse. Let's not get carried away."

I climb out of the car, ignoring Slade's burst of laughter.

"Do you want to grab something to eat at the main house?" I can smell the aroma of something cooking as he asks.

"Honestly, I'm still full from earlier. What I could use is a nap."

"I could use a nap too. Want some company?" Slade asks, walking around the car to us as he pockets my keys.

"That depends if nap means nap or if you're talking in code."

He grins and grabs my hand. "I think you have a dirty mind, Miss Montgomery."

I roll my eyes at him and look at Jagger. "You want to come too?" I flush when I realize what that sounds like. He just chuckles before grabbing the bags from the back and handing me the one containing the book I bought from the awesome little bookstore.

"I'd love to, but I've gotta run these packages to Oz, and I need to see Hawk about something. Go nap. I'll catch up with you later."

He leans down and kisses my cheek before closing the truck and leaving me and Slade alone. Slade takes my bag from me and turns me so I'm pressed against the car as he leans over me. "I really am sorry about earlier."

I reach up and cup his jaw with my hand, feeling the spiky stubble against my palm. "You don't need to be sorry. You weren't a dick to me. You just needed time to regroup."

He stares down at me, and I can see him measuring his

words as he chooses what to say. What he does say shocks the absolute shit out of me.

"I enlisted when I was eighteen, right out of high school. I wasn't like Jagger, who dreamed of becoming a soldier. I never knew what I wanted out of life until a recruiter came to our school and talked about what life was like in the armed forces. His words just resonated with me. I signed up, much to my family's disappointment, and left for basic training a week after graduation."

"Your family didn't want you to be a soldier?" I ask gently, trying to be careful with my words.

"They wanted me to follow in my family's footsteps. My father is a lawyer. My brother was a lawyer, too, before he was killed in a car accident while I was deployed."

I stroke his arm in comfort, but I don't interrupt him.

"Even my sister became a lawyer, which was surprising because my dad is like his dad—old school, believing a woman's place is in the home. I think he only made the exception with Dawn because he needed someone to carry on the family business after Cliff died."

He stops talking and looks around. I follow his gaze and notice a camera on us.

"Come on." He tugs my hand and leads me out of the garage, around the back of the building, so we don't have to go inside.

Now that he's pointed out the first camera, I can't help but notice the others as we make our way back to the house.

"I always wondered how I got so close to the house if you guys were so strict about security. It's because you could see me on camera, right?"

"We had eyes on you the whole time," he confirms.

"What if I'd had a gun?" I keep my words light, but I still feel him tense. I don't want to push the issue, but it's something that bothered me from the start.

"I'm not asking that to be a dick. But having a vision of a woman, a woman who I now care about, being killed tends to make me nervous about things like that. Yes, you're all big and strong, and you subdued me within seconds, but what if I was prepared and came in guns blazing? I could have hurt someone or worse."

"We are really good at our jobs."

"I don't doubt that for a second. But unless you're all bullet-proof, I think there is always room to tweak things."

He sighs and nods, opening the door to the house and holding it wide for me to enter. I kick off my shoes near the door and walk over to the sofa before plunking myself down with a big, dramatic sigh.

"Have I told you lately how much I love your sofa?"

"No. Should I be jealous?" he asks, moving to sit next to me.

"If you're asking if I'd pick this sofa over you, then—" I pause and bite my lip, as if contemplating it.

He growls and grabs me, flipping me so I'm flat on my back, and he's leaning over me. "I guess I'll just have to remind you why you should always pick me."

He glides his lips over mine, teasing me with a soft kiss until I open for him, and he slips his tongue in to play with mine. I grip the back of his T-shirt, loving how his weight feels pressed down on me.

Before we can get too carried away, he pulls back until our lips are barely touching, his eyes finding mine.

"There's more."

"God, I hope so."

He chuckles, bracing himself on his forearms.

"Not that, though that will come soon. I mean, there is more to what I was telling you in the garage. I just don't want you to look at me differently."

"I'm the least judgmental person you'll ever meet, Slade. I've been on the receiving end of it too many times myself."

He nods almost absently before swallowing. "I told you I enlisted. What I found in the army was what I never knew was missing before. I made friends—good friends like Jagger. Found a purpose. I thought I'd be a career soldier for sure."

"What happened? What took the stars from your eyes and replaced them with shadows? Did you lose someone?"

"I lost myself."

He smooths my hair away from my face before kissing me gently again. Dropping his forehead to mine, he hesitates for a moment before continuing.

"There was a man—Major John Elks. I was never a fan of his. Everyone's a hard ass in the army—you've gotta have tough skin to survive—but Elks was a cruel motherfucker. I didn't come into contact with him much, but I heard the stories, you know? I'll admit, I didn't think much about the man at all. I was living my dream life. I had a job I loved, good friends, and women willing to drop their panties at the sight of my uniform. I should have paid more attention."

"What did he do?"

"He murdered his wife and framed me for it."

His words hit me like bullets, the shock of them leaving me speechless for a few minutes.

"He what?" I whisper, unable to process what he's saying.

"I went to the bar, picked up a woman who was just looking for one night. She was dressed for the occasion and wasn't wearing a wedding ring. I should have asked. But she probably wouldn't have told me the truth anyway."

"Let me guess. She was his wife?"

"Yeah. I'll spare you the details. We slept together, and then we went our separate ways. I didn't know anything was wrong until the MP came knocking the next day.

"He strangled her to death and blamed me for it."

"I don't understand. Him blaming you shouldn't matter. It should have been easy enough to clear your name. Witnesses you met in the bar or, I don't know, something."

"There were witnesses that saw us in the bar, but it just proved I was with her, not that I didn't kill her. When they questioned me, I denied knowing her because they framed the question in such a way that I had no idea what they were talking about."

My face must show my confusion.

"They asked me if I knew Major Elks' wife. I told them I'd never laid eyes on her before in my life. Of course, at that point, they already knew I had. They had the CCTV footage from the bar."

"Okay, but that wasn't your fault you didn't know her as the Major's wife. You weren't lying. But let's play devil's advocate here. Let's say you knowingly slept with his wife but lied about it because you knew it was wrong. That still does not make you a murderer."

"No, what it made me was a scapegoat. Elks found out his wife was having an affair with a soldier who was killed in action a month before I slept with her. The story goes that he felt he couldn't do anything about it because the man was dead, so he decided to forgive his wife. However, when he turned up at the bar that night to find her, and she was all over me, something in him snapped. He recognized me. So, he let her fuck me in their bed while he watched, and I had no fucking clue."

"Jesus, that's messed up."

"You have no idea."

He pulls back and sits up, running his fingers through his hair in agitation. Hating to see him looking like this, I crawl into his lap and wrap my arms around him, his arms automatically going around my waist.

"After I left, he waited until she fell asleep, then killed her."

"You left a lot of details out there. I have a stronger stomach than you might think."

"He raped her—brutally—before choking her to death. Then he pulled the condom I had used with her from the bathroom trash and emptied it inside her."

He swallows hard, squeezing me a little tighter.

"They found my skin under her nails where she had raked them down my arms and back, my DNA all over her sheets—" He shakes his head. "Trust me, they've convicted people with less."

"But you obviously know what the Major did, so it worked

out. Still, I'm so sorry you had to go through something like that."

He looks down at me, his eyes strained, as he tucks my hair behind my ears. "We found that out after the fact."

"After the fact? What are you saying?"

"I'm saying I served ten years of a life sentence before they realized they had the wrong guy."

CHAPTER TWENTY

Jagger

I lost track of time talking to the guys. E is like a dog with a bone right now, wading through all the shit Judge Jones had his hands in. I tried to help him but ended up getting in the way. I'm convinced the man is part machine.

When I walk back into the house, I'm surprised to find Slade and Astrid asleep on the sofa. I thought for sure napping was going to turn into fucking.

I stand there for a minute and just watch them. Astrid is tucked against Slade's chest, and the man himself has his arms wrapped around her like he's worried she might slip away. They look so peaceful that I leave them and head to the kitchen to make something for dinner, deciding on pasta with a spicy tomato sauce and a salad.

I chop the onion and the chili peppers, my eyes drifting to

Slade and Astrid often, a weird feeling running through me. I'm not saying I'm jealous because I don't hold any animosity toward either of them, but there is a part of me that feels left out.

Jesus, fuck. I sound like a baby.

Shaking it off, I go back to cooking, making an extra special effort to ignore them until I hear Astrid stirring. She gently pulls herself free from Slade's arms before leaning down and pressing a kiss against his forehead. The move surprises me. Slade had been a dick to her when she first arrived. I'm glad she managed to put that aside and offer him affection, something he doesn't get from anyone except Salem.

"Hey, are you hungry?" I ask her quietly when she gets closer.

Instead of answering, she walks around the counter and straight into my arms, pressing her face against my chest.

"What's wrong?"

"Slade told me what happened to him."

"Wait, he talked to you about it?"

She looks up at me and frowns. "Yeah. Why? Is he not supposed to?"

"No, it's not that. It's just that Slade is pretty private. He doesn't usually share with anyone."

"I think he was trying to explain why he reacted the way he did today in town."

I don't say anything for a minute, stunned that he opened up at all. I'm one of the few people who knows what happened because I've been there from the beginning.

"He told me how he was framed and sent to prison. He didn't get around to the part where he was exonerated, though."

"Honestly, the whole thing was a shit show. Here. Sit while I stir."

She sits on the stool closest to me as I toss the chopped ingredients into the pan and lower the heat.

"Slade always claimed that he was innocent, and I never doubted him for a second. I know him better than he knows himself, and he's just not capable of something like that."

"I didn't think for a second he was. But how did it get so far? Isn't the husband the first person the police look at?"

"To the outside world, they had the perfect marriage."

"But surely the truth would have come out during the trial?"

I scoff. "Like I said– shitshow. Elks told the court how much he loved her, how he would never hurt her, how they were trying for a baby. It was total bullshit mixed with fake tears. And the guy she was having an affair with before she hooked up with Slade was dead, so he couldn't testify," I tell her. "Add in that Elks was supposedly out of town when it happened, and Slade was found guilty. But there were a lot of inconsistencies in Elks' story that threw the timeline off completely."

"If there were inconsistencies, how—" I cut her off.

"It was easier that way. And don't forget, he was a major with more powerful friends and the money needed to grease the right pockets. What kills me is that anyone who knew Slade should have known how smart the man is. If he had killed her, he sure as fuck wouldn't have left his DNA all over the place."

I shake my head. "I've never felt so helpless in my life. Most of Slade's so-called friends abandoned him. His family disowned him. He was convicted in a court of public opinion way before he saw the inside of the courtroom."

"How did it all come out in the end?"

"Elks got drunk and tried strangling his new fiancée. She went to the police and pressed charges, and the media caught wind of it. After that, lots of shit came out.

"Unearthed security footage from the parking lot Slade passed through has him timestamped as being there at one. This place was ten minutes from the Elks' residence, but Slade was on foot that night because he'd been drinking, so it had taken him over an hour. That meant he left their place before midnight. Yet the coroner places the time of death between 12:30 and 1:30 a.m. A neighbor remembered seeing the lights on in the bedroom and a person moving around inside when he returned from his shift at the hospital at 1:15 a.m. But the neighbor was never questioned by the original investigating officers. He also remembered seeing Elks' car in the driveway, which should have been impossible."

"I can't even begin to process how this could happen."

"It's the military. Rank is everything. It was a fucking mess. And then, when the truth came out, they tried to bury it. But with social media being what it is, it was impossible once it had been exposed."

"Did the asshole get arrested?"

"He killed himself before he went to trial, confessing every-thing in a note."

"What a fucking coward!" she snaps, angry on Slade's behalf.

"Now you can see why he has such a hard time trusting people. The army turned their back on him, the legal system fucked him, his family washed their hands of him when he needed them the most—"

"He had you. Trust me, one true friend is better than a hundred fake ones."

"Truer words have never been spoken." Astrid jumps at the sound of Slade's voice, turning to look at him.

"Hey," she says quietly, looking worried.

"I'm not going to yell at you for talking to my best friend about it. It happened. You needed to know, but now it's over." He shrugs and presses a kiss on her shoulder before looking at me. He's not okay. One look, and I can see the truth.

"I got time for a shower before dinner?"

"Sure, man, go ahead."

He heads off without looking back, silence filling the room.

"He's not okay, is he?"

"Would you be?"

She looks from me to the hallway.

"Go. Dinner can wait."

She hesitates before sliding off her stool and making her way to the bedroom. I add the rest of the ingredients to the sauce, wondering if I've made a mistake telling her to go to Slade. The man can be unpredictable, especially while he's hurting.

Turning the stove off, I head to my room and find it empty. I look at Slade's door and see it slightly open, so I make my way over and pause before pushing into the room. I don't see them, but then I hear the shower. Walking to the bathroom, I stand in the doorway and watch as Slade picks Astrid up and presses her against the wall of the shower.

The rushing water drowns out most of their sounds, but I can just about make out her whimper. Her legs wrap around his hips as he adjusts himself before thrusting inside her. He holds still for a moment, giving her time to adjust. It also gives me time to pop open the fly of my jeans and ease my hard cock out. I stroke it up and down, my eyes never leaving the erotic scene playing out in front of me.

Again, I find myself on the outside looking in, but this time it doesn't bother me as much. Watching them together does something to me. I'm not even sure what it is. I've watched porn just as much as the next guy, and I've seen Slade fuck women before. But none of it affected me the way this does. And it's not even what they're doing. It's who they are and what they mean to me.

It's because they're mine, even if it's in completely different ways.

I keep stroking my dick, watching Astrid throw her head back as Slade sucks her neck, neither of them bothered by the water beating down on them. They are so lost in their own world, they're completely oblivious to me. I'm tempted to pull out my phone and start recording so I can show them later, but nothing can make me tear my eyes away from them right now.

The tattoos on Slade's back almost come alive with every thrust—the fairy and her demonic lover caught in a moment of weakness. I step closer, not wanting to disturb them but unable to stop myself from getting a better look. I squeeze my cock harder as I stroke, willing myself to hold on as long as they do.

When Slade roars, I know he's filling her with his cum. Flashes of Astrid in the future with a swollen belly rush through my brain, threatening to push me over the edge, when her eyes open and clash with mine. She comes with a whimper, gripping Slade tighter as her gaze keeps me captive.

And still, I keep stroking, locking my knees when my legs start to shake. Astrid taps Slade on the shoulder, and he turns and spots me. He lowers Astrid to the floor before whispering something in her ear. She nods, and he opens the shower door for her to step out.

Her body is slick with water, her skin flushed with heat, but her eyes are what have me sucking in a sharp breath. They mirror every filthy fantasy I have for us. She walks toward me, dropping to her knees before looking up at me again. I move my hand from my cock and into her hair, yanking her closer until she opens her mouth and takes me in.

I'm too far gone to be gentle, too close to the edge to hold back, but when her hands move around to grab my ass, I realize she's not looking for gentle at all. My grip tightens in her hair as I thrust deeper, holding still only for a moment to see if she can handle it.

When the little minx doesn't gag, I throw caution to the wind and start fucking her mouth with reckless abandon. Her nails dig into my ass, urging me on as Slade watches us with a hunger of his own. When she starts humming around me, I can't hold on any longer. I thrust in and hold her in place. She has no choice but to swallow my cum as it fires out of me. Like the good girl she is, she drinks it all down, licking her lips when I slip my cock free.

"You, Astrid Montgomery, are a dangerous woman."

CHAPTER TWENTY-ONE

Astrid

S itting on the back porch with a cup of coffee in my hand, I stare out at the mountains and wonder how anyone can wake up and see all this beauty and not be affected by it. There's a light mist making everything hazy, but the warm sun bathes the mountains in gold everywhere it touches.

"You look lost in thought." I jump when I hear Salem's voice and nearly drop my cup.

"Shit, I'm sorry," she apologizes, reaching for the cup.

"Don't worry about it. I was in my own little world and didn't hear you walk up. Are you looking for me or one of the guys?"

"You, actually. I feel like I haven't seen you at all lately."

"I know, and it's my fault. I've been busy with work. We're down to the last stages, which means there is a lot of back and forth between me and my team while we work out the bugs. E's been a godsend, though. If he didn't work for you guys, I'd be tempted to steal him away."

"Something tells me he wouldn't put up much of a fight."

I smile. But I've seen the way the guys are together. He likes me, but he'd give his life for them. That's a heck of a difference.

"So, did you need me for something specific, or is all the testosterone getting to you?"

She chuckles and sits down beside me. "Maybe a little of both. But mostly, I just want to talk to you."

I feel myself tense up on instinct, but when she reaches out and pats my leg, I relax a little.

"It's like a whole different world out here." She sighs, looking at the mountains I was just staring at.

"I know. And I say that having a pretty spectacular view of my own back home. But there is something about the mountains touching the sky that makes the world seem so much more infinite."

"I agree. It's scary and peaceful."

I nod and wait for her to ask what she came here for.

"I've never talked to anyone before who was like me, except for my mom and Penn, but it was different. My mom... Well, that's a long story. And Penn might be gifted like us, but he seemed somehow removed from the world. I was a little girl the first time I met him and found it hard to relate to a man in his twenties."

I nod. "Though I guess as similar as our circumstances were, they were also completely different."

When I don't continue, I can feel her shoulders drop. I

might feel bad for her if it wasn't me that she wanted answers from. It gets tiring after a while when people expect you to reveal all your dark secrets but refuse to spill their own.

"My gift runs in the female line of my family. I don't know what happened to my father. It was always just my mom and me until she got sick. We moved around a lot. As an adult, it's hard to hide my gift. But as a child who didn't understand that she was different, it was impossible."

I sip my coffee, knowing exactly how she feels. When I started getting visions as a child, I didn't have the capacity to understand them, so naturally, I told an adult. Nobody ever believed me, and the more I told the truth, the more I was persecuted for it. Eventually, I just stopped telling people. At least until I figured out what I was seeing wasn't just night-mares but premonitions.

"How did you meet Penn?"

She bites her lip. "We met in passing when I was seven or eight. But he seemed familiar to me, and I didn't understand why. My mom spoke to him like she'd known him for years, so maybe I'd met him and just didn't remember. Anyway, he was the only other person I met who was gifted. He made me feel a little less lonely and a lot less like a freak. He taught me things about my gift that I didn't know I could do."

She pauses, her hands squeezed into fists. And I get the feeling she just skated over something important. Not that I'm one to talk. But it does act as a gentle reminder that she doesn't truly trust me yet. I can't say it doesn't hurt, though. I know it makes me a hypocrite because I haven't told them everything there is to know about me. But how do you cut yourself open and reveal all your dirty secrets to people you can't trust?

"Anyway, we moved again, and I haven't seen him since. I was surprised when you said he sent you to find me. I thought he'd have forgotten about me over the years."

I look at her like she's nuts. "You can literally heal people. Trust me, that's not easy to forget."

"You don't know how much I wish that wasn't true," she whispers.

"Except I do." I slide my free hand over and grab hers in a silent moment of unity. No matter what happens in the future, here and now, we're the same.

"How about you? How did you meet Penn?"

I feel my stomach swirl as acid burns in my gut. She must sense my need to run because she holds my hand tighter. I take a deep breath and blow it out slowly before taking a chance and giving her a snippet of my past.

"He stopped me from shooting myself," I whisper, staring at those mountains, wishing I had half the strength that they do.

Her hand squeezes mine to the point of pain, but I don't pull away. It helps ground me, keeping me in the here and now instead of drowning in my memories. I turn to look at her and see tears in her eyes, but there's no pity, only understanding.

"All I see is pain and death." I never got to be a dreamer because all I saw were nightmares. "I wish, for once, I could get a glimpse of someone's happily ever after. But alas."

"You've never had a vision of something good happening?"

I shake my head. "No. Not once. I'm not a psychic, Salem. I'm a harbinger. I try to warn people." I snort out a laugh. "Well, you saw how well that worked out for me. And your guys had a better reaction than most."

"People are scared by what they don't understand."

"I know. Trust me. But what do I do with that? If I keep my mouth shut, people die. And if I speak up, people—" I shake my head, not voicing the shitty things people have done to me over the years. There are some things that are just mine.

"That day—the day Penn saved me—I was so mad at him. Taking my life wasn't something I just decided to do on a whim. I'd thought about it for a long, long time. I brought nothing but misery into people's lives. I'm the screech of tires on a wet road, the knock at the door at four a.m., and the last tortured breath leaving someone's lungs. Nobody wants to believe what I can see. But that doesn't stop them from avoiding me like the plague because wherever I go, death follows."

We're both quiet for a moment as I compose myself.

"I'd just had enough, and then bam, Penn. Looking back, I'm pretty sure he used his mojo on me, but some of the things he said made sense."

"Like what?"

"Like people could only hurt me if I let them. They only had power over me if I allowed it. Nobody owed me anything, so in the end, the question became less about other people and more about myself. Could I live with the decisions I had made? The answer to that was yes. My pain came from other people's actions, not my own, and by taking my life, I was giving them all the power. So I took it back. I stopped going out of my way to help people. If I had a vision and I thought I could make a difference in the outcome, I'd say something. But sometimes I know I'm not there to change the future—just witness it for some reason."

I think about the woman from the diner, knowing she falls into that category.

"I live a quiet life now, and I keep to myself. I never want to feel like I did that day again."

"And then Penn came back," she whispers.

I nod, looking at her. "I don't know how he found me. I was a different girl, living a different life. But he walked up to my door and knocked like he visited every day. He told me about you—about what you could do. He said—" I snap my mouth shut. I hadn't planned on telling her the next part. She looks at me warily, like I've wounded her, so I give in.

Fuck it. "He said there were others like me. Others like us out there. That I wasn't alone and that we were all struggling to find our way in a world that both revered and loathed us."

Her mouth drops open at that.

"You're surprised?"

"You weren't? I mean, I knew about my family and Penn, and then you came along, so I figure there might be a few others. But you're making it sound like there's a lot more than that."

"I don't know how many there are, but I doubt it's too many. Think about how hard it is to hide those parts of you. Now imagine if there were thousands of us living around the world with strange and often uncontrollable powers. It would get out eventually."

"Maybe it does? We all see these bizarre stories in the news that we write off as crazy. Maybe there's an element of truth in all of them."

"Maybe not all of them. I read about a woman giving birth to an octopus yesterday. There are some things I really need to remain fiction."

She giggles, breaking the tension.

"Anyway, as Penn was leaving, he grabbed my hand, and the vision of you flashed in my head."

She swallows before looking at me. "But how did you know it was me?"

"I didn't. Penn did. His gift somehow enabled him to see what I was seeing."

She frowns before shaking her head. "He's powerful. I knew that as a child, but that's not the nature of Penn's gift. Unless he has developed a new one over the years, then that's not something he can do."

"Well, he must have because he saw the same thing I did, which is why he told me I had to find you," I tell her, feeling somewhat defensive because I'm not lying.

"I'm not explaining this properly. I believe Penn saw what you did. I just don't think it was Penn's power that allowed you to share the vision. It was yours."

I shake my head right away. "I've never been able to share my visions with anyone before."

She looks away again, tense once more. "When I heal, I push energy into the person I'm helping. I have to be careful that I don't drain myself, though. If I give too much, then I don't have enough natural defenses left to heal myself. Penn showed me something else about my gift, something I knew nothing about.

He said there is a duality to all gifts. He was born with the ability to read other people's emotions, but he figured out how to manipulate them too."

"Motherfucker. I knew he mojoed me!"

She cracks a smile at that before continuing. "He taught me that I could do something similar. Instead of pushing energy into a person, I can draw it out."

She lets that hang in the air as I realize what she's saying. Her voice cracks as she continues, "I can draw someone's life force into me. It charges me up like a battery, and then I can pass that energy into someone else if I need to. It's not something I do lightly. It terrifies me, that feeling of being full of power. I can easily understand how corruptible it could be."

"I don't know you that well, Salem, but you're a good person. You radiate kindness. I don't think you need to worry about the power going to your head. But knowing from experience how people can be, I feel better knowing you have a way to protect yourself that others can't take away from you."

She slumps in relief. I guess she expected me to paint her out to be the monster she clearly believes herself to be.

"I hope you know I would never judge you for who you are or what you can do." She looks at me with hope in her eyes. "There are enough people out there willing and waiting to hate us for the things we can do. Don't be one of them too."

She nods.

"When Penn saw your vision, I think it was you pushing it on him, not him drawing it out."

"Like I said, it's never happened before," I remind her.

"But Penn is special. That might make him more open to it."

I suck in a breath. "You think I might be able to do it with other gifted people? Like you?"

She shrugs. "I don't know. It's just a theory, and not an easy one to test. You've touched me a few times now and haven't had a vision."

She's right. I have touched her, and I haven't seen anything.

"It's not unusual for me to go weeks, even months, without one. You have to remember that I only see horrible, mostly violent things. It's like my subconsciousness calls to all that negative energy somehow."

"As someone who relies on energy to heal, I get it more than you think."

I nod. "So if nobody here has any dark things due to happen to them, then I won't pick up anything. That being said, and it's really important I say this now, I don't see everything. Don't ever think you're safe just because I didn't give you a heads-up. I don't understand why I see some things and not others. I don't control them—they control me."

"I know it wasn't easy for you to come here and share what you saw. And I know we made it ten times harder, even if we did it with the best of intentions. I just want to say, whatever happens, thank you for trying."

I tense before looking into her eyes. "Nobody ever believes me. That's not me feeling sorry for myself. It's the truth. And if people don't believe me, they dismiss what I say until it's too late. I'm hoping that you'll have a little faith in me, enough to stay away from Christmas lights."

She offers me a smile, but it doesn't fill me with confidence.

"Well, Christmas is still four months away. So, I'm good for now. I'm sure nearer the time, Oz and Zig will lock me in the bedroom for my own safety." She chuckles, but her hand drops to her stomach. She strokes it lightly, reminding me that it's not just Salem's life at risk but her baby's too.

"Hopefully, I'll get another vision that will give us something more to go on before then. I mean, what's the point of having this gift if I can't change the things I see?"

She doesn't answer for a second before she swallows. "Sometimes it's not the event you need to navigate, but the aftermath."

Her words slice through me like a knife. I've lived through more aftermaths than any one person should have to. But staring into Salem's sad eyes, I know one thing. Losing her would change everything. And Oz and Zig would burn the world to ashes in retribution.

CHAPTER TWENTY-TWO

Slade

"You need to get out more, or at least take a fucking shower. You stink." I scowl at E as I hand him a plate with a sandwich on it.

"I'm so fucking close. I can feel it."

"E. Evander," I snap when he ignores me. Reluctantly, he turns and looks at me. "I know this is important to you. We all do. But we need you in fighting form. That means you need to look after yourself too. Eat this, take a shower, and take a nap. And so help me God, if you argue with me, I'll send Salem in next."

His eyes widen at my threat before he squeezes them closed and groans. "Fine," he concedes, opening his eyes. He takes a bite out of the sandwich and glares at me. "Happy?"

"Ecstatic."

I take a seat on the sofa and look up at the wall of screens in front of him. Staring at it for two minutes gives me a headache. Fuck knows how he can stare at it for hours.

"You need a break after this."

He shrugs but doesn't disagree, probably knowing he won't win in an argument right now.

"I'm close. Judge Jones was even dirtier than we suspected, and we already assumed he rolled in shit like the pig he is. Every trail I follow leads to another. By the time I'm done, this man will be lucky if he ever sees the outside of a prison cell again."

"That bad?" Ev doesn't shock easily, so when he looks at me with wide eyes and a jerky nod, I look at the screen again. "Any players involved we should be wary of?"

"Tons. But I'm working through which ones might pose a threat and which ones are most likely to just crawl under a rock once their puppet master's strings have been cut. This guy has lived and practiced all over the map, so I have thousands of pieces to try and fit together."

"Any chatter to suggest he's looking for the wife?"

"Ex-wife, and no. But that doesn't mean he isn't looking."

"You're going above and beyond. You always do in cases like these. But you can't save everyone, E." I stand up and walk over, giving his shoulder a squeeze. I know Evander's mom was the victim of domestic violence, so these cases always hit him the hardest.

"I can try. And sometimes, that's enough." He slides the plate onto his desk before he gets to his feet. "Thanks for the food. I'm going to take that shower now."

I back up so he can walk past me, cursing myself for saying anything. Everyone has their crosses to bear. This is E's. Why the fuck I think I have any say in how the man lives is beyond me. It's just that I know what it's like to hold everyone at arm's length, and sometimes I see echoes of that in E. And he's not the only one. Astrid is as prickly as a cactus, but it's easy to see, once she lets you close enough, that it's all a defense mechanism. She wants to be loved so badly. I see it in the way she watches Oz and Zig with Salem. But the fear of being hurt is like a hand fisted in the back of her shirt, tugging her back.

With a sigh, I leave the security room and jog downstairs to the main part of the house, finding a few of the guys lingering around the kitchen. When I look at my watch and see it's lunchtime, I get why.

"Hey, have you been to see Ev?" Crew asks, walking over to me with a beer in his hand.

"Yeah, I managed to get him to eat a sandwich and take a shower. He'll probably jump straight back to work afterward, but it's better than nothing."

"I'll make sure he comes down for dinner even if I have to carry him down here myself."

"Good luck with that."

"Good luck with what?" Wilder asks, walking into the kitchen with a bag of chips in his hand.

"E," I simply say.

He grunts in understanding. He looks around the kitchen and frowns. "Where's Salem? I swear she told me she was on her way over here to start lunch."

"When was that?"

He looks at his watch. "A couple of hours ago."

I turn to the living room, taking in Greg and Jagger, who are watching the football highlights on the TV. "Either of you seen Salem?"

Jagger looks over at me and nods. "She knocked on our door as I was leaving earlier and said she wanted to talk to Astrid about something. I thought she'd be back by now. Want me to go check on them?"

"No, I'll go. I'm surprised her men haven't gone looking for her," I joke, knowing that Oz and Zig are even more possessive now that Salem is pregnant.

"They're checking out the perimeter cameras. Apparently, two of them went down in the same area this morning." He must see me tense because he shakes his head. "Ev reported some kind of technical issue, but he doesn't think it's any cause for concern."

I don't mention how distracted he's been working on tracking down all of Judge Jones's dirty deeds. E's mind works differently than ours. He's like a computer himself, with fifty tabs open and multiple programs running in the background. I just nod and head out. I don't question the odd feeling in my gut. I can look into that later. Right now, I need to find the girls and make sure everything is okay.

When I get to the house, I shove the door open. Finding the kitchen and living room empty, the feeling in my gut tightens. I make my way to the bedrooms, but when I pass the side door, a shadow from outside catches my attention. I take a detour outside and find both women sitting on the porch.

They turn at my approach and smile. I don't know what my

face looks like because while Salem's smile remains firmly in place, Astrid's slips away.

"What's wrong?" Astrid asks, climbing to her feet, knocking over the cup that was on the porch beside her.

"Nothing. We didn't know where Salem was. She was supposed to be making lunch," I reply, the relief at finding both in one piece making my words come out sharper than they need to.

Astrid's shoulders slump as Salem jumps to her feet. "Oh shoot. We lost track of time chatting. I forgot what I was supposed to be doing."

"That would explain why the men are wandering around the main house like starving zombies. It's like they've forgotten how to fend for themselves now that you've spoiled them."

Salem laughs before turning back to Astrid. "Thanks for the talk. I didn't know how much I needed to get everything off my chest until today."

Astrid offers her a soft smile and a nod before Salem heads down the few steps.

"I'll walk you over," I tell Salem, but my eyes are on Astrid as she wraps her arms around herself in a defensive posture.

I frown, not knowing why she's holding herself back from me and finding I don't like it one little bit.

"It's fine, Slade. I'm pretty sure I remember the way." Salem laughs, and I pull my eyes from Astrid and turn to Salem.

"I'd feel better knowing I delivered you safely."

"Lord, spare me from overprotective males. Fine, better get a move on before the boys revolt." She looks over at Astrid, taking her in, before her eyes flick to me and back to Astrid.

"I'll make you up a plate and put it in the fridge for when you want it, Astrid."

"Thank you," she whispers before I jog down the steps to join Salem. The sooner I can drop her off with the others, the sooner I can come back and find out what's bothering Astrid.

I hold my elbow out for Salem to slip her arm into before walking her back to the main house. "Everything okay with you guys?"

She looks up at me and smiles that secret smile of hers. "Why wouldn't it be?"

I make a face that lets her know I think she's full of shit.

She laughs and shakes her head, the tendrils of her light brown hair blowing across her face. "It's nice, you know, having someone to talk to about things."

"You have a house full of people up there who would hang off every word you say."

She stops, making me stop with her. "You don't want me talking to Astrid?"

"Don't be stupid. I just meant that you always have someone ready to listen to you. None of us would ever judge you. You have to know that by now."

"I do. Of course, I do. I love all you guys because of it. But it's not the same as talking to someone who has lived it. It's a bit like you listening to me whine about wearing high-heeled shoes. You might sympathize, but you've never worn the devil's version of a torture device, so you don't really get it."

I can't help but chuckle at her analogy. "Point taken."

We walk in silence for a little while before I broach a

subject, I'm unsure I should. "Do you find it odd that Astrid hasn't had another vision?"

She shrugs. "I don't have any idea how Astrid's visions work beyond what she said. And before you ask, if you want more information, talk to her. I don't want her to think that the talk we had this morning was a fact-finding mission. That's not fair to either of us, and it will cheapen what I hope will become a close friendship."

I hold up my free hand in mock surrender. "Calm down, mama bear. I was just asking. You like her, though, don't you?"

"Of course, I like her. It's hard not to." She pauses for a minute before continuing. "She's strong. You have to be to live with what she has and still be standing. But there is something so innately fragile about her too. Like her strength is steel shutters locking the world away from the soft-hearted parts of her. I haven't had an easy life, but Astrid has scars so deep they make mine look like paper cuts."

"She could just be showing you what she wants you to see."

"I guess. But then she could say the same about us, huh? After all, you take her to bed every night and hold her in your arms, but right here and now, you are asking me about the woman's character. Sounds to me like you should be careful about throwing stones, Slade. One might bounce back and smack you in the face."

She doesn't look at me as she walks off, heading up the ramp to the main part of the house. I hear the cheers as the door opens. I stand there and wait until the door closes behind her before making my way back home.

I mull over Salem's words and sigh, feeling like a dick. She's right, though she was nicer about telling me I'm a dick than I would have been had the roles been reversed. I need to be able to trust what I see instead of always looking for some hidden backstory that might come along and throw a wrench in the works.

I make my way around the back of the house, but Astrid isn't on the porch anymore. I open the door and slip inside. Standing still, I listen for movement when I hear sniffling coming from Jagger's bedroom. I walk toward it quietly and stand in the doorway, taking in Astrid sitting on the bed with her bare feet tucked up underneath her as she gazes out the window.

Sensing my arrival, she looks my way, swiping a tear that runs down her cheek. A slash of pain stabs my chest as I make my way toward her. Part of me expects her to retreat, but when I sit beside her, she leans into me and lets out a soft sigh when I wrap my arm around her. We sit in silence, the sound of our hearts beating in tandem the only noise in the room.

Her soft voice breaks the silence. "When I was four years old, I was kidnapped by a man who blackmailed my father."

Her words suck all the oxygen out of the room. I want to fire a million questions at her, but Astrid is such a closed book, I don't want to risk ruffling her pages.

"He had me for three days. I don't really remember it. I vaguely recall being scared and confused, but that's about it."

"They catch the fucker?" My voice sounds thick and choppy, like I've gargled with glass.

She shrugs. "Nobody spoke about it afterward. Everyone forgot it happened and moved on with their lives."

"That's fucked up."

"I was so young. I'm not sure my brain could process it. Not that time anyway."

I freeze at her words before pulling her until she is sitting on my lap. I cup her jaw and tip her head back so she has no choice but to look at me.

"What do you mean, *that time?*"

"I was taken again when I was seven. That time by a group. They were a little more organized. They had me for twenty-four hours. All of which I spent locked in a dog cage."

"Did they hurt you?" I ask, afraid of the answer.

"They were a little rough with me, but they left me alone once they had me. Their only interest was money. Once they were paid, they dropped me off at a park."

I shake my head in shock. Getting kidnapped once is a horrific ordeal for a kid, but getting taken twice is insane.

"Did your parents get you counseling?"

She huffs out a laugh. "Of course. Therapy is socially accept-able among the wealthy. Broken, traumatized little girls, not so much.

"When I was taken at fourteen, things were a little different."

I stare into her eyes, unable to process the words she's saying.

"They wanted money too. It was always about the fucking money. But I wasn't a little girl anymore. My body had changed —developed—and money wasn't the only thing on their mind."

"Astrid, no," I whisper, my hands sliding to her hips, holding her in place.

"One of the men grabbed my arm—his bare skin touched

mine, and I got a vision. I saw him hurting and killing a woman, and I knew that's what would happen to me too. The only thing keeping me safe was the knowledge that they might have to provide proof of life.

"The leader… he handcuffed me to a chair and left me there. My arms were restrained behind my back and through the wood, making it impossible for me to get them free. Still, it didn't stop me from trying."

She lifts her wrist and rubs it absently. I take her hand in mine and gaze down at her wrist and notice, for the first time, silvery, faded scars.

"I didn't stop trying, not when the screaming started and not when I felt my skin split open and blood run down my arms. I could hear my vision playing out in the room next door, and not even the pain from my torn skin could distract me from the horror that was happening to her or from the knowledge of what was waiting for me."

She takes a shuddering breath as I wrap my arms around her and pull her against me, holding her tightly as my heart gallops in my chest. "Shh… You can stop now. You don't have to tell me anymore."

She continues as if she didn't hear me. "When he came for me, I switched a part of my brain off, taking myself somewhere very far away. I could be there when he did those things to me. I was so lost in my mind that I didn't realize there was a rescue team there. They shot him and dragged him away. I was in someone's arms and on a helicopter when my brain finally registered that I was free."

She lifts her head from my chest, a few more tears slipping

free. "He never got the chance to do what he wanted to me. That woman's screams are just some of many that haunt my dreams. Her torment gave the team time to find me. Her death kept me alive. It was a lot for me to process, especially when, a few months later, I found out that my father refused to pay the ransom. He said that people thought he was soft. Because he had paid the first two times, people thought he was an easy target. He decided to *take a stance and not reason with terrorists*," she mocks, the anger and pain clear in her voice. "And he came to that decision while his daughter was in the hands of a psycho. The team that rescued me came for the woman who died. Her husband hired them to bring his wife home, and instead, they found me."

"I don't even know what to say, Astrid. None of that should have happened to you. Jesus, baby, you are so fucking strong." I soothe my hand up and down her spine, feeling her shiver under my touch. "If I ever meet your parents—" I shake my head, biting my lip at the last minute. It doesn't matter what I think. They are still Astrid's parents.

"I'm telling you this because when you found me and Salem together, you looked at me as if you had expected me to hurt her."

"No. Astrid—" She places her fingers over my lips.

"Your reaction to seeing me was different than your reaction to seeing Salem. I know I have my own issues to deal with, but you felt cold, and I had to fight back an overwhelming urge to run. I realized then that I hadn't told you much about me. How can you build trust with someone when you don't know anything about them, right? And after you opened up to me about prison and stuff, I wanted to be brave and let you in a little." Her voice cracks at the end, so I pull her close and press a soft kiss to her lips.

"Thank you for trusting me."

She smiles, small but true. My thumb smooths over the scars on her wrists, my eyes darting down to them before drifting up to her face. "That's why you don't like being restrained. It triggers the memory." Guilt weighs me down. I'm an utter bastard.

She nods absently. "I'm good most of the time, but handcuffs take me back there and to that feeling of helplessness."

I roll her until she's beneath me and press my body against hers, smoothing my hand over her hair. "I have an idea. It will involve trust."

She looks at me warily. "Okay."

I climb off her and disappear into my bedroom. I open my nightstand drawer and rummage around until I find what I'm looking for. I grab them and head back to Astrid, finding her exactly where I left her.

Holding up my hand, I let her see what I have. Her breathing falters for a second, her face paling as she takes in the handcuffs. Raising my other hand, I show her the key. Walking slowly to the bed, I tug open the drawer and place the key inside before closing it.

"I want to cuff one of your wrists to the bed. I'll leave the other one free. I don't want you incapacitated. I want you to know you can reach for that key any time you want to."

"If I can reach the key, why bother locking me up at all?"

"One, because I want you to be able to work through your fear. Two, because I want you to enjoy the experience."

"Enjoy the experience?" Her eyes widen at that. She looks from the cuffs to the door to the nightstand. "And you won't stop me if I want to take them off?"

"Nope. I'll sit back and hope you'll give me the opportunity to work on it with you again someday."

She blows out a shaky breath before nodding slowly. "Okay, Slade. I trust you."

Those three words hit me harder than any *I love you* ever could. This woman has love to give in spades, but trust she guards like a dragon watches over its treasure. It's precious, and I vow in this moment to make sure she has no regrets.

"Good girl. Now stand up and strip for me. I want you completely naked and at my mercy." I give her a devious smile, feeling her nerves snap tight. But my brave girl only hesitates for a second before climbing from the bed and doing as I command.

I watch her remove her T-shirt first, followed by her bra, her large breasts begging to be sucked now that they are free. Her eyes latch onto mine as she slides down her shorts and underwear, letting gravity do the rest for her. She steps out of the clothes at her feet, standing before me like a fucking goddess.

"Lay down on the bed," I order, my voice thick with arousal.

My dick is hard enough to pound nails at this point, but I don't undress. If I get my dick out, I'll end up fucking her into the wall. And while that sounds like fucking heaven, that's not what she needs from me right now.

She lies in the center of the bed, sucking in a breath when I lean over her and suck one of her rosy nipples into my mouth.

"Hands on the headboard, princess."

She reaches up and grasps the headboard with both hands, thrusting her chest out farther in a silent invitation. I keep my eyes on hers as I reach up and clasp the metal handcuffs around the bedframe before easing one around her wrist. As soon as I click it into place, her breathing turns ragged.

"Keep your eyes on me, Astrid. Nothing is going to happen that you don't want to." She nods rapidly, but her breathing is still too fast.

I slide down her body and spread her legs wide, looking up at her from between her thighs. "You're doing so good. How about a reward?"

Before she can reply, I lean down and close my mouth over her clit before sucking. She gasps and bucks her hips. I hold her still as I feast on her, never slowing down, not wanting her mind to wander to that dark place. I circle her clit with my fingers before flicking it with the flat of my tongue.

She jerks her arms, the clank of metal against metal yanking her out of her lust-fueled state for a minute. Not giving her fear enough time to take over, I glide two fingers between the lips of her sex, teasing her. Once my fingers are coated with her arousal, I thrust them inside her, curling them to hit that spot inside her she likes so much.

She murmurs my name, her focus returning to me as her free hand reaches down to grasp my hair. I should reprimand her for letting go, but the bite of pain as she tugs hard on the strands almost has me coming in my pants.

I pound my hard cock against the bed, seeking the bliss of release, much like Astrid is as she grinds her hips against my mouth. I slide my fingers in and out of her slickness as I suck on her clit, feeling her tighten around me. I lap, suck, and lick her pussy like a dying man seeking the elixir of life.

She cries out my name, tearing at my hair as she holds me in place. I can feel how close she is, so when I slip my fingers free and she curses me, I grin against her. Her curses turn to moans when I start fucking her with my tongue, my fingers now stroking her clit.

"Such a good girl, Astrid. Do you want more, pet? Or do you want me to stop?"

"Stop, and I'll kill you," she snarls, making me chuckle.

Without warning, I thrust three fingers inside her and nip her clit lightly with my teeth, the shock setting her off like a firework on the Fourth of July. She screams, and her legs lock around me, holding me in place as I swallow down her orgasm.

I soften my touch, my tongue licking gently over her sensitive skin as I help her through the aftershocks. I lift my head and grin at her. "How was that?"

"You missed your calling as a therapist. I think you just cured me."

"Really?" I laugh, loving the lightness dancing in her eyes.

"I'm not sure. Maybe we should do that again, just in case."

This woman has no idea what she's doing to me. For now, it might be best to keep it that way. It wouldn't take much for her to wrap me around her finger, and nothing good ever came from letting someone else have power over you.

CHAPTER TWENTY-THREE

Jagger

I'm surprised to find Slade alone on the sofa when I get back. He looks up at me as I enter and takes a sip of his beer.

"Where's Astrid?"

"She's taking a nap."

"She seems to need a lot of naps lately."

He smirks, but it quickly fades away. He places the bottle of beer on the table and leans forward. "She told me a little bit about her past."

I walk over to the sofa and sit on the arm, facing him. "What did she say?"

He looks down at his beer, as if deciding whether he wants to spill her secrets. A tendril of jealousy weaves through me at the knowledge of how close they are getting. Not gonna lie, it sucks ass standing on the sidelines, even if I'm the one who's holding back. I know Slade needs her more than me, more than he knows. I just didn't realize how it would make me feel.

"She was kidnapped."

His words snap me out of my thoughts, my mouth dropping open, not expecting that at all. "What the fuck? Are you serious?"

He nods, his hands tightening into fists. "The kicker, though, is she wasn't just kidnapped once, but three times." He frowns before looking toward the bedrooms. "Or three times that she told me about. I want to believe that's it, but... Fuck!"

"How is she not a basket case?"

He shakes his head and shrugs. "I don't know, man. Especially knowing a little of what she went through."

My blood turns to ice. "Explain!" I bark.

He blows out a breath, running his hands through his hair in frustration. "The last one was the worst, though she was young enough the first two times that she doesn't remember much. You know her father refused to pay the ransom the last time? She's only here because someone else was taken by the same guy, and the rescue team sent to retrieve her took Astrid with them when they found their target dead."

"She died? Jesus fuck. Did Astrid see this? How old was she?"

"She was fourteen. She didn't see it, but it happened next door, so she heard it just like, like—" His eyes widen, and he curses. "Shit, no, she did see it. She had a vision. So even though she didn't watch the act itself, she didn't need to. She'd already witnessed it. So, when the screaming started, she knew exactly what was happening, and there was nothing she could do to stop it."

I think about how we kept her locked up here when she first arrived and how she tried to make a run for it. How her reactions were both fearful and resilient. At the time, I was confused. But now her actions make sense.

I rub my eyes, feeling tired all of a sudden. "We need to let the others know about this."

"Why? It doesn't change her reasons for being here," he tells me with a sigh.

"It does, doesn't it? It has to."

He opens his mouth but closes it again. We sit in silence, staring at each other, both of us thinking about Astrid and what this means.

"She told me in confidence. I know we need to tell the others, but I can't help but feel like shit for sharing what isn't mine to share. She trusted me."

Again, I feel that slash of jealousy because he's right, especially knowing all this. Gaining Astrid's trust must feel a lot like winning the lottery.

"We still have to tell them," I remind him quietly. "They were upfront about Salem."

"Yeah, but she was on board with that."

He looks toward the bedroom again before cursing and climbing to his feet.

"We can wake her if you want and explain."

He shakes his head and runs his fingers through his hair again, making it stick up on end. "If she says no, I'll have to break her trust and do it anyway. This way, at least, I can claim ignorance."

"It's a fine line, Slade."

"What choice do I have? You said it yourself," he snaps back, moving to the chair and grabbing his jacket from the back of it. And now I feel like shit.

"You want me to come with you?"

He thinks it over for a second. "No, stay with her. I'll text you if I need you."

"Alright. Look, I know you feel like crap right now, but it's for the best. We can sit down with her and explain. She might not like it, but she'll understand."

"Yeah, sure she will," he murmurs before heading out and closing the door behind him without a backward glance.

I wander over to the window and stare outside, contemplating where to go from here. I feel caught in limbo. I've been waiting for Slade to catch feelings for Astrid, and now that it's clear he has, I'm wondering where I fit in. It's not her body I'm worried about. I know he seems happy to share that with me. But what about her heart and all the other things that make Astrid who she is?

The little peek she gave him about her life before makes me wonder if she is separating us into two sides. Does she feel the same way for me that she does for Slade? Or am I just the bonus she gets for fucking Slade?

I grab Slade's beer from the coffee table and down it. She hasn't been standoffish with me—at least not since the beginning. I've never felt like she wants me to fuck off when Slade is around, either. But not once has she pushed for more or opened up to me like she did with Slade. Is she keeping her distance because she doesn't want me like that, or has she picked up on the fact that I've been holding back?

"What a clusterfuck," I grumble, rubbing my hand down my face, knowing I created this damn mess myself. If I keep one foot out of this relationship, can I complain that she's holding back too?

I take the empty beer bottle and toss it in the trash before making my way to the bedroom. I stand in the doorway and watch her sleep. She's tucked into a ball, almost protecting herself, something I note she doesn't do when she sleeps beside me and Slade.

Testing that theory, I slip off my T-shirt, wanting to feel her skin against mine. I climb onto the bed beside her and maneuver her so I can slide my arm underneath her. As soon as I do, she rolls into me, her hand sliding over my chest as she lifts her head and opens her eyes a little.

"Jagger?"

"Shh, I just want to hold you for a little while. Go back to sleep."

She doesn't argue with me. She lays her head on my chest, her white hair fanning out over my skin as she lets out a sigh of contentment. If her actions are anything to go by, the problem is me. When she's not awake and sensing my distance, she doesn't hold back. She's open to me without feeling the need to protect herself. I need to give her a reason to take the leap and give me a chance.

I need her to know I won't let her fall in vain.

When I was fifteen, my father died. I stepped into his role as family protector and provider for my mom and two sisters. We lived in a trailer park, and money was always tight until I enlisted and could send more home to them. It's been ingrained in me to put others before myself. But since Astrid came along, I find myself wanting to be more and more selfish.

I must drift off because the sound of my phone chiming with a message, followed by another one right on its heels, has me opening my eyes. Looking outside, I see it's still light, so I couldn't have been sleeping for long. I turn to the clock, but it flashes. I guess the power must have gone out at some point.

I ease out from under Astrid, who is still dead to the world, and climb off the bed, grabbing my T-shirt on the way out and putting it on. I pull out my phone from my pocket as I walk down the hall, checking the time. It's only three p.m.? Fuck, it feels later than that. I'm not usually one for napping, so I guess that's thrown me off. Though, I don't regret the hour spent alone lying with Astrid in my arms.

I see two messages from Slade and tap on his name.

Come over.

Leave Astrid there.

I frown as I read the second one, glad she isn't awake so I don't have to make an excuse. I slip my boots on and lace them up before opening the door and closing it quietly behind me. It's warm outside but overcast, making me wonder if we might get some rain later.

I'm so lost in my own world that when I open the door to the main house, I don't pick up on the atmosphere right away. Not until I realize it's completely silent and all eyes are on me.

"I take it Slade filled you in. It's messed up, I know."

I move to the table where the others are sitting. All except E, who is standing at the island looking a little pale, and Salem, who is nowhere to be seen.

"She's napping right now, thank God," Zig answers, reading my unasked question.

"Did Astrid say anything to you since I've been gone?" Slade questions.

"No, she's still asleep. Why?"

Slade looks at me with an expression I've seen too many times before. Pure lethal rage.

"Who the fuck pissed you off?"

Slade drops the bomb. "Ev found a link between Judge Jones and Astrid." It's the last thing I expected him to say, and it takes a moment for me to realize the implication.

"What the fuck?" I seem to be saying that a lot today. I look over at Ev as he grips the edge of the island so hard I'm worried he'll crack it. "Ev?"

"I don't have all the details yet, so I really do think we all need to keep our shit together until I do."

"Fuck that, Ev. I know you have some kind of hero worship going on with the woman, but she's a fucking liar and a killer. I don't want her anywhere near my woman and kid," Oz snarls. When nobody disagrees with him, I stalk toward Ev, fisting the front of his T-shirt. "Tell me what the hell is going on. I've just held that woman in my arms for the last hour, and now you're telling me that she's the enemy?"

"I never said that. I said—" I shake him, but he yanks himself free. "I stopped working on Astrid's file while I was wading through Jones's shit. That didn't mean I wasn't running it in the background. I just wasn't actively pursuing anything because I thought we had all been won over by her."

"Speak for yourself," one of the guys grunts, but I don't turn around to see who.

"Anyway, a name popped up when I was going through Jones's old cases. Six years ago, he was working as a DA. He, as well as a couple of colleagues, from what I've found so far, were paid to hush things up."

"Hush things up? What things?"

"There was a school shooting. It didn't receive nearly as much coverage as other shootings because the students come from some of the richest motherfuckers in the country."

"What does that have to do with Astrid?"

"With Astrid Montgomery? Nothing. With Astrid Oakes, everything. Because she was one of the perpetrators arrested."

I draw in a ragged breath that burns my lungs. "No. I don't believe it."

"It seems whoever paid Judge Jones off managed to keep her name out of most of it. And the things they couldn't erase, they had buried. That's why I'm asking for more time before you all tar and feather her."

I shake my head. I don't buy it. None of it makes sense. I turn to look at Slade, who is staring at me like he wants to smash everything in the room. "You can't believe this."

"She has scars on her wrists from a set of handcuffs." He huffs out a laugh and stands up, pacing back and forth. "I have to say, the kidnap story was a nice touch. It sure did tug at my heartstrings. I guess she knew I wouldn't be as sympathetic if I knew the cuff marks were from resisting arrest."

"She told Salem that she met Penn Travis the first time when he stopped her from shooting herself. Salem saw it in a different context, and I did too, at first," Zig cuts in. "But after finding out about this, I've gotta question if Astrid was actually the bad guy looking for a way out. We've seen how the perpetrators tend to take themselves out at the end of their sprees, too fucking cowardly to face what they've done."

"And why does this Penn guy keep showing up at fucked up times?" Oz snarls. "If he was responsible for blowing up the clinic, we know he has no morals at all. He didn't care about the staff or patients there, so I sure as hell doubt he'd care about a bunch of high schoolers. The only people he seems interested in are Salem and Astrid, so it's not hard for me to believe he'd step in that day before she could turn the gun on herself. Hell, he probably had a hand in the carnage himself."

I stare at the tiled floor in shock. None of this seems real. "Why come here then?"

I stare at Oz and Zig.

"You don't think she came here to warn Salem, do you?"

Oz shakes his head. "I think she came here to take her. She's just waiting for us to let our guards down. And we nearly did, dammit."

"When I couldn't find Salem earlier, I had this feeling... Maybe deep down, I knew something was off. Fuck!" Slade shoves his hands in his hair and pulls it.

"So, what now?"

"Ev needs to finish digging. We need all the evidence we can get on this. We also need to find this fucking Penn guy. I have a feeling he's closer than we think," Zig answers.

"Anyone else find it odd that she hasn't had a single vision since she's been here?" Crew asks, crossing his arms.

Wilder grunts, leaning forward. "If she was lying about them, wouldn't she at least have faked a couple to give herself more credibility?"

"The more she lies, the deeper the hole she digs for herself. Pretending she's having a vision could just as easily blow her story to pieces as verify it," Hawk points out.

Greg, who up to this point has been quiet, looks around the table with a scowl before standing up and knocking the chair backward.

"What?" Oz growls at him. "If you have something to say, then fucking say it already."

"Why? You've already made up your mind. I need to take a walk before I say something I can't take back. You might want to consider it yourself."

He storms out toward the garage, slamming the door behind him.

"He's right. We need to keep our mouths shut until I have more to go on. I'm not comfortable rolling with this without all the facts." Evander straightens up, making his way around the counter.

"Tell me she didn't do this, Ev. That's all I need. None of the rest matters." Not to me, anyway. Whether she came here to do as she said or came for a more sinister reason, she hasn't done anything yet that I can't stop. But if she was responsible for the mass killing of kids, I'm done. There is no coming back from that.

"I can't. All I know so far is that she was arrested for the murder of nine classmates and three teachers. Charges were pressed and then mysteriously dropped before her name was scrubbed from the files altogether. If it wasn't for Jones's files, I wouldn't have found that much. I need more time," he urges. When nobody says anything else, he curses and walks back upstairs to his room. I'm sure he'll keep digging until he uncovers every secret Astrid thought she had buried.

The need to hit something—to fucking rage—eats at me. I glance over at Slade and see the same anger reflected back at me. We trusted her, despite all the reasons we shouldn't. Shame on fucking us.

"Are we supposed to play nice or lock her up until Ev's done?" Creed questions.

"I don't trust myself to be around her right now. Not without lashing out," I admit.

All eyes move to Slade, but he shakes his head. "I don't want to even fucking look at Astrid right now. If I never see that bitch again, it will be too soon," he snaps.

The sound of a whimper has all our heads whipping around toward the backdoor, where Astrid stands, staring at us all in horror.

CHAPTER TWENTY-FOUR

Astrid

I feel myself shut down, as if a wall of ice encases my heart, locking it away from everyone. I can hear them talking, but I can't focus on their words. What's the point? Nothing I say now will matter. Everything I thought I knew—thought I felt— has been ground into dust. Why do I keep doing this—putting myself out there, hoping for a different outcome—when nothing ever changes?

"Lock her in her room until E is done," an angry voice snaps.

The roaring in my ears makes it impossible for me to tell who spoke before a hand wraps around my arm and drags me away. I stumble, barely able to see through my tears. I don't bother to hide them. I let them flow, so when these assholes look back and realize what they've done, they'll remember this moment. When they dream of me, they won't see the smiles I bestowed on them over the last few weeks. They'll recall this moment when it all fell apart. They'll remember the pain and anguish in my eyes that they put there as they stomped all over the heart they promised to be gentle with.

I hope it fucking haunts them.

Jagger doesn't say anything to me as he guides me back to the house and takes me to his room, shoving me down to sit on the bed. He takes the handcuffs from the nightstand drawer and hesitates for a second before snapping one cuff around my wrist. He tightens it, but not so much that it hurts, before attaching the other to the bed.

I don't give him the satisfaction of a reaction, even though any trust Slade had infused into me has withered to dust. My lack of flinching must make him think my fear of handcuffs was a lie, too, because his expression turns thunderous.

"I don't know you at all, do I?" he growls at me.

I look up at him, and when he sees my hollow expression, he's the one who flinches. He looks unsure for a moment, but then his phone beeps, and the moment is broken.

He pulls his cell phone out and reads the text, his jaw clenching at what he finds. "I'll be back."

Good for him. I just don't care.

He doesn't wait for a response. He leaves me and heads back to the others, who remained seated around that table like kings, judging my worth and finding me lacking.

I look around the room that's been my home for the last few weeks, and a bubble of laughter escapes me, hurting my ears with how jagged it sounds. I remember how hopeless I felt the first time they locked me in here, but that's nothing compared to what I'm feeling right now. Looking down at my chest, I expect to see slivers of glass sticking out of me. That would at least explain the pain—making each breath feel like I'm being stabbed over and over.

After a few minutes, when I'm sure I'm alone, I turn to the nightstand drawer and use my free hand to open it. I rummage around until I find the key to the cuffs and snort at the irony. Jagger wasn't here when Slade cuffed me. He doesn't know that Slade put the key in the drawer to keep my panic at bay. I never needed it because I gave him all my trust—trust I'm now taking back.

I twist the key in the lock and watch as the cuff falls from my wrist, leaving the other attached to the bed, before walking over to the closet. Grabbing my bags that I never unpacked, I shove the few things I have scattered around inside my tote, including my laptop and toss it over my shoulder, then pull the handle up on my suitcase. They never asked me to stay, I realize now. They never told me to hang up my clothes or offered me a drawer or two of my own. I was always just a warm body to pass the time with while they decided whether I was lying. If I were anything more to them, they'd know all this is bullshit.

Learning from the last time I tried to escape, I head straight for the front door. Jagger flew out of here so fast that he wouldn't have bothered rearming the place. They rarely do now that they trust me. I huff. Trust. Right. It was just a fucking illusion.

Creeping along the side of the building, I scan where I remember the cameras are and wait for them to rotate before running to the next spot. It takes me longer than if I ran straight for the garage, but it's better to stay undetected for as long as possible. Hell, a five-minute head start could make all the difference.

I slip through the back entrance of the garage and keep myself low. If I'm lucky, the camera on the far side won't spot me, but with the closer one being fixed, it's harder to avoid. I glance at my car, but I don't head for it. They haven't given me the keys back yet, and now I realize they never intended to. Well, fuck them. I don't need the car. I've figured out that with how fast people come in and out of this place, using whatever vehicle they like, the keys are either already in the cars or they are hanging somewhere inside here.

I look around the room and find what I'm looking for—a metal cabinet with three rows of keys. Making my way over while keeping as low as possible makes my thighs burn. I promise to all that is holy that if I make it out of here alive, I'll get fit. I'll start doing more cardio or something. Maybe take up hot yoga or Zumba. If I'm constantly going to be on the run, I should at least make sure I'm fit to run. Plus, when the zombies come—and given how shitty my life is right now, I say zombies will be an actuality—I don't want to be the juicy, plump girl who looks like a tasty snack. Right now, all that's keeping me going is my anger. I refuse to let these bastards hurt me any more than they already have. I know it's a lie, though—that once I'm safe, I'll fall apart. But I need the lie.

Focusing on the keys, I grab the one with the Audi emblem

on the fob. There is only one Audi in here, so that takes the stress out of finding the car that matches the key. I hurry toward it, not bothered about being stealthy anymore. The urge to go fast pushes me. I know they'll notice I'm gone soon, and then they'll come for me, worried I'll spill secrets about their precious Salem and the layout of this place. I want to be far away from here before that happens.

I throw my things in the back seat before climbing into the car, adjusting the seat, and starting it. Checking my mirrors, I pull out of the garage. I see two men talking near the main entrance of the house as I leave, but they are too far away for me to make out who they are. Thanks to the tinted glass, they can't tell who's driving, either. Neither of them runs toward me, so the Audi leaving isn't triggering any alarms, thankfully. And on that note, I put my foot on the gas and hightail it out of there before my luck runs out.

My stupid tears start again the farther away I get. When I make it to the main road, I swear my breath stutters in my chest for a moment when I remember how damn proud of myself I was when I found the turn to the mysterious Apex ranch. Well, fuck them. Fuck them all. I wish Salem the best. Hopefully, she keeps her guard up because, despite everything, I truly don't want anything to happen to her. But it's time for me to go.

I'm not noble enough to stay here and be chained up like a dog on the off chance I might be in the right place at the right time to save a woman that probably won't even miss me now that I'm gone.

"Jesus!" I hiss when I realize how jaded and bitter I sound. I don't want to be this person. I worked too hard to beat back the demons that I spent years trying to drown in the bottom of a vodka bottle. I can't help but be pissed that I let Jagger and Slade in enough to make me slip back into old habits. The feelings of worthlessness and of being used and ridiculed make themselves known once more—like old friends from another life you wish you could just forget about.

I shake my head, trying to displace my wayward thoughts, but my self-loathing has a grip on me that refuses to relent. I'm angry—so angry that I need a stronger word to describe how beyond angry I am. Not just with Slade and Jagger, but all of them. The person I'm pissed at most, though, is me. I knew better, but stupid girls make stupid decisions. Well, not anymore.

I pull up to the first ATM I come across and withdraw as much money as it allows before moving on to the next. I do it until I have a sizable wad of cash in my hand, thankful I have a high withdrawal limit from my bank. I drive to the small café that sits at the start of a hiking trail I passed on the way here that's apparently popular with tourists this time of year. I order a few sandwiches and a couple of bottles of water to go before making light conversation about how I'm going to wander the trails.

The waitress looks at my face and frowns. I have a feeling this woman can see right through my bullshit. "You okay? The trails can be dangerous if you're not familiar with them. I'm not sure I'm comfortable letting you wander around on your own, especially when it looks like your heart might have taken a beating. Broken hearts make it easy to get caught up in your head, and that's when you look up and find yourself lost."

I shake my head sadly at her. "I'm already lost. But I promise I won't go far. I just need to be alone for a little while."

She looks at me skeptically. "You're not going to do anything stupid, are you?"

I shake my head. "I think I've reached my lifetime quota of stupid decisions."

After a minute, she reluctantly nods her head and offers me a quick wave goodbye. I walk to the back of the parking lot, closest to the trail, where I parked. Grabbing my bags from the car, I shove my food inside my tote and head toward the trail, making sure to keep my suitcase hidden from view. Once I'm out of sight of the diner, I loop around and head in a straight line parallel to the diner until I reach the road. I cross the street and head toward the bus station that's about a mile from here, pulling my luggage behind me.

By the time I reach the station, I'm huffing and puffing, and even though it's early evening now and the temperature has dropped, I'm coated in a layer of sweat.

When I walk up to the ticket counter, the woman sitting behind the glass partition takes one look at me and frowns. "Are you okay?"

"I... I... need a ticket."

"Where to?"

"Anywhere away from here."

She reels off the places, and I pick three at random. I buy tickets for each destination, so if questioned, she won't be able to tell anyone exactly where I went. With a thank you, I head to the restroom and park my bags beside me so I can lean on the counter. I gaze in the mirror and wince. Yikes, no wonder I've been getting some looks—well, more than usual. My eyes are swollen and bloodshot from crying, my usually fair skin is bright pink from being exposed to the sun for too long, and my hair is a tangled mess.

Turning on the faucet, I run the water before splashing some onto my face, relishing the soothing coolness of it. Once I feel more clearheaded, I take a few minutes to use the facilities before rummaging in my bag for a hoodie. I slip it on and tug the hood over my hair. From the small front pocket of the bag, I grab my tinted glasses and cover my eyes. With my head throbbing like it is, I chastise myself for not putting my sunglasses on earlier when I was in the damn sun, but my mind was clearly on other things.

Blowing out a breath, I head out to the waiting area. I sit in the corner next to an older lady who is knitting. The chair on the other side of me is empty except for a baseball cap. The owner of the cap is asleep in the chair next to it. I sit with my bags, anxious to put some distance between me and this place. My leg bounces up and down nervously as time seems to crawl by. Finally, a bus comes in that I bought a ticket for.

I quickly glance at the sleeping man beside me, and before I can question my actions, I snatch his cap and cover it with my bag as I head to the bus. I fidget as I wait to board, trying to keep cool and not draw attention to myself. I'm clearly not cut out for this life. I'm a nervous wreck already. What am I going to be like a week from now? Will they even try to find me, or will they just cut their losses and let me go? If they do come, what will they do with me? I have so many questions I don't have the answers to that it makes my stomach churn and my head pounds harder.

By the time I make it to the driver and hold my ticket out for him, my hands are shaking so badly that he can't read it. He reaches out to steady it, and his pinkie brushes against mine. Maybe it's because my defenses are down—my mind too preoccupied with everything else that I'm not shielding myself like I usually do—that a vision hits me hard and fast.

I see the driver with his pants around his ankles as he thrusts himself into a woman who is pinned over one of the bus seats. One of his hands grips the back of the seat for balance, the other is over her mouth as he fucks her brutally. Her screams are muffled by his hand, but there is nothing to stop the flow of tears from her terrified eyes. I look around the bus, wondering why nobody is helping her, when I see it's completely empty except for the two of them. A quick look outside shows it's pitch dark and eerily isolated.

I snap back to the here and now and yank my hand back.

"You okay?" the driver asks, the picture of concern. His words feel like oil on my skin after what I've just seen.

"I'm fine," I reply gruffly.

He waits for a second before nodding his head for me to find my seat. I turn and blow out my breath, feeling sick to my stomach.

It's visions like that one that haunt me, not just because the act is so heinous but because I have no time frame for when it could take place. It could happen tomorrow, two weeks from now, or two years. Even if I managed to track down the person in my vision, how would I make them understand what I saw?

And if, by some miracle, I did convince them, then what? They get to spend the next however long it takes to come to fruition, terrified, always looking over their shoulder.

Calling what I have a gift is a joke. I can't help anyone. All that's going to happen is that I'll slowly go insane. Now I remember why I keep myself isolated.

I push my way to the back of the bus, keeping my head down, not wanting anyone to remember me. When I trip over someone's bag lying in the aisle, I look up and gasp when I stare into the eyes of the woman getting raped in my vision. She glares at me as I right myself and continue on, throwing myself into the back seat, my heart thundering in my chest.

I place my bags beside me to stop anyone from sitting next to me. While everyone is distracted, I tug my hood down and put the baseball cap on before pulling the hood up over it. Leaning back, I study the woman four seats ahead and across from me and try to figure out the best way to approach her. As much as I want to blurt out the truth, it's not really an option. If she thinks I'm crazy, she won't listen to me, or worse, I scare her. My biggest fear is that my actions are what cause the vision. For example, if I do nothing, will she climb off the bus a stop before mine? What if it's me freaking her out that makes her stay put, figuring she's safer on board than outside with me? What if my words push her into the very situation I'm trying to avoid? I try to relax, knowing I'm going to be here for a while, so nothing is going to happen yet.

I keep my eyes on her for most of the journey, except for when they drift to the front of the bus and the driver watching her in the rearview mirror. As my stop gets closer, my anxiety increases as the bus slowly gets emptier. When the person sitting behind the woman gets off, I take a chance and change seats. I'll only get one shot at this, and I pray to God that she heeds my warning before I hear about her on the news.

I blow out a breath, lean forward, and start whispering to her.

CHAPTER TWENTY-FIVE

Slade

"How much longer is this going to take?" I cross my arms impatiently as Ev types God knows what into his computer.

"As long as it fucking takes, Slade. A lot of this stuff has been buried."

"You think it's a government cover-up?" Zig questions. It's not hard to make that leap. They know about Salem, after all. If there is even a slim chance of Astrid having visions, then it stands to reason they know about her too.

I look from Zig to Oz and see them staring at the screen, trying to follow along with Ev, but the man works at speeds that are beyond us.

"I can't see anyone else having the means or funds," Oz agrees. "Erasing something like that, something that should have made national news, is nearly impossible. I'm looking for other options, but right now, all I see is the government."

"Then you're not looking in the right places." Ev turns to look at the three of us.

"It would be one hell of a bargaining chip to hang over her head," Zig adds.

Ev crosses his arms and shakes his head. "You guys have already decided Astrid's guilty, so what's the rush? Could it be that you're not sure that she's guilty of the assumptions you all jumped to after all?"

None of us say anything to that. I, of all people, don't want any of this to be true. That's why we're standing here while Ev keeps digging. I can't be around Astrid right now, not until I know for sure. Like Greg said, I'll end up saying or doing something I'll regret. Something more than I already have. I can't deny, though, that the feeling of betrayal made me react without thinking.

Could Astrid—my Astrid—really have done this?

"Alright, I'll bite," Oz drawls. "Who else could have covered Astrid's involvement up? And if they were skilled enough to hide parts of the story, why not hide it completely?"

"Her parents are loaded. Who the fuck do you think covered it up?" Ev sighs, rubbing his eyes. "And I'm guessing they didn't cover it all up because they didn't have to. They just needed to hide enough to bury the truth. Though some people won't see the truth even when it's right in front of them, which I don't get.

"Take you, Zig. You've always had a feeling when something wasn't right, right? A knowing, or a sixth sense, if you like. And you listen to it every time because it's rarely wrong. Nobody can see it. Nobody can feel it except you. And yet we don't question it because we believe you. You've earned our loyalty again and again.

"Astrid doesn't have that. Nobody stood in her corner. Because they couldn't see what she saw until it was too late to stop it. After that, it didn't matter what she said or did. Everyone had already made up their mind about her, just like now. She was the crazy girl who should have been locked up, but her rich parents didn't want to deal with the stigma of having a mentally disturbed child. Instead, they normalized her issues." He says normalized with air quotes.

"What the fuck does that even mean?"

"It means, according to some of the files I found, instead of letting the world think Astrid was a crazy girl who claimed to see the future, her parents made her out to be just another spoiled rich kid doing what other spoiled rich kids do best–act out. What that actually did was make things a thousand times worse for her. Can you imagine what it must be like to see what she sees? The awful, horrible things, and yet nobody believes you when you say something. These same naysayers are the ones who vilify her when her visions come to life. Imagine being mocked and jeered on top of having to deal with what she sees, and even her own family pretends she's nothing but a joke. All she needed was for one person to stand up for her." He's practically growling now, and it's making my hackles rise.

"If you've got something to say, Evander, just spit it out. I'm not a mind reader," I snap.

"Wouldn't matter if you were. It's all just a bunch of bullshit, right? Salem can heal people with her touch, but Astrid—"

"I never said I didn't believe she was gifted. I'm not sure either way yet, because she hasn't had a vision the whole time she's been here."

"Imagine that," Zig mutters under his breath. "Look, I get what you're trying to say, Ev. And a part of me thinks it's cool that you want to have Astrid's back like that, but I'm not sure she deserves it. Salem earned our trust by saving our lives. Astrid has yet to prove anything."

"And that's how you measure someone's worth, huh?" Ev shakes his head, turns back to his screens, and resumes typing as he talks.

"Salem can prove her gift. We've seen it work with our own two eyes," Oz points out.

"Yet I believed her before I saw the video. Remember, I wasn't there the day she revealed it to all the guys. I saw the footage and never questioned its validity. I deal in facts and truths, but I never had a doubt when it came to Salem's gift. I get that same feeling with Astrid."

The room is quiet at that. I stand back and try to think through everything Ev is saying. What does he see that I'm missing?

As if he can hear my thoughts, he replies. "It's not that I see more, it's that you're wearing blinders. You think you're all believers now because of Salem, but you all just openly admitted it was only because she could prove she was gifted. Astrid can't prove her gift is real until her vision comes true.

Part of me wants to lose my shit over that because you seem to all be forgetting that if her vision does come true, Salem dies."

"She's not going to fucking die," Zig snaps. "We'll take precautions. No fucking fairy lights, and we'll postpone Christmas no matter how Salem protests," he argues, but Ev laughs bitterly.

"You're taking precautions against the things Astrid saw, but you still don't believe her without proof?" He shakes his head. "You can't have it both ways. But then this must be how it always is for—oh shit!"

"What? What is it?" I step forward as Ev types something else, and the large screen on the wall flares to life.

"Bingo, I'm in."

I spot the national headlines that Ev showed us earlier about the school shooting that Astrid was implicated in before her name disappears completely from the following copies. I dismiss them for a minute, trying to find what it was that caused Ev's reaction. And there it is, on page five of a local paper.

"Psychic Teenager Saw School Shooting Two Weeks Before It Happened"

Something heavy presses on my chest as I move closer, seeing more articles about the eerie claims of the then sixteen-year-old Astrid.

"It says she went to the police, and they sent her away with a warning about wasting police time," Oz reads.

"Jesus, the officer who sent her away was the same guy who arrested her the day after the shooting."

"How come that didn't flag up before?" I choke out, vomit rushing up the back of my throat, but I swallow it down.

"Like I said, she changed her name, and her parents' influence made all this disappear."

"This doesn't prove she wasn't involved," Oz says quietly.

"She had an airtight alibi." Ev turns and points to the far corner of the screen. "That's how they hid everything so easily. Because she was innocent. The police would have looked like fucking idiots if this came out. She was in a cell while the massacre happened after being arrested the night before for causing a disturbance. She was waiting for her parents to post bail, but they never turned up. Eventually, her guardian, who is also her lawyer, came and collected her."

"So why all this if they knew she didn't do it?" I wave my hand angrily over the original newspaper articles. Angry at them, angry at me, and angry at all of us for believing this bullshit.

"She knew too much. They didn't believe she was psychic, so she had to be the killer or an accomplice who was in on the plan all along. That was the only way she could have known the details like she did. The police really had it in for her. So did the grieving residents of her hometown," Ev says quietly as he flips to the next screen.

Photos of a black and blue Astrid lying in a hospital bed, her face so swollen it looks deformed. I wouldn't know it was her if it wasn't for the mass of white hair.

"She was attacked?" I snarl.

"Over and over again. The town was grieving, and she made the perfect scapegoat. She never went back to school. And as soon as the case was dropped against her, her parents moved her away. It might have been the one good thing they did for her because they seemed conveniently absent for everything else. Saving the world took precedence over saving their only daughter, I guess." Ev turns to look at us, his face hard.

"You know what this means? That even though she might have been miles away, locked in a cell when it happened, she saw it all as if she was there. She saw her classmates gunned down—teachers who she knew most of her life lying dead in the hallways. She saw it all, but no one believed her. I bet she still sees it every time she closes her fucking eyes." He turns back to the screen.

"One of the detectives, James Allen, filed a complaint about the handling of her case. He had been there when she made her initial report. He was also one of the detectives who took state-ments from the families of the victims." Ev points to a report and enlarges it so we can read the messy writing more clearly.

"Claire Delaney taught AP Chemistry. She got dressed in a white dress that morning, but when she went to leave the house, she spilled coffee all over herself and changed into gray pants, and a pink shirt." He flicks to a crime screen photo of the teacher lying in a pool of blood before highlighting a section of the officer's report.

"Astrid described her outfit, gray pants and a pink shirt, two weeks before this went down. She talked about seeing a lone shoe at the bottom of the stairs, as if it fell off when someone was running away, too scared to come back for it." He points to another photo, and sure enough, there is a black high-heeled shoe at the bottom of the stairs.

"I could read you a dozen more details that seem insignificant, but these are all things Astrid couldn't have known about without seeing them. Sure, she could have planned everything down to the last detail. But she wouldn't have known about the little things like spilled coffee, pink shirts, and lone shoes."

I take a step back as the full impact of what he's saying—what he's been trying to say all along—hits me.

Looking me in the eye, Ev shakes his head before looking at Oz and Zig with the same disappointment. "We just did to her what they all did."

"Wait, it's not the same," Zig says, but there isn't much conviction in his voice.

"Might as well be. Because from where I'm sitting, yet again, there was nobody in her corner."

I shake my head. "You're wrong. This time she had you and Greg." It should have been me and Jagger, but thank fuck for them.

"Doesn't matter. I was the one who brought your attention to this shit before I had all the facts."

"You were just doing your job, and you told us to wait until you could dig further. This isn't on you," Oz tells him as his eyes move to mine. "It's on us. We fucked up. We need to go talk to her. Apologize."

"We all do," Zig agrees.

"Let me and Jagger talk to her first. She'll accept your apologies, that's just who she is. But what me and Jagger did... I'm not sure she'll be quite as forgiving."

I turn and leave the room, heading back downstairs. I try to think about what to say, how to explain, how to justify my actions. But I have nothing. What we did, what I did, was so out of order it's not even funny. I just shit all over what we were building, treating her like a liar and a fraud.

I scrub my hand down my face as I spot Greg and Jagger at the table. "Where is everyone else?"

"Salem woke up. Crew and Wilder took her down to the orchard. She doesn't know what's going on, but she keeps asking where Astrid is, and we didn't know what to tell her," Greg replies, his voice void of emotion. "Hawk and Creed are doing a supply run."

I look at Jagger and feel my shoulders slump. "We need to go talk to Astrid. We owe her one hell of an apology."

"She didn't do it, did she?" Jagger doesn't sound surprised. "I mean, we had all that information in front of us, telling us she was guilty. But once I sat down and thought about it, it just didn't sit right." He jumps to his feet and heads out the door toward our place.

I follow behind him, growling when he pushes the door open. "You didn't lock it?"

He turns to look at me and winces. "I cuffed her to the bed."

I blink and come to a dead stop before I sprint toward the bedroom.

"What the fuck?"

I swing the door open, and sure enough, the room is empty, the discarded cuffs still hooked to the bed.

"How the hell did she get out of those?" Jagger yells, coming to a stop behind me.

"The key was in the drawer of the nightstand. I was trying to teach her how to face her fears."

"Motherfucker! And you didn't think to tell me that?"

"Oh, fuck you. If you would've locked the fucking door, then we would've known she had left because she'd have tripped the alarm. You're just as much to blame as I am."

I open the closet door and find her bags gone. Shoving the bathroom door open, I see her toiletries are missing as well.

"Call Ev. Tell him Astrid's gone. Get him to check the cameras. I'm going to look for her in case she's hiding somewhere."

I hurry past him but stop when he calls my name. "It was bad. What you found out, it was bad, wasn't it?"

I nod. "Yeah, it's about as bad as it can get. Yet I can't help but feel like what we did was a hundred times worse."

I leave after that, not wanting to stand around talking when Astrid could be getting farther and farther away. I search the area closest to the house before moving out. The property is massive, so there are plenty of places to hide, but I'm not sure she is hiding.

"Slade!" I stop and turn when Jagger and Greg jog over to me.

"You find her?"

"Ev spotted her on camera. She left about an hour ago in the Audi."

"Fuck!" I yank my hair.

"We need to go after her."

"I hate to say this, boys, but she might not want to be found," Greg states.

"No. I don't believe that. I can't let her go like this, G. She needs to know I was wrong. That we all were. I don't want her spending another second blaming herself for trusting us when we were the ones that fucked up. We need a chance to fix it."

He blows out a breath. "Good luck. You're going to need it. You were both complete bastards to her." He slaps me on the back and nods to Jagger.

I'm not going to argue because he's right, so I just nod.

"You need to tell me everything and do it fast," Jagger orders as the two of us head to the garage.

I yank the keys for the Range Rover off the hook and toss them to Jagger. I'm too wired to drive. I can't focus on the roads and Astrid. I tell him everything Ev found out about Astrid, and by the time I'm finished, Jagger looks like he's been punched.

He looks at me, his hands gripping the wheel. "Maybe we should let her go. We've done nothing but fuck up since we met her. She deserves better than us."

"She does. But I'm too much of a bastard to let her go. And do you really think there are men out there that can keep her safe like we can?" I look out the window. "You were right about me being drawn to her. Right from the start, I knew she was going to change my fucking world. And that fucking terrified me, Jagger. So instead of manning the fuck up and taking what I wanted, I destroyed it."

"I spent ten years behind bars because I trusted the wrong people, and I've barely got my life back on track. Then all of a sudden, this...this pint-sized fairy princess comes into my life, threatening it all. What was I supposed to do? Even when I let her in, it wasn't all the way. Hell, I'm not sure I let any of you all the way in."

I blow out a breath and keep my eyes ahead as we pass

under the large wooden Apex sign. "I guess it's true what they say about not knowing what we have until it's gone."

"I don't think we ever really had her, Slade. All three of us held parts of ourselves back for various reasons. I know you're kicking yourself right now, but you weren't alone in this. Astrid could have told us, but she didn't. And I followed along with everything, whether I agreed or not, because that's what good soldiers do, and the last time I went against orders and listened to my instincts, I led my team into a fucking ambush. They died because I trusted my gut, and my gut was fucking wrong."

"Come on, Jagger. That's bullshit, and you know it. What went down that day wasn't your fault. It was shitty orders from a shitty captain who had never stepped foot in the sandbox in his life. You had a feeling something was wrong, and you acted on it. I'm sorry you lost your team, man, more than you'll ever know. But I can't help but be thankful. If you hadn't listened, we could have lost you too. You think if you made a different decision, then they might all have somehow survived despite the situation you were all thrown into. I don't. I think, as fucked as it sounds, you were all destined to die that day. You're only here because you listened to your gut. Stop beating yourself up for shit that was beyond your control. I need you to learn to trust yourself again because you're the only damn person who can rein me in," I admit, making him laugh.

"Well, then, we're both fucked."

CHAPTER TWENTY-SIX

Astrid

I sit in the twenty-four-hour diner with my hands wrapped around the steaming mug of coffee and smile as Glory, the woman in front of me, hangs up her cell phone.

"My sister is coming to pick me up. She's just getting off work, so she'll be about twenty minutes."

"Okay, good. Do you mind if I sit here while you wait?" I don't want to assume that just because I spared her from the bus driver that we're friends.

Her dark eyes latch on to mine and narrow a little, making me squirm in my seat. She leans forward, her inky black hair falling over her shoulder as she talks. "Girl, from what you just potentially saved me from? You can move into my damn house if you want to."

I grin before taking a sip of the surprisingly good coffee.

"So, this friend of yours, she didn't report him?"

I swallow, hating the way my skin feels too tight all of a sudden. That's the thing about lies. Once you tell one, you end up having to tell more until, eventually, you've planted a field of lies you have no choice but to cultivate. They'll flourish for a while. But when the root is twisted with secrets, at some point, your deception will come to light like a weed slipping through a crack in a sidewalk.

I knew I couldn't just get off the bus and leave Glory to her fate, just like I knew I couldn't just tell her the truth. I made up a story about having a friend who had been raped by the driver and how I heard him talking with one of his buddies about getting a taste of Glory's dark meat later.

At first, she was shocked and suspicious. But when she looked into the rearview mirror and saw the driver's eyes on her, she knew. She knew in the same way a lot of women do. She sensed the evil in him and saw a premonition of her own. Not like mine, of course. But she knew what could happen if she shrugged it off.

In the end, she took a chance on me, and we both got off together. Three stops early for me, five for her. Her stop would have made her the last person on the bus.

"He is a family man, goes to church. She is a party girl who gets drunk and wears tight dresses."

Glory's face hardens. It's a story everyone has heard before. In these cases, it's almost always a case of the victim trying to prove her innocence and the predator casting doubt.

I push a little harder, not wanting her to ever hesitate to run if she sees this man again. "She reported him to his bosses. They told her she was mistaken. She doesn't have a whole lot of faith in the police, so she didn't even bother them with it."

That part of my story I can at least draw from experience. I've had my fair share of trauma over the years, but nothing makes my skin crawl quite as much as the sight of a police uniform, no matter how irrational that is.

"You know, I have a daughter. She's only two, but it's things like this that scare the crap out of me about the future. I know one day I'll have to talk to her about the things men can and will do to pretty young girls, given the chance. I'll teach her about keeping her drink safe, about not taking unmarked cabs, or walking alone at night, or anywhere off the beaten path. I'll buy her a rape whistle and teach her how to throw a punch, and I'll pray every fucking day that she never ever finds herself in a situation where she finally understands why I taught her all those things."

"Not all men are bad." I want to laugh at the irony of the broken-hearted girl saying that shit, but it's true. The men of Apex might not like me very much, but I've seen the way they are with Salem. They'd sooner cut off their arms than hurt her.

"I know. But some days, it feels like the scales are really fucking unbalanced."

We sit quietly, drinking our drinks, as the rain begins to fall outside. The sounds of the diner making themselves known—cutlery scraping on plates, soft chatter—and I can hear Eminem's *Lose Yourself* playing in the kitchen. I can't help but think how appropriate the song is when the silence is broken.

"I'm coming back after visiting an old friend for the week-end. I can't drive, and I sure as shit can't afford a plane ticket, but you look like that's not an issue. What's your story?"

You gotta love someone who doesn't give a fuck about social etiquette.

"I'm not sure I'd even know where to start. Let's just say it involves men and me finding out that, yet again, they can't be trusted."

"Girl, I feel that. I'd suggest, given our combined experiences, we just try batting for the other team. But I do love me some dick."

I choke on the mouthful of coffee I had been sipping and barely manage to refrain from spitting it all over her. I can't help but laugh at her grin.

"Thanks, I needed that."

Lights flash through the window we're sitting next to, drawing our attention, and Glory's phone buzzes with an incoming text.

"That's my sister." She slips her hand in her pocket and pulls out a twenty and tosses it on the table. "These men you mentioned—are they bad men, or are they good men that did a shitty thing?"

"Not sure there's much of a difference right now."

"Right now, you're too wrapped up in your pain to think clearly. But tomorrow or next week, when the anger burns out, will your answer be the same?"

"I don't know."

"Then figure it out. I'm not saying you need to have a man to be happy. That's the biggest crock of shit I've ever heard. It's nobody's job to make you happy, that's all on you. Having limits is good. But ask yourself this, do the moments of happiness outweigh the moments of pain? If the answer is no, then walk your fine ass out of here with your head and middle finger held high. But if the answer is yes, then you have to decide if you can forgive them. My mama used to say, love is like an investment. The more you give, the bigger the risk. But the rewards can be limitless. You can give them your heart and put everything you have into living a thousand more happy moments with them, or you can cut your losses and walk away. But if you walk away, do it knowing you'll be giving those happy moments to the next woman who comes along."

She walks to the door and nods goodbye as she pushes through it, her words surprising me. She's right. I'm too raw right now to look beyond my pain. But when I'm not, what happens then?

I watch Glory climb into the car and pull the door shut as the rain starts coming down in sheets. I stare until the taillights disappear from view before I signal for the waitress to come over and refill my coffee cup.

"Can I get you anything else?"

"No, I'm good for now, thanks. My friend left this for you, though." I reach over and hand her the twenty, which she slips into the pocket of her apron with a smile.

"Thanks. Holler if you need anything." She turns and walks over to another table.

Glancing around, I spot a man in the far corner eating a piece of pie. Near the door are a couple of what look like medical students or nurses in scrubs, wolfing down waffles and coffee—that, by the looks of it, they desperately need. Everyone is so lost in their own lives they are too busy to pay attention to me. I'm glad I kept the cap and hoodie on, though, because thankfully, I look just as forgettable as the next person passing through.

I lean back and close my eyes for a second to think. If Apex is tracking me, they've probably figured out I've hopped on a bus. Which means they'll know I purchased three tickets. If they cover all destinations, getting off the bus early means I'm not where I'm supposed to be, and I've bought myself some more time. The question is, where do I go from here? Do I get a hotel room for the night while I think this through, or should I contact Mandy, my lawyer, and see if she can discreetly get me out of here so Evander won't be able to track me?

With a groan of frustration, I sit up and rub my palms over my thighs. No, fuck this. What am I doing? I'm acting like a freaking criminal, and I'm not. No matter what the Apex guys think, what happened with the school shooting had nothing to do with me. As much as Officer Dickface would like to have proved otherwise, I was completely cleared of any wrongdoing.

Not that it erased the vision from my memory. It's ingrained in my brain. Every detail was crystal clear, as if it were playing out right in front of me. Not all visions are that clear, though. Glory's was, but the one about Salem was much hazier. I don't know the ins and outs of why some are so much stronger than others. I've never met someone with my particular gift, so I have no one to compare notes with. The only thing I've been able to gather is that my proximity to the victims is key. Salem was hundreds of miles away when I had my vision of her, whereas I was close to Glory and the victims of the school shooting when I had the visions of them.

I bite my lip and think back to other instances, other visions, other memories. I strip back all the parts I usually think about—the fear, the dread of the scene playing out, the worry about the aftermath, the anger, and the guilt. Instead, I focus on the images themselves, and I'm surprised to see my theory might hold some weight. There is definitely a difference in the quality of the visual when distance between me and the victims is a factor. There's less information, too, like something interferes with the frequency I'm tuned into.

"How have I not noticed that before?" I mutter to myself and take a big gulp of coffee.

With a sigh, I think back to what Glory said. In particular, the part about knowing if Jagger and Slade are bad men or good men who did a bad thing. Even though they hurt me, I can't just slide them into the evil category. They were protecting their brothers and Salem. The fact that I don't fall under their protection hurts, but it doesn't make them bad guys. Maybe it just makes them the wrong guys. At least for me.

With that figured out, I have to question my reasons for running and hiding. No, not the running. That part is justified. I had to get away from them. But why am I hiding? I don't think they'll hurt me. Lord knows they've had plenty of opportunities if that's the way they wanted to. So, if it's not fear, why hide at all?

I sip my coffee slowly as I sift through my feelings. It isn't until I slide my empty cup onto the table that the answer comes to me. I don't want them to find me because I don't trust that

I'm strong enough to say no to them. I don't want them to charm me with their words and offer me apologies that fall flat. I deserve better than what they gave me. I know that. But knowing what's good for me and remembering how good they can make me feel are easily blurred.

There are women out there that ooze confidence. They take no shit and stand up for themselves. And if the man fucks up, they walk away and find a new one to play with. I'm not that girl. I don't throw anything away. Hell, I still have clothes I wore in high school and stuffed toys from when I was a toddler.

Constantly being reminded about how unwanted and unlovable I am didn't affect my ability to love. It affected my ability to recognize good love from the toxic kind. As a result, I always end up with someone who treats me like dirt—a part of me believing that's what I deserved. When they used me up and threw me away, I took all the blame and hated myself for a while before repeating it all over again with the next man. It's a vicious circle that I play out on an endless loop. Jagger and Slade are just the latest in a long line.

I know this situation is different. For starters, I know they don't love me. They never offered me any promises, just sex, and I naively thought it was enough. But the rational part of my brain knows that even if all this hadn't happened, we would have just been prolonging the inevitable and fallen at the next hurdle. The problem is that my heart got involved without me realizing it, and it's too late to go back.

What I feel is all that matters. And I feel a lot. Too much for it to be considered normal this soon. I'm not saying I'm in love with them yet. I think I'm just in love with the idea of them and the potential of who we could be together.

I bite my cheek and pull a couple of bills out of my pocket and place them underneath the edge of my mug. Climbing to my feet, I look from the med students to the trucker, who looks ready to leave, and walk over to him.

"Hi, sorry to bother you, but I was wondering if I could borrow your cell phone. I lost mine, and I need someone to come pick me up. I'll pay you for it."

He looks me up and down—his gaze is neither creepy nor judgmental—before he nods and stands, pulling out his cell and holding it up to his face to unlock it.

"Thank you so much." I take the phone and move back toward the table I had been sitting at so nobody can overhear me and place my call.

It rings four times before an irritated voice answers. "Who is this?"

"It's me, Astrid."

"Jesus fucking Christ, Astrid. I've been going out of my mind. You were supposed to check in. I was two seconds away from making a missing person's report."

I hold back my snort as Mandy yells. She's been so concerned that it's taken all this time to report me missing when I've been gone for weeks.

"Well, as you can hear, I'm fine. I need a car to pick me up and drive me home."

"Okay, which car and which home?" She sighs.

"Any car. Call me an Uber or a cab. You'll just have to prepay them for me since I have no idea where an ATM is around here." And I don't want to use the cash I already have in case something goes wrong and I need it. Call me paranoid, but I'm not taking any chances.

"And where is here?"

I reel off the name of the diner and the town I'm in and tell her which house I want to go to. When I'm finished, I wait for her to speak again, knowing she's taking this all down.

"You want to head home from there? It won't be cheap."

"It's not like I can't afford it. Just get me out of here."

"Can I reach you on this number?"

"No, the phone belongs to a trucker who looks ready to leave."

"A trucker? Fuck me!" she curses again. "Hold on."

She keeps me on hold, but I hear her typing away and talking to someone on another line before she comes back. "Cab will be with you in five." She repeats the registration number she was just given, like I'll remember it, before telling me she will call me tomorrow and hangs up.

"Yeah, bye, Mandy," I mutter as I walk over to the trucker and hand him back his phone. As my fingers brush his, a vision slams into me.

I grip the edge of the table as my legs buckle. The sound of smashing glass and the squeal of tires so real it's like I'm there. I take in every detail I can before the vision fades and I'm back in the here and now.

"Is she okay?"

I look up at the voice and see one of the medical students leaning over me. Shit, when did I end up on the floor? The vision might have been over quickly, but it kicked my ass.

"I'm fine. Sorry to freak you out. I got a little dizzy for a minute. Low blood sugar," I state sheepishly.

She looks at me, unsure, before telling me to drink some juice and returns to her table.

The trucker reaches out his hand and helps me to my feet. "Are you sure you're okay?"

I nod but stop myself, taking in the red and black checkered shirt he's wearing, the same one from my vision. "I will be if you promise me something. I can't tell you why and I can't tell you when, but I need you to trust me. No questions asked."

Tears well in my eyes as I pray desperately that he'll hear me out.

"There's a large truck carrying wood supplies. The company is called EN Holms Logistics. The cab part is green, and the name is scrolled across the top and side of the truck in black writing." I shake my head for getting off track. "When you see it, speed up and move to the inside lane. The man behind the wheel is going to fall asleep," I choke out, gripping his arm when he moves to step back.

"He'll clip the back of your truck. You'll spin and hit the guardrail before falling through it. Your truck will catch fire, and you won't be able to get out because you're gonna be pinned inside. I know you don't believe me. If I thought I could get you to take a different route, I would, but I'm begging you." My brain flashes to the dog-eared photo of a pregnant woman and two young boys that falls out of the visor when the truck flips.

"If you won't do it for me, do it for your wife and sons. Please."

I release his arm and hurry away, yanking the door open as a yellow cab pulls up in front of the building. I climb inside just as the diner door opens, the trucker standing in the doorway with the light illuminating him from behind. He looks almost angelic. I only hope he listens to me, and this is the closest he gets to becoming an angel for a long time yet.

CHAPTER TWENTY-SEVEN

Jagger

We found the Audi at the café near the edge of town. A waitress there remembered the pretty girl with white hair. One, because she looked like a fairy princess, and two, because she mentioned walking one of the trails to get some alone time. After we both ran out of there in a panic, trying to figure out which way she went, I realized we'd played right into Astrid's hands.

"This isn't Astrid. She wouldn't come here when she had no idea what she was facing."

Slade looks at me incredulously.

"Yes, she would. That's exactly what got her into this mess in the first place. She drove halfway across the country to a strange place filled with strange men to try and convince them of something unbelievable while hoping it didn't sound like a threat. All while praying we didn't kill her."

"Okay, when you put it like that, it sounds bad. But what I mean is this—" I wave around the area. "Does Astrid strike you as the nature type? Or the hiking type, for that matter?"

Slade looks around and frowns. "No. Astrid is much more the play-video-games-and-watch-cats-do-the-funniest-things kind of girl," he admits, making me chuckle, which turns into a sad sigh.

"I can't believe we thought this woman was a threat." I hang my head in shame before lifting my eyes to my best friend, and I see the same guilt I'm feeling reflected back at me. After a moment, the guilt shifts to determination.

"Okay, so where would she go?"

"As far away from us as possible." I rub my eyes, trying to think like Astrid would. But a pissed-off Astrid is a whole different kind of woman than the usual Astrid.

"She has nothing tying her here, so my guess is she'd go where she feels safe."

"Without her car?"

I shrug. "It's not like we left her much choice." I look at my watch before scanning the area, noticing that it's getting quieter now.

"My guess is the bus or train station. And since the bus station is closer, we might want to start there."

He nods as he heads back down the trail, picking up speed when the car comes into view. By the time we get to the bottom, we are both jogging. I jump into the driver's seat as Slade climbs in beside me. He doesn't even have his seat belt on before I'm reversing out of the parking spot and swinging the truck around.

"What do we even say to her?" he asks, sounding lost. I don't blame him. I'm feeling the same way.

"We start with sorry and go from there."

Somehow, I don't think sorry is going to be enough. My mind keeps flashing back to her face as she stood in the doorway listening to us talk shit about her. I've never been great at figuring out a woman's emotions, but Astrid never tried to hide how she felt, even when it confused her. In that moment, though, a child would have been able to read the heartbreak in her eyes.

When we pull up outside the bus station, Slade jumps out before I've even shifted the truck into park and runs inside.

It's virtually deserted when I enter the building, not like the big city stations, where it would still be chaos at this hour. I look around and spot Slade running toward the restrooms, clearly not finding Astrid among the waiting travelers. Scanning the area again, I head to the ticket counter, hoping to catch a break.

I reach the counter and lean against it. Sensing my presence, the woman behind the desk lifts her head and gulps loud enough for me to hear through the safety glass. Normally, I would find her reaction funny. I'm well aware that I can come off as intimidating, and I'd try to downplay it, but I don't have time for subtlety today.

"Hi, I'm wondering if you can help me."

"Um… I can try."

"Did you see a young woman come through here with long white hair and pretty purple eyes?"

She freezes, which is all the confirmation I need.

"I'm sorry, sir. I can't give out that kind of information."

"Can't or won't?"

"Both. I'm sure if she wanted you to know where she was heading, then she would have told you herself."

"So, she did come through here," I muse.

The woman opens her mouth but closes it again quickly, looking flustered.

"I'm not trying to cause any problems, I swear." I sigh and run my hand through my hair as I see Slade heading back this way. When he spots me, he heads over.

"The woman I'm looking for, her name is Astrid." I decide honesty might be the best policy here. "My friend and I—" I point at Slade as he steps up beside me. "We messed up. We hurt her feelings by jumping to conclusions about something. She didn't deserve that. What she does deserve is an apology."

"You're probably right. If you call her up and she says it's okay to give you the information you want, then that's fine. Don't worry, I can wait," she tells me before popping her gum.

I look at Slade, who shrugs and subtly shakes his head.

I'm sure the woman is thinking Astrid won't answer, and she'd be right. But, like fuck am I going to admit it's because we never bothered to get her number.

"I'm sure you know she won't answer. My girl knows how to hold a grudge, and honestly, she should. Please, I'm not asking you to do anything other than point me in the right direction. If she turns me away when we find her, then I'll back off. But I have to at least try."

She sighs, and I'm doubting this is all because of company policy and Astrid and has more to do with her own experience. Some guy fucked up and hurt her, so now we're all in the doghouse. I can't blame her. Haven't we been treating Astrid the same way? We drew on our collective experiences instead of opening our fucking eyes and seeing what was right in front of us.

"Look, even if I wanted to help, I can't. The lady was a smart cookie and bought three separate tickets, I'm guessing in case this, right here, happened and I crumbled under your man's smolder there." She nods at Slade, who is glaring at her. I have to bite back my grin as Slade looks at me.

"Smolder?"

"Don't pretend you don't know what you're doing. The only reason there are no panties on the floor here is because that baby mama over there is asleep, and the other girl is distracted by the tongue down her throat. As for me, I'm immune to bullshit."

She crosses her arms over her chest as Slade leans forward and lowers his voice a notch. "I get it. I'm sorry we bothered you. We're men." He shrugs. "We fuck up. That's what we do. It's in our DNA. You know that, right?" he asks, obviously getting the same impression as me. We were fucked before we opened our mouths, thanks to our appendages.

"The difference between us and the others is that we're man enough to own it. Man enough to get on our fucking knees and beg for forgiveness. And if we're lucky enough that she can forgive us, we'll spend the rest of our lives worshiping her like the goddess she is."

"Took it a little far at the end there," I tell him out of the corner of my mouth.

He looks at me before smirking. "Go big or go home."

I turn back to the woman and notice her cheeks are flushed as she looks at Slade a little starry-eyed. She shakes her head and coughs to clear her throat.

"I'm sorry. Like I said, I can't tell you where she went. What I can say is that only three buses have left here since she bought her tickets, and one of them was heading to Washington, which was not one of the destinations your girl may have been heading to."

"Thank you," Slade tells her with a wink, tapping the desk lightly before we both turn and leave.

I pull my cell phone out and call Evander, who answers after two rings, like he's waiting for my call, which he probably is.

"You find her?"

"No, but I'm hoping you can. We know she bought three tickets at the bus station. Three buses left in the time frame that she was here. Discounting the one to Washington, can you find out where the other two were heading?"

I can hear him typing as we exit the building.

"Okay, the other two buses were heading to California and New Mexico. Running a cross-check brings up properties for Astrid in both those states. Let me just hack into the bus station cameras."

"We're on our way back now, so text us if you find—"

He cuts me off. "Found her."

I've said it before, the man is a machine.

"She took the bus destined for California. I'll see if I can follow the bus using street cams, but I'm not making any promises."

He hangs up, so I relay the info to Slade.

"What do you want to do?" I ask, and he looks at me as we climb into the truck.

"What do you mean, what do I want to do? I want to go get our girl."

"I'm not being a dick here. I'm just asking. We need to be all in or all out. I'm not disrupting this woman's life anymore unless we're keeping her."

I turn the key in the ignition, letting Slade think about that as I pull out of the parking lot. We could go home now and stay there. We could let Astrid get on with her life and learn from our mistakes so we don't fuck up if we're lucky enough to find someone again. But that someone won't be Astrid. I picture her with another man and a kid on her hip, and I grip the steering wheel tightly, wanting to punch my hand through the windshield.

"Between us, we have so many fucking regrets. I don't want Astrid to be one more," I admit.

"She's that girl. You know when you hear people talking shit about the one that got away? That's Astrid. She'll be the woman we measure all others against."

I look over at him and see the determined set of his jaw.

"If we go all in, I won't hold back anymore," I warn him. He hasn't said anything, but I know he's noticed.

"We'll have to earn her trust back. It won't be easy, and she'll fight us every step of the way."

"Don't tease me with a good time, Jagger."

I laugh, and he joins in, the sound lighter than I've heard from him in years.

"So, we're doing this?"

"Fuck yes. First, though, I think we need to plan shit out. Let her think she's safe from us."

I nod. "Alright. What are we going to do about the others, though? It's not just us that let her down. We all did."

"They'll have to fix that damage themselves. I want her to be happy here with us. But, Jagger, if she can't find it here, then we need to decide what we're willing to give up. I owe the guys everything. This is the only place that's ever been home to me. But for Astrid, I'll walk away. I just didn't know I'd follow her until she was gone."

The last thing I want to do is leave Apex. Like with Slade, these guys are my family. But we can't expect Astrid to make all the sacrifices here. We don't know much about her life, but she doesn't hide that she's taken a few hits and has had to heal alone. It's time someone stepped in front of her and took the blows.

It's time we stepped up and put her first.

"I meant it when I said I was all in. I want her here. I want to give the others a chance to apologize and get to know her. But if she can't find happiness here after what we all did, then we go wherever she feels safe."

"Deal."

When we pull up to the house, Greg is waiting outside.

"You didn't find her?" He looks in the back seat as he asks, already knowing the answer.

"No, but we have a rough idea where she's heading. Can we use the plane? Once Ev has a lock on her, we want to head out."

Greg looks between Slade and me, crossing his arms over his chest. "It's going to take more than some sweet-talking to win her over."

"I know."

He looks at us for a few minutes, and I feel like everything hinges on what he says next.

"Fine. Take the plane. You can call when you need it to return. I'll give you some time to sort your shit out."

"Thanks, G." Slade nods at him and goes to leave, but stops when Greg holds up his hand.

"Some scars run deep. What we did—what you did—marked her. You know that. But it hits differently when you leave that mark on scar tissue that's already been damaged."

"We fucked up, we know. We're going to make it right."

"I hope so, boys. I really do because I'd hate for you to be the thing that finally breaks her."

CHAPTER TWENTY-EIGHT

Astrid

I sign off on the changes before sending the email, excited that at least the game is all done now. Thank goodness all the promotion and shit falls to someone else because I feel like I could sleep for a year.

Standing up, I stretch my arms above my head, wincing when my back cracks from sitting in one position for so long. My new cell phone starts vibrating across the table, so I reach for it, blowing out a breath when I see it's Mandy. I'm tempted to ignore it. But she'll only come over, and it's much harder to get rid of her then.

"Hey, what's up?"

"The annual fundraiser is in two weeks. Your parents' absence will be noticed, so you need to go."

"I'm not going, Mandy, and you know why. Someone will

recognize me, then the press will be all up in my shit again. I've had enough of dealing with the media vultures to last a lifetime."

"People will ask questions, Astrid. It's been years—" she presses, but I interrupt her.

"Well, then maybe it's time to tell them the truth."

"And risk everything else coming out?" She sounds horrified.

I pinch the bridge of my nose and walk over to the glass doors, gazing out at the inviting pool. "I don't care. I'm not a child anymore. There is nothing these people can do or say that will be worse than what's already been said and done."

"You say that now, but we both know that's not true. Last time, it was a gun. Next time, it might be a cocktail of prescription drugs. Your age might have changed, but mentally, you didn't. You'll always be a victim of your circumstances, which is why it will be easier to deal with the fallout if we steer the direction in which it topples."

"As always, your compassion astounds me, Mandy. But last time I checked, you worked for me. Oh, I know you were brought on by my parents, but I've been paying your fees since I turned twenty-one."

She doesn't say anything, but her snort sounds every inch as condescending as her voice usually is. For years, this woman has treated me like something she would scrape off the bottom of her Louboutins, and I let her. After all, she has been the one constant in my life. But my loyalty to her is built on my guilt and gratitude. Gratitude that was twisted in my brain as a child to make me feel like I owed her. Lord knows she cultivated that feeling so she could bend me to her will. Maybe if the last few weeks hadn't happened, I'd have let her get away with it, like I always have.

But something in me has changed. I can't say it's because I'm being overly emotional. If anything, I feel numb. My whole life feels like a fucked-up game of Jenga, but instead of building a tower out of bricks, we built one from lies. Each day, the lies shift as we pull them out and move them to fit while we wait for the whole thing to come tumbling down. Well, fuck that, and fuck her. I'm ready to kick the tower over.

"You have my answer, and now I have to go. I have a meeting." I hang up without saying goodbye and dial another number.

"Hello, is this Detective Allan?"

"Astrid?"

I swallow down a lump in my throat and drop to my knees, letting my tears flow down my face. I haven't spoken to this man since the day I turned eighteen. The fact that he still has me programmed into his phone shouldn't make me feel this raw inside, but it does. For a girl who has been forgotten about for everything but the chaos swirling around her, it means everything.

"Yeah." I cough to clear my throat when my voice comes out barely above a croak. "Yes, it's me."

He exhales loudly. "Jesus, it's so good to hear your voice. I think about you a lot."

I smile through my tears, swiping at them with my free hand as I tuck my knees up under my chest. "I just wanted to say thank you. I don't know if I ever told you that before."

"You told me. But there was nothing you needed to thank me for. Are you okay, honey?"

I nod, even though he can't see me. "I will be."

"Want to talk about it?"

I laugh, remembering another place and another time when he said those exact same words to me. I told him my biggest fears and my darkest secrets, and he didn't run away. He didn't tell the world, and he sure as hell didn't treat me like some kind of freak afterward. In fact, he risked his job and his family for me. I'm not sure I've ever trusted anyone more in my life, and the only thing he asked in return was for me to be happy.

"Well, it started like this..." I tell him everything that's happened to me over the last couple of months, skimming over Salem and her gift and leaving out everyone's names. They pride themselves on their privacy, and I won't invade that just because of the way they treated me.

Stooping to someone else's level won't make me feel better. Taking the high road sucks sometimes, but at least the view is better from up here.

"Holy shit, you don't do things half-assed, do you?" I hear a screen door opening and closing behind him before I hear the creak of a swing.

"Okay, well, I'm guessing you want some help figuring it all out?"

"Yes, but I have something else I want to talk to you about too."

"Okay, color me curious. Let's start with your lawyer. I get that your hands were tied when you were a kid, but you're an adult now. She did her job, and I know you feel like you owe her for that, but she was paid a fuck-ton to do it. She isn't your friend, honey. She never was. I know that because she could have stepped up, but she didn't. She did what she had to do for her, not you. If you were anyone else..." He drifts off, but I know what he was going to say. If I were anyone else, he would have had me removed from that house a long time ago. But my situation made everything a fuck of a lot harder.

"She knows a lot. She could go public with it all. And if she does, your name might come out." Which is the main reason for my call.

"I don't think she'll say anything because it's against the law, and she'll get crucified. But even if she does, I'm not a detective anymore."

I blow out a breath. "So, the rumors were true. I tried to follow you online, but you don't have much in the way of social media."

"I'm too old for that shit. I'll leave that to my grandkids. I'm a private investigator now, specializing in cold cases."

"Really? Do you like it?"

"I do. Less bureaucratic bullshit, and there is something really satisfying about giving a family closure. But enough about me. I say fire the lawyer. Get a new one to handle your estate and all the shit from your parents. Hell, you should hire an assistant while you're at it. If you're anything like the girl I remember, you're still running yourself ragged."

I chuckle because he's not wrong. "Okay. And thank you. I needed to know you'd be okay before I pushed Mandy any further."

"Push. I'm tougher than I look and mean enough to push the

fuckers back. If you need me, say the word, and I'll hop on a plane."

Goddamn, these tears are relentless. But seriously, he doesn't even know where I live. After everything I've been through lately, this is exactly what I needed. To be reminded that I matter.

"Thank you." I sniff. He's quiet, letting me have a moment to get myself together.

"Now, let's talk about these men, shall we?"

"We don't have to. They don't really matter in the grand scheme of things. It was stupid to wish for something normal anyway, right?"

"Not stupid, honey, but unrealistic. Do me a favor. Don't aim for normal. Aim for exquisite because you, my dear, are far too good for normal. You deserve something magical—something breathtaking. They had the whole world in the palm of their hands. They have to be class A jackasses to let you slip away."

I sigh. "There is a part of me that thought they'd come looking for me. In the deepest parts of my heart, I wanted them to track me down and tell me they were wrong, that they made a mistake, and that they chose me. It's stupid, I know. But for a little while I…"

I hold my hand to my chest, feeling my heart beat methodically beneath my palm despite the cracks in it.

"I almost had everything I wished for," I whisper.

"I still have connections. Do you want me to track them down and shoot them for you? Because I will," he growls, making me smile.

"I'll be okay." And I will. This conversation is just rein-
forcing everything I've been thinking about since I made it
home two weeks ago. "But thank you. Nobody has ever cared
enough to commit murder for me before," I tease. "But I
wouldn't want you to get arrested for me. Trust me, it's no fun."

"Please. I'm an ex-cop. I know how to get rid of a body," he
deadpans as the buzzer for the gate rings. I ignore it because
I'm not expecting anyone.

"Good to know. That kind of leads me to what I was going
to say next. I had an idea about how we could help each other."

He's quiet for a moment. "Help each other how?"

I lean my head against my knees and remind myself that this
is the right thing to do. It's time. "I still get my visions, but
convincing people of them is even harder than watching their
deaths play out."

Needing air, I climb to my feet and walk over to the glass
doors and push them open. The heat envelops me immediately,
banishing the cold that has been seeping into my bones at the
memories of my visions, and I take a deep breath.

"I saved a woman from getting raped." I let that hang
between us as I walk across the deck, the wooden planks hot
beneath my bare feet.

"All my visions usually come true. Do you know what that's
like? To see evil at work and be helpless to stop it? When I
would say something, nobody listened. So much fucking hate
comes my way that the actual guilty parties end up looking
innocent. After I moved here, I thought it would be better. I hid
away a lot, and when I did go out, I was careful to avoid
contact. After a while, I almost convinced myself that my gift

was gone, that whoever cursed me with it realized I was too weak, so they took it back."

"You were never weak," he chastises, his voice gruff, giving me comfort. "I don't know why you can do what you do, but I wholeheartedly believe it was given to you because you might just be the only person alive strong enough to handle it."

"I almost didn't, though, did I?" I whisper.

"Almost only counts in horseshoes and hand grenades. You did not fail anyone, Astrid. It was the people around you that failed. Maybe that's why things played out the way they did. They were tested, and they were found lacking."

I suck in a breath at his words. He curses and apologizes, but I shake my head, gazing out at the stillness of the pool.

"No, I understand what you meant. I might have still been fucked up, but when my life was in chaos, a safe place where I had someone to shield me would have made all the difference. You know how I know that? Because once upon a time, you were that shield for me."

He makes a noise that sounds like he's fighting back tears, which makes my own start flowing again.

"I'm crying like a baby here." I laugh, wiping my cheeks, when I hear him grumble, "me too."

"Anyway. Once I started coming into contact with people again, the visions returned. It's basically why I've been a recluse all these years. But the woman I saved from being raped? I couldn't not try to do something. I knew if I told her the truth, she'd ignore me. So, I did something I've never done before when it comes to my visions. I lied. I told her the man who I saw raping her had raped a friend of mine and that I overheard him bragging to his friends about what he wanted to do with her."

"That was risky and easy enough for her to disprove if she asked questions."

"I know. And in a case of my word against his—or anyone's—I'm always going to lose with a reputation like mine. But rape and murder aren't the same.

"Women have a built-in creep radar. Most of the time, we ignore it, though. We don't see the signs until it's too late or we're in too deep. But there are always a red flag or two. You just have to pay attention. She listened to me and watched him, and she saw him looking at her. And on a crowded bus…" I let myself drift off because the rest is obvious.

"A red flag," he huffs. "So many times, people ignore their instincts or brush them off because they think they are overreacting. When, in reality, they aren't reacting enough. I'm glad she listened to you, though. You did good."

"It felt good. I've never stopped a vision from happening before. I never gave much thought about how I was delivering what I saw. I just always wanted people to know. But this time…" I take a breath. "My lie saved her, and it felt right. Like something just clicked into place. And I thought, I did that. I saved her, and because I lied, Glory went home safe and sound, and I saved her daughter from living in the aftermath. So, I started thinking, I have this gift, and if you're right, it was given to me for a reason. But all I've been doing is hiding like a coward—"

"Tell me what you need." Just like that. Dear God, this man…

"I used to wish you were my dad. Did I ever tell you that?"

"Oh God, you're killing me, kid. I would've been honored to be your father, Astrid. I really, really would have."

I smile, feeling lighter. The sadness will always be inside me. My body and mind were shaped by tragedies that ripped me apart at the seams and changed the very fabric of what made me…me. But I'm done being afraid.

"I need your help. I have resources, or the money for resources."

"Okay."

"I can fund a team of people, buy you a freaking plane if that's what it takes."

"Okay."

"I—Wait, what?"

"I said okay. Let's do this."

"But… don't you want time to think about it? I mean, do you even realize what I'm asking?"

"First, she tries to talk me into it. Now, she tries to talk me out of it. Women are so confusing. No wonder I'm divorced."

I wince. "I'm sorry. I'm happy, don't get me wrong—ecstatic, actually—but I didn't think it would be this easy."

"We both know that what you're asking will be anything but easy. But that doesn't stop it from being the right thing to do. I'm divorced, Astrid. My kids are grown, and I can visit my grandchildren whenever I want."

"You said you love what you do—"

"And I do. But you don't get multiple visions a day. I'm still going to have plenty of time to work on cold cases. They kind of go hand-in-hand, actually."

I snap my mouth shut, feeling completely overwhelmed.

"Astrid?"

I take a few deep breaths to get my shit together.

"Astrid, are you okay?"

"Would you like to come visit me? We can iron out all the details and—"

"Just tell me when and where."

With a grin, I tell him I'll deal with his plane tickets and rent him a car. He tries to argue with me, but I don't back down. The man is doing enough for me already. When I hang up, I place my phone on one of the loungers around the pool and pull my cover-up off, placing it on top of my cell phone.

I wasn't sure that was the direction I was going to go when I called James. My main reason had been to warn him about Mandy and what she might do or say when I fire her. But listening to him reminded me that there are good people in the world, people who still want to make a difference. And underneath all the layers of hurt and mistrust, I know I'm not ready to give up being one of them.

I check my watch and set an alarm so I don't forget when to reapply my sunscreen before walking to the edge of the pool. I take a deep breath and dive in, leaving all my worries behind me as the cool water envelops me. I swim the length of the pool, kicking off the side and swimming back, my mind gradually emptying of everything as I focus on my movements.

When my alarm goes off, my arms feel like wet noodles. Instead of reapplying sunscreen, I decide to take a shower and maybe read for a while. I swim over to the steps and climb out, wringing the water out of my hair, and curse myself for forgetting to grab a towel. Turning to head back inside, I freeze when I realize I'm not alone.

The swirling thoughts and unwanted emotions return with a blast so strong I stumble as Slade and Jagger's eyes take in my bikini-clad frame.

"What are you doing here?"

CHAPTER TWENTY-NINE

Jagger

I take her in, forcing myself to stay where I am instead of rushing to grab her. The purple bikini makes her violet eyes seem even more vivid. Though I try to keep my eyes on her face, I'm only human. Her curves make my mouth water and my dick hard as I picture her thick thighs wrapped around my head as I eat her until she comes.

"We came for you," I tell her, taking a step closer.

"Then I'm sorry you wasted the trip."

Slade walks toward her, and she holds her ground until she realizes he isn't going to stop. She steps to the side and holds her hands up, but he doesn't stop until he's right in front of her.

"Astrid."

Her name on his lips flips a switch in her. She steps forward and shoves him. He tries to catch his balance, but he's too close to the edge of the pool. He falls with a splash, Astrid's hands covering her mouth in shock as I laugh.

When Slade surfaces and looks up at her, he shakes his head with a grin on his face. "Guess I should be grateful I wasn't standing at the top of the stairs."

The comment seems to sober Astrid right away. "It's not funny. I could have hurt you. Christ, I don't even recognize who I am anymore."

"Hey, it's fine. He's okay. And let's be honest, he deserved it. Would it make you feel better if you pushed me in too?"

"No, it wouldn't."

Slade swims to the side and hauls himself out, water running from his jeans and plastering his T-shirt to his body.

"There is nothing here for you."

"You're here," I tell her, walking closer, knowing there is no way of getting past me.

"I came here to get away from you. I thought you'd be happy." She turns to look at Slade. "I thought you couldn't stand to look at me." Her anger forces her words out, but it does nothing to hide the crack in her voice as her pain bleeds through.

"I'm sorry. So, fucking sorry." He reaches for her arm, but she yanks it away.

"Yeah, me too. But don't worry, you're safe from me. I don't own a gun." She digs the knife in a little deeper.

Slade growls and reaches for her again, pulling her to his chest and wrapping his arms around her as she tries to fight him. She thumps his chest, sobbing and cursing us both before the strength goes out of her.

"Let's get her inside. She's been out in the sun long enough," I say, closing the distance between us.

Slade nods, letting go and taking a step back so I can sweep Astrid up into my arms. Slade strips off his T-shirt and tosses it on the deck before popping open the button on his jeans and peeling them down over his hips. I leave him to it and carry Astrid inside.

"I hope your parents aren't here, or they're going to be scarred for life," I joke, trying to lighten the mood because I know Slade will walk in at any moment, buck fucking naked.

"My parents are dead. There is nobody here for him to scar but me. But wait, you guys already did that."

I forgot, with how sweet she had been recently, just how sharp her tongue can be when she's on the offensive.

"I'm sorry, Astrid. I didn't know." I head to the stairs and carry her up. I don't bother asking which room is hers, not expecting her to tell me anyway. Instead, I choose the first room I come across, kicking the door open lightly with my foot.

Taking a breath, I instantly know this is Astrid's room. I can smell her unique scent of oranges and something subtly floral. Spotting the open door to the bathroom, I carry her inside and gently lower her to the ground.

As soon as she's on her feet, she tries to shove past me, freezing when she sees Slade, who I can sense standing behind me.

"Really?" she snarls before yanking a towel off the rail and tossing it at him.

"Aw, don't be like that, princess. I know you missed my cock as much as I missed your hot, slick pussy," Slade answers.

I roll my eyes to the ceiling, just about managing to stop myself from swinging around and punching him in the face. "You are not helping, jackass," I snap at him. He grins unrepentantly when I look over my shoulder to glare at him.

"Is this some kind of joke to you? Do you think it's funny? Newsflash, assholes, this is my fucking life," she yells before her shoulders drop.

"Go home, both of you. Leave me to my joke of a life."

Slade's eyes flash when he realizes he pushed too far. He shoves past me and pulls her to his chest, holding her tightly. She keeps her arms at her sides. She might not be pushing him away, but she's definitely not a willing participant.

"I'm a dick. Ignore me." He pulls back and cups her jaw, tipping her head back and staring down into her eyes. "How about you take a shower and put something on, and then we can talk?" he urges gently.

"I, honest to God, don't want to hear what you have to say. You're sorry. Great, super. But honestly, so fucking what? I trusted you. I trusted you both, and you stomped all over it. And what? Now that you're standing here—two weeks too fucking late, might I add—throwing out innuendos and sorrys like confetti, I'm supposed to just smile and spread my legs. I'm supposed to just pretend you didn't hurt me, that you didn't break my heart?" She ends in a whisper as I walk up behind her and slide her hair over her shoulder before placing a kiss on the skin I expose.

The pain in her voice lets me know it will take more than an apology to fix what we broke.

"We don't expect you to just pretend nothing happened. We fucked up. We own that. All we're asking is for a chance to prove ourselves to you. Let us earn your trust back," I murmur as my lips skate along the skin of her shoulder to the spot where it meets her neck.

"No. I'm sorry, I can't." She pulls away from us both and walks from the bathroom to her bed, wrapping her arms around herself protectively.

I look at Slade, who stares at Astrid with a fierce expression on his face.

"You won't even give us a chance to explain?"

"You mean like you did me?"

Slade licks his lips and smirks. "I deserved that. Want to know the biggest difference between me and you, though, sweetheart?"

He steps closer, and with the bed behind her, Astrid has nowhere to go.

"You're a giant asshole?" she asks with a sweet smile.

"That and I never quit. I never give up. And when something is mine, I'll fight to the death to keep it."

Tears spring to her eyes, but she shakes her head. "Good thing I was never really yours then."

Slade motions for me to move. We spoke about this, preparing for every possible outcome, so we came prepared. As I step aside, Slade rushes her and tosses her on the bed. She lets out a surprised scream, but by the time she has her head together enough to fight back, Slade already has her positioned where he wants her. Grabbing her arms, he shoves them up the bed, leaving enough space for me to maneuver around him as I grab the cuffs out of my back pocket and clip one of the bracelets around her wrist.

"What the hell? Guys, stop," she yells. She's no match for Slade, who doesn't give her an inch.

Threading the chain of the cuffs through the bars, I snap the other bracelet around her other wrist. Slade climbs off her once he sees that she's been restrained.

"Guys, this isn't fucking funny. Let me go." She thrashes on the bed. It might make me a dick knowing she's freaking out, but my body can't help but react to her writhing around half-naked as the sheets get tangled up beneath her.

"I don't know, this kind of feels like old times," Slade jokes, his eyes moving to mine. The tightening of his jaw is the only outward sign that he's not as unaffected by everything as he's pretending to be.

"I'm going to go take a shower and let Jagger talk to you for a minute. We both fucked up, and we both want to make it right. I know you don't trust us, but we're willing to put in the work so that one day you'll forgive us."

She starts cursing us out again, but Slade just looks at me. Though no words are spoken between us, I know this is him telling me to stop holding back, to man up and take what I want, or to back off for good this time. He must find what he's looking for in my eyes because he nods and heads to the bathroom, closing the door behind him.

I turn my attention back to Astrid, who has stopped moving now. Her hands gripping the headboard for dear life.

"Let me go, Jagger. You can't force me to forgive you. That's not how it works."

"Says who?" I ask, leaning over her.

"Says me. And if you're working the Stockholm angle, I'd quit while you're ahead. I think I'm immune to being held hostage at this point."

I pause at that comment, hating that she would dump me and Slade into that category, knowing what she has experienced. But I can't exactly blame her for saying it, either.

Okay, time for another tactic. "You know, I wanted you from the second I laid my eyes on you," I admit, crawling up her body, pushing myself between the cradle of her thighs.

"I told myself that Slade needed you more than me, that I could give you my cock but hold back my heart. I watched you get closer, saw you soften his edges, and wished I was him. I've never been jealous of Slade. He's been my friend for so long that I don't know where one of us starts and the other ends. But seeing him falling in love with you a little more every day made me want to kill him. Not because I didn't want him to worm his way into your heart, but because I was afraid there wouldn't be enough space there for me too. I thought if I held back, it wouldn't hurt as much if I had to give you up. If you only wanted one of us in the end, I knew it had to be him. But now..."

She looks at me with wide eyes, her chest heaving. I reach inside my back pocket and pull out my switchblade and flip it open.

"Knowing what it feels like to lose you, I was a fucking fool to think I'd survive." I slip my knife into the front of her

295

bikini top and slice through the material, exposing her breasts.

"Jagger." Her voice trembles, a mixture of shock and trepidation.

"I won't hurt you, baby girl."

"You already did."

I don't ask her to trust me. I prove it by gliding the tip of my knife around the edge of her areola. Flicking the tip of her nipple with my tongue, I drag the blade down between the valley of her breasts to her navel, circling her belly button before slicing through the material at her hips. I fold the knife away and slip it back into my pocket before pulling the now-ruined scraps of damp fabric from her body and tossing them to the floor.

"Never again. I swear on my life, I will never doubt you again." My words are my vow. As the tears run down her cheeks, I know she hears it too. She just doesn't believe it.

Sliding down her body, I spread her legs wide, relieved when she doesn't fight me. But I don't like that desolate expression on her face. My girl is fire and sass, chaos, and calamity, all tied up in the body of a fairy tale princess. Right now, the woman in front of me is hollowed out and empty. We did that to her. We took everything that made her shine bright and snuffed it out with a callousness that burned its way into her soul like a fucking brand.

I use my thumbs to open her up and swipe at her wetness with my tongue. She might not like me very much right now, but her body still knows it's mine.

"I know you don't trust the words you hear, and that's okay.

But I'm going to make sure you feel every fucking promise I make to you."

I dip my tongue inside her as she arches her hips off the bed and gasps. She looks like heaven spread out before me and tastes like sin. I suck on her clit and slide my fingers up and down her wet pussy until they are slick with her arousal. When she whimpers, I thrust my fingers inside her, hearing the door click open as she screams.

I look out the corner of my eye and see Slade watching us from the doorway, his hand on his cock as he takes in the look of rapture on Astrid's face. He stays in the shadows so that she can't see him watching her. I might be the one with the taste of her on my lips, but he's the one drinking her in.

I feast on her, keeping her on the precipice of coming before pulling back. I tease her until she's deliriously begging me for more. Only then do I free my weeping cock from the confines of my jeans. I shove them down my thighs with my boxers, line up my cock with her greedy pussy, and thrust inside her.

She comes instantly, squeezing my dick so hard it's almost painful. Seeing her come undone like that for me—no, *because* of me—unravels what little control I have left.

I pull out of her and push her legs together before pushing them down so her knees are pressed against her chest. Only then do I ease myself back inside her. She's even tighter this way, if that's possible. I feel myself getting sucked into oblivion, her pussy like a siren's song to my punch-drunk cock. I'm not wearing a condom, and I know I should give her the choice after everything that went down between us. But I don't. I can't. The borderline compulsive need to mark her as mine, to coat her insides with my cum, the fucking need to breed her overrides everything. It's all too much. I erupt, filling her as I thrust inside her a couple more times and hold myself still, the tip of my cock brushing against her cervix.

It's only when her legs begin to shake uncontrollably that I manage to pull back and regain some composure. I ease out of her and spread her legs wide, feeling my dick twitch as I watch my cum run out of her.

"You're mine, Astrid. I might have fucked up what we had before, but I can be a better man. Today, tomorrow, and every day until you realize it."

"Until I realize what?" she whispers.

"That I'm not going anywhere."

CHAPTER THIRTY

Astrid

As soon as he pulls back, I slam my legs closed and turn my head, feeling shame trying to edge its way through my anger. But then I remind myself that I have nothing to be ashamed of. If they want to fuck me, then have at it. That's all I'm good for, right? So, I'm more than happy to go along for the ride. But if they think I'll ever willingly hand them pieces of my heart again, they're delusional.

I avoid looking at Jagger as he strips out of his clothes. My eyes move instead to Slade as he walks out of the bathroom, stroking his cock. I clench my thighs together, remembering how it feels to have him inside me. It doesn't matter that I've just been fucked by Jagger, not when Slade looks at me like that.

This is why I ran. I didn't trust myself with them. The power they have over me makes me feel weak and needy. And being handcuffed to the fucking bed while they do whatever they want to me only adds to it. The worst part is that I get off on the helplessness of it all. After everything I've been through and the traumas I've endured, I never would have thought that having someone else take control would feel so freeing. There is even a part of me that likes being manhandled. I don't want to get hurt, but I'd be lying to myself if I didn't admit that being pinned down and fucked hard makes my toes curl.

A hand on my throat or a fist in my hair has brought me the kind of bliss that can only come with giving yourself over to someone completely, trusting them not to take things too far. They gave me that. The weird girl who nobody liked got the chance to be free between two of the most unlikely sources. But fucking with my heart and fucking with my body are not the same thing.

"Your turn now, huh? You going to fuck the attitude out of me?" I snap when he doesn't move.

He stands there, trailing his eyes over my body like a warm caress, igniting the embers that Jagger stoked before him. Slade ignores me as he takes the key to the cuffs from Jagger and sets me free. Before I can scramble off the bed, he scoops me up and carries me to the bathroom. Once inside, I notice he's filled the tub and added my favorite bubble bath. Gently, he lowers me into it before he tucks a strand of hair behind my ear.

"I'm not going to fuck you. Not just yet anyway. I'm going to look after you, and you're going to let me."

I huff out a laugh and roll my eyes. "And why would I do that?"

"Because I need to fix what I broke. I hurt you over and over. I know I did. And I'm so fucking sorry."

"I don't believe you."

His hand grips my jaw tightly—not enough to hurt but tight enough that I can't pull away. "I didn't want to love you, but you pulled me in anyway. I never knew I needed you until you were gone, and I couldn't fucking breathe without you. You can be pissed at me all you want. I'm pissed at you too, but it won't change how I feel about you."

"You're pissed at me?" I gasp in surprise.

"You ran away," he snaps, his other hand splashing down into the water. "You gave up on me."

My mouth gapes open like a fish out of water. "You're certifiable. Absolutely fucking crazy."

"I'm crazy about you. And if you think I'm going to let you leave me again, I'll show you what crazy really is."

"Have fun with that. I'm going to bring our bags up and find some food for us all," Jagger calls from the doorway.

I look at him and glare. "You don't need to bring your bags in. You're not staying. Neither of you are."

"Oh, good. We'll just pack you a bag then, and when you're dressed, we can leave." Slade smiles as Jagger disappears.

"Leave? And where the heck do you think I'm going?"

"Home with us."

I shake my head. "This is my home. You need to call your doctor and get him to change your meds or something. I don't know what's going on, but I'm not playing these games with you anymore. You want to fuck me, Slade? Go right ahead.

Want me to suck your dick? Just pass me a cushion for my knees. But anything else is off the fucking table."

He snarls, his hand moving from my jaw to my throat, which he grips as he leans in and nips my mouth with his teeth. "Oh, I'll fuck your tight pussy and fill it with my cum. Then I'll fuck that pretty little mouth of yours too. Make you choke on my cock while you drip all over my fingers."

My pussy spasms at his crude words.

"And after that, I'll slide into your ass as Jagger slips into your pussy. We'll take you together, over and over, until all you can think about is having us inside you. But I don't just want your body, Astrid. I want it all. Every tear, every curse word, every mark you scratch down my back—I want your dark, your light, and all the shadows in between. You can say what you want to me, punish me with your words. Go ahead. I deserve it. But I won't leave you. I'll fight for us because I'm not the kind of man who runs away from his problems."

"Fuck you," I snarl, knowing that dig was meant for me. "You made it clear what you thought of me. Why the hell wouldn't I leave?"

"Why the hell wouldn't you stay and fight? Am I not worth it?" he yells. He releases me and falls back on his ass, cocking his head to the side as he repeats the question. Only this time, there is a sickening realization to his words that—despite my anger—I don't like hearing. Not one little bit.

"Am I not worth fighting for?"

"Aren't I?"

He frowns and takes in my face as the shutters fall down over his eyes. If I hadn't caught the flash of panic, I'd have thought from his blank expression he didn't care. But now I realize this face is nothing more than a mask.

"Don't hate me." It comes out as an order, but his voice cracks, and his pain bleeds through. And god-fucking-dammit, it feels like a knife to the gut.

"I don't hate you. I hate what we do to each other. What we turn each other into. We're toxic together."

"We can start fresh. A blank slate."

"There is no blank slate for us, Slade. Not for you, not for me, not for Jagger. Too much has happened to us. Our pasts have already shaped us. The prologue of our story began years before we ever became an us. We can't just skip over that to get to the good part. Not in real life."

He closes his eyes for a moment, letting my words sink in. For a second, I think he's going to nod and agree, give up at the latest hurdle, and walk away. I'm surprised that it still hurts as much now as it did before.

Only when he opens his eyes, there's a look of pure possession blazes from the depths of them. I know then I've underestimated the lengths this man will go to.

I can't see my own future, but I don't need to be psychic to see how this is going to play out. They're going to win. They're going to break me down, and I'm going to let them. Because as much as they've hurt me, I'm more alive with them than I've ever been before.

"I love you."

I swallow hard at his soft words.

"I'm in love with you, and nothing you can say or do will change that. You know what I think?" He leans closer, his fingers now skating over my collarbone. "I think you love me too. You love both of us, and it terrifies the fucking hell out of you. We might not have started on the same page, but we'll finish together. By the time we're done, we'll be so intricately woven together you'll never be free."

He leans closer and kisses me softly. "I don't have all the answers, Astrid. I wish I did," he says before pressing his forehead against mine.

"All I know is I was meant to love you."

"Then why"—I sob quietly— "does it hurt so much?"

"It hurts because you care. Because it's real."

I close my eyes and breathe him in, my emotions crashing around me as I topple off the cliff of anger into the jagged rocks below. I keep my eyes closed as my tears fall. I taste them on my lips before they drip from my chin into the water below.

"Astrid." The sound of my name on his lips like the sweetest torture. Pleasure laced with poison, his lips skimming down my throat and hovering over my rapidly beating pulse. A threat and a promise that this man has the ability to kiss me sweetly and rip out my jugular with one aimed strike.

He moves, and I hear the pop of a bottle being opened before his soapy hands start to glide over me, starting at my shoulders before working their way down my back. His actions are commanding yet soothing, allowing me to slip into an almost trance-like state.

"Lie back, pet. Let me take care of you."

I do as he asks without thought or fight, keeping my eyes closed—refusing to pull myself from my dream-like state and let reality invade.

His hands smooth over my collarbone and down to my chest as he washes my breasts with a touch so tender it almost brings more tears to my eyes. His hands move down my body until he reaches my legs. He hooks his hand under my bent knee and lifts my leg over the edge of the bath, opening me up for him. A soft sigh leaves my lips before I can pull it back, his fingers stroking over my sensitive clit before dipping inside me.

"I like taking care of you. I never got to do that for anyone before. My siblings were older than me. And when I enlisted, I was one of the youngest. Same when I went to prison. I knew how to take care of myself, but what did I know about taking care of someone else? Hell, I'd never even had a dog before. Then Salem came along, and she was so…" His voice trails off, searching for the right word.

I know what he means, regardless. There is something endlessly sweet about Salem. No matter what life threw at her, somehow, the enormity of her gift seemed to round out the sharp, jagged edges someone like me picked up along the way. I can't help but be a bit jealous.

"Salem is easy to love," I say quietly. Unlike me. But I don't say that out loud. Opening my eyes, I look at him and find him staring at me, his eyes finding mine.

"She is. Loving her was effortless and safe. I could care for her like a sister. She was never mine, so I never had to worry about causing her any damage. I knew Oz and Zig would keep her safe from everyone, including me."

I reach out my hand and touch his cheek. The bleakness in his eyes calls to the hollow parts of my soul, urging me to act as a balm and soothe him the way he can soothe me.

"And then there was you. You are anything but safe and easy. But God, I wanted you more than I wanted air, and it pissed me off."

I can't help but grin at that. A part of me revels in the fact that a nobody like me can have such a profound effect on someone like him.

He turns his face into my hand and kisses my palm. "Loving you is like trying to hold fire. So fucking beautiful, yet touching you opens me up to an endless world of pain. I wasn't ready for you. I'm supposed to be a badass mercenary. And yet here I am, kneeling before a fairy tale princess, scared out of my fucking mind."

He pulls back and offers me his hand. I look at it for a moment, trying to see all the strings attached to it. In the end, I let my heart guide me and slide my hand into his.

He pulls me up and reaches over to grab a towel before wrapping it around my body. He lifts me out and pulls me tight to his chest.

"I'm scared," he admits once again. I can't lie and say I don't find it incredibly sexy that he's just opened himself up and shared his weakness with me.

"Scared, I'll fuck up again. Hell, I'm scared I'll get it right. But I won't run, Astrid. I'll fight. And right now, I need you to fight too. Fight for what the three of us could have. Fight for me, even knowing I'll mess up again, and you'll have to kick my ass for it." He lowers his mouth until his lips hover over mine. "Fight for you, for the lonely, invisible girl you used to be. I see you, Astrid. I see you."

His whispered words are my undoing. My legs crumple as

sobs wrack my body. He lifts me with ease and carries me out into the bedroom, where Jagger is waiting, his concern clear on his face. Slade places me in the center of the bed and climbs in behind me as Jagger lies down in front of me.

I don't put up a fight as they fit themselves around me like puzzle pieces clicking into place. And that's how I fall asleep, cocooned in their warmth, letting it slowly melt away the ice I've encased myself in since the day I left them.

CHAPTER THIRTY-ONE

Slade

It's been two weeks since we got here. Two weeks of building bridges that we so stupidly set on fire. Two weeks and not a single person has come by to visit until today.

"So, who is this guy?" I ask, holding my coffee mug tight enough to crack.

Astrid looks up from the melon she's chopping to glare at me from across the kitchen island. "He's my friend."

"If he's such a good friend, why hasn't he come to visit you? How come he didn't know you were missing when you were at Apex?" I fire back, knowing if I'm not careful, I'll undo all the hard work Jagger and I have put in since we've been here.

Astrid is stubborn as the day is long, but we've been wearing her down slowly. I find that even someone like me can have the patience of a saint if the prize at the end is worth it. Of course, there have been hiccups along the way, and I know today is going to be trying for all of us.

"He used to be a detective."

My body goes solid as Jagger enters the room, sweat dripping down his body as he grabs a bottle of water from the fridge. "What's wrong? Why do you look like you're constipated?" He stares at me before looking at Astrid.

"It seems Slade doesn't approve of my friends."

"I didn't say that. I said he couldn't be much of a friend if he hasn't been here for you."

Jagger's eyes narrow. "He?"

Astrid throws a piece of melon at him. "I cannot handle it when you're both acting like crazy possessive cavemen."

Jagger walks around the island and pins her against it, wisely taking the knife from her hand and laying it down. He wraps his hand around the back of her neck and slams his mouth down over hers.

My dick goes rock hard in a nanosecond.

I have no interest in Jagger sexually, not even a passing curiosity. But watching him take control of our girl gets me every fucking time.

"You have no idea how possessive we can be, baby girl. We've been holding back so we don't freak you out," he admits, pulling back so he can look down at her.

"Were you always this insane?"

He winks at her before stealing a piece of melon and popping it in his mouth.

"You can pretend you don't like it all you want, Astrid. But we both know if I peeled those tiny little shorts over your ass, pulled your panties to the side, and slid my fingers through your slit, I'd find you wet. Admit it, you like how possessive we are with you," I growl, my dick begging for relief.

She mumbles something to herself I can't hear, but I don't miss the blush spreading across her chest and face.

"His name is James Allan. He used to be a detective," she says, quietly resuming her chopping.

My eyes snap up. "He was a part of the investigating team surrounding the shooting."

She flinches, but Jagger wraps his arms around her from behind, tugging her back into his chest. The knife clatters to the counter as she grips his forearms, her eyes on mine. So many shadows in those pretty haunted eyes.

"I think it's time we talked. I know we still have a long way to go to earn your trust back, but this isn't about that. This is about us having the tools to help you exorcise some of those ghosts, princess."

She blinks slowly, her teeth sinking into her lip. She huffs and pulls free from Jagger and heads over to the window seat, which offers a perfect view of the landscape outside.

"What does it even matter if you don't believe me anyway? You won't be the first. Sure as hell won't be the last." She wraps her arms around herself as I look at Jagger, and we both go to her.

We did this. Seeing her like this, trying to protect herself from us, guts me. But that's the penance we'll pay until the day she reaches for us instead of hiding.

"Tell us everything, Astrid. We're not going anywhere. Not

without you," Jagger promises as we sit on either side of her, offering her our support.

She nods absently as her mind drifts to the past. "I had a vision of the school shooting two weeks before it happened. One of my teachers handed me back a paper she had graded, and our fingers touched." She closes her eyes and takes a deep breath before blowing it out.

"To this day, it's still one of the most vivid visions I've had. I didn't know why at the time, but I'm starting to think that the visions are clearer when the victim is close."

"She was one of the victims?" Jagger asks softly.

Astrid nods. "She was one of three teachers killed that day. She told her students to hide while she blocked the door. The lock was broken," she chokes, reaching out to grip my hand. "She sacrificed herself to buy the others time. I saw the best and worst of people in my vision. When I came back to myself and found the teacher hovering over me with concern written all over her face, I knew I had to say something. I could live with the mocking and the ridicule, but I couldn't live with their blood on my hands."

She turns her gaze to the window. "Nobody believed me. Not the teacher, not the principal, not the kids in my class. They thought it was a joke. They listened to my words, but they didn't hear a damn word I said. I couldn't make them hear the truth. It was like I was screaming at the top of my lungs but it all fell on deaf ears."

I use my thumb to draw circles over the back of her hand, keeping her grounded in the here and now as she takes a walk through the nightmares of her past.

"The police didn't believe me either. So, I decided I needed to be louder, more in their face to make them take notice, to hear me. I vandalized the school, smashed the windows of a police cruiser. But that just made them see me as a problem. They arrested me and threw me in a cell the night before the shooting and left me there. Nobody came for me. As the first shot was fired at school, I started screaming. I screamed until my throat bled, and I lost my voice. Everyone ignored me. And then the phones started ringing," she whispers, tears slipping down her cheeks.

The phone calls I can only imagine were from the terrified kids trapped in the building with a killer.

"A lot happened after that, but most of it is a blur now. I shut down, just going through the motions. Even when I was arrested as an accomplice, I sat there and did nothing. Then Detective James Allan came out of nowhere. He knelt down in front of me, held my hands, and said, 'I've got you, Astrid.' And he did."

She pulls her hand free and wipes her face. "Mandy, my lawyer, eventually came and bailed me out. But it was James who virtually attached himself to my side, keeping the vultures away. My parents flew home, threw money at the issue, and had their PR team spin things. Then they left again. I'm not sure of all the details. I was barely functioning.

"When the charges against me were dropped, I thought things would get better. But people hated me. The whole town did. They took no responsibility for the fact that they ignored me. Instead, they laid the blame at my feet for cursing the town.

"I was attacked more than once. A few times, I needed to

312

stay in the hospital for a while. One day, I just decided enough was enough. I stole a gun from the police officer who was asleep outside my door and left against the doctor's wishes. I headed home, and when I got to the bridge that separated our town from the rest of the world, I climbed the railing and held the gun to my head. I figured I should join those I had failed to save."

I jump up, my heart in my throat, vomit swirling in my gut, at the realization that we almost lost her before we had her.

"God, Astrid." Jagger's voice is rough and filled with the same emotions I'm feeling.

"Penn saved me that day. I don't know how he found me or if it was just fate, but he talked me down, and I never thought about giving up like that again.

"When I got home, Mandy was there. She informed me that my parents had been killed in an attack at one of the hospitals they'd been helping out at. They had planned for the possibility, so arrangements had been made, and my orphaned state was hidden from the world. After all, what difference did it make? I'd been alone for years, and Mandy was my guardian, so no one questioned her presence when necessary. The house was sold, and I moved here. Their deaths were kept secret to keep me safe and to keep their obvious neglect quiet. James was the only one, aside from my lawyer, who knew. He kept the secret, knowing I needed a fresh start away from the town that hated me. Being thrown into the foster system, especially for someone who came with the kind of money and problems I did would do way more harm than good. He could have lost his job if anyone found out he knew and did nothing. He also helped suppress any information that came out about me. He stepped in when I had nobody." She looks at me, wanting me to understand.

I lean forward and kiss her temple.

"Then I'll be honored to shake the hand of the man who protected my girl."

WHEN THE GATE buzzes an hour later, Astrid jumps to her feet and heads to the door. After Jagger and I managed to break in here with such ease, we upgraded the security measures. But I'd still rather get one of our guys over here to overhaul the whole system.

"Let me get the door, Astrid."

"You know I've managed to open the door all by myself for years, right, Slade?"

"That was before you had me." I kiss her cheek, and when I see a rental car pull up, I open the door and slide my hand around to rest on my gun.

"Oh, for fuck's sake," she huffs as Jagger steps up behind her and tugs her back.

"Keep being mouthy, and I'll put you over my knee. I don't give a fuck who's here to witness it," he warns her.

"Caveman," she grumbles as a huge fucking mammoth of a man climbs out of the car.

The guy looks to be in his late forties early fifties, and though his dark hair shows signs of aging with the sprinkling of salt and pepper at his temples, his fit body clearly does not. He walks around the front of the car toward the door, catching sight of me. He gives me the once-over before his eyes fall on Astrid, and a smile spreads across his face.

"Astrid."

"James!" she squeals before pulling free from Jagger's hold and running into James's arms.

He swings her around and places her back on her feet as I growl, not liking the sight of another man's hands on her.

"I take it they apologized." He looks from Astrid to me.

I cock my eyebrow, surprised she mentioned us at all.

"Slade." I offer my hand when Astrid doesn't answer. He reaches for it and gives it a shake before offering his hand to Jagger.

"Jagger," Jagger offers, his voice tight.

"I'm James, but I'm guessing you know that. Astrid, you might want to let me go before one of your men tries to gut me."

She whips her head around and glares at us. "Don't even think about it. If you lay one finger on him, I'll kill you both."

"Threatening murder in front of a cop, no less?" I tsk.

"Ex-cop," James corrects. "And just saying, ex-cop to ex-soldier, you hurt her again, and I don't give a shit who you are, nobody will find your bodies."

"Oh, my God. I give up." Astrid throws her hands in the air before stomping into the house.

I sweep her up before she gets too far and carry her over to the sofa, where I sit with her on my lap with my arms wrapped around her. Jagger drops down beside us, while James sits in the chair opposite with a grin on his face.

"Happy looks good on you, kiddo."

"I'm hardly a kid anymore."

"You'll always be a kid to me."

I don't know if he's saying that for our benefit, but I nod in acknowledgment at what he's implying. He has no interest in Astrid in any other way than parental.

"I'm glad you figured everything out."

"Figuring it out. They're still in the doghouse," Astrid huffs, even as she snuggles into me, her ass wiggling in my lap, making my dick hard.

"Yeah, looks like it," he says dryly.

I laugh, seeing why Astrid likes the guy.

"Would you like something to drink, James?"

"No, I'm good for now. Thank you, though."

After that, we make small talk for a few minutes, and I watch as Astrid smiles and laughs. I love seeing her like this, relaxed and happy. I just wish I got to see it more often. I must get lost in that thought because the next thing I hear has me snapping to attention.

"Honestly, if you've changed your mind about what we talked about, that's fine. I'm happy I got to come out and see you anyway."

"Wait, no. I'm not changing my mind."

"Talked about what?" Jagger and I ask at the same time. Clearly, he missed something too.

James doesn't answer, letting Astrid take the lead. Again, my opinion of the guy grows.

"It's fine, James. They know about my gift. I just haven't had a chance to talk to them about this because I wasn't sure if they would still be here," she admits, making me tense.

Feeling it, she turns her head and looks at me, regret in her eyes. "I know what you've both been saying, but I've still having trouble trusting that you mean it. I figured eventually you'd get sick of me and go home. You have jobs and lives that don't include me."

"Like fuck. You are our life. Obviously, we haven't been doing a good enough job showing you that, baby. We will be wherever you are. If you really don't want to go back, then we'll stay here with you."

"He's right, Astrid. If you want to stay here, we'll make it work. We don't care what we have to do. We just want you."

She sniffs a couple times before bursting into tears.

I pull her tight to me as Jagger cups her head.

"What the fuck?" he murmurs, but James just laughs.

"I think she just figured things out."

"Baby?"

She lifts her head, her watery eyes losing the ever-present wariness she's had the last few weeks. "I'm sorry."

"You have nothing to be sorry for."

She turns so she can see Jagger, too, touching his chin with her fingertips. "I do. I'm sorry I ran. I'm sorry I made you work so hard for it. I don't know what I'm doing."

"You're protecting yourself just like you've always done. But that's our job now, okay?" Jagger kisses her fingertips before focusing back on James.

"What do you two have cooked up?"

I kiss the tip of Astrid's nose as we both turn to look at James, whose sole focus is Astrid.

"I didn't know what I expected when I came here, but this is exactly what I wished for. I've been worried about you for so long. I couldn't have picked better for you if I'd created them myself."

"You're not bothered that she's with the two of us?"

James frowns. "Astrid's special. She was always going to need something special in return."

Yeah, I can definitely see why Astrid likes him.

"I asked James to work with me," Astrid blurts out.

"Doing video games?" Jagger asks, surprised. He's not the only one. James doesn't look like much of a gamer.

"No. At the moment, he's a PI that specializes in cold cases. But I need someone, or a team of someones, to help me with my visions." She bites her lip, still wary about talking about them with us.

"How?"

She explains about the woman on the bus and the trucker in the diner and how she wants to figure out a way to communicate what she sees to the probable victims in a way that they'll believe.

"I know it sounds stupid, and maybe it won't work at all. It's never going to be easy explaining to someone that they are in danger and how I know that, but I want to try. I have to try." She takes a deep breath when she's done.

I nod my head. "I know, princess. And I think it's a good idea. I can't imagine having to go through what you do or how helpless it all must feel. I'm not sure how we can help, but anything you need from me and Jagger, just ask. Hell, I'm sure any of the Apex guys will help."

"Really?"

"Really, Astrid."

She blows out a relieved breath just as the buzzer for the gate goes off. She frowns at me.

"You're not expecting anyone else?"

She shakes her head, and Jagger pulls his gun and heads to the door. Astrid gets to her feet, but before she can move, I'm standing in front of her, and James walks over to stand beside me so that she's completely covered.

"Oh, fuck," Jagger curses.

"What? Who is it?" I snap as he opens the door, and a familiar face appears.

"What, family can't visit now?" Oz complains, and I'm stunned because it's not just Oz at Astrid's door. No, it's the whole Apex family.

CHAPTER THIRTY-TWO

Astrid

I'll admit, I'm a coward. I stay hidden behind James and Slade, wondering if I could sneak away without anyone noticing. When Slade is nudged out of the way and I find Ev looking down at me, I know I'm screwed. His puppy dog eyes make my own well with tears a second before he picks me up and squeezes me tightly.

"I'm so fucking sorry, Astrid."

I nod against his T-shirt, which I'm soaking with tears and probably snot.

"It's okay," I whisper. I missed him. I just didn't realize how much until now because all my feelings were wrapped up in Slade and Jagger.

"It's not, but it fucking will be," he promises before setting me down and handing me off to someone else.

I lift my head and see Greg smiling widely at me. "Damn, you're a sight for sore eyes."

I hug him tightly before looking back up at him.

His smile slips, and he scowls at me. "No more running. You took ten years off my life. I'll teach you how to use a gun. That way, if those bozos piss you off, you can just shoot them instead."

I laugh as James speaks up from behind me. "I like him."

"I do too." I introduce Greg to James before a hand on my arm steals my attention. I look at Crew and Wilder, and my stomach drops like a rock.

"We're sorry. We fucked up. We all did, but that's what families do. You're not supposed to run away, though. You're supposed to put salt in our coffee and Nair in our shamp—" Crew starts, but Wilder hits him in the stomach.

"Jesus, Crew, don't give the woman ideas."

I can't help the small smile that tugs at my lips before it drops. "I'm sorry. I've never really had a family before."

Wilder opens his mouth to ask but shuts it again before pulling me in for a quick hug and stepping back again so Crew can hug me too.

"We fucked up. We never made you feel like family but we'll do better, I promise. Thank you for putting these two out of their misery. I've never seen two grown men mope so much in my life."

"Hey, we did not mope," Slade complains.

"We kind of did," Jagger admits.

"Fuck you, Jagger. You were mopey. I was sad in a manly

way," Slade retorts, and I burst out laughing at his ridiculousness.

"Jesus, he sounds like you, Oz," I hear Zig say as I look at the trio standing closest to the door.

Zig, Salem, and Oz stand watching me, waiting for my reaction as Crew and Wilder slip away. Salem is the one to step forward first, her lip wobbling as she moves toward me.

"I'm sorry," she whispers and starts to cry.

I close the distance and wrap my arms around her. "You don't have anything to be sorry for."

"I told Oz and Zig a little about what you told me. It's my fault for loving idiots."

I laugh, holding her tighter. "True, but I forgive you anyway. It turns out I love my own set of idiots," I whisper so only she can hear.

"Astrid." I know Salem feels me tense when Zig says my name.

I swallow before letting her go and facing him and his brother.

"We're—" Zig is cut off by Oz scoping me up and squeezing me tight enough for the air to rush out of my lungs. "—sorry. For fuck's sake, Oz, she can't breathe. I can't apologize if she's dead." Zig pulls me from Oz's arms and holds me to him, thankfully a little more gently than his nutjob of a brother.

I narrow my eyes at Oz and start chanting. His eyes widen before he looks around. "What's she doing?"

"Oh no. I've seen this before. You're cursing him, right?" Salem shakes her head. "Thank goodness I have another lover."

"The fuck, Salem? That's just plain mean. And what do you

mean, curse? Jesus, is it hot in here? I swear I feel a little faint."
Oz wipes his forehead with the back of his hand.

"Don't worry, it won't last forever."

"Won't last forever? WHAT THE HELL DID YOU DO TO
ME?" His eyes open even wider before he grabs his cock.

"Nope. Not today, Satan." He runs away, and I can't hold
back any longer. I double over in laughter.

"You two are mean." Zig chuckles.

"He deserves it." I shrug, looking up at Zig.

Taking a deep breath, I do something I've never done before.
"My whole life, I have been treated like an afterthought, a freak,
or a liar. I've been kidnapped more times than I'd like to admit,
I've been used, beaten, and forgotten about. I've done things I'm
not proud of, but I've never treated anyone like you all treated
me. I understand it was in the name of love, and I was a
stranger, but you never gave me a chance. I was guilty until
proven innocent, and even then, I was still the bad guy. You
hurt me.

"I've hidden from the world because of my gift, tried to stop
the visions, but I... They make me who I am, good or bad. Yes, I
ran instead of staying to defend myself, to fight, and for that,
I'm sorry. I was hurt and mad. And I've never had anything to
fight for before. But like I've been told a few times today, family
fucks up, but at the end of the day, we are still family."

Zig looks at me for a second, then shocks the shit out of me
when he wraps his arms around me. He pulls back and looks
into my eyes. "I'm so sorry, Astrid. More than you'll ever know.
And you're right about it all." I suck in a breath at that and
smile.

"I think I've heard enough sorrys to last a lifetime. How about we just start over?"

He smiles and holds his hand out for me to shake. "Zig. I'm the leader of this rag-tag group of losers and the hotter twin."

"The fuck you are," Oz yells from somewhere behind me, making me smile.

I slip my hand into Zig's huge one and shake it. "I'm Astrid. I have visions about death and—" I try to think of the most important thing he needs to know about me as I survey the room. My eyes land on Slade and Jagger, who are watching me with smiles on their handsome faces.

"And I'm theirs," I tell him, not taking my eyes from them.

"You sure are, Astrid. And that also makes you ours." Smiling, I turn back to look at Zig.

"So, will you be coming home?"

"Um, Zig, she has a mansion and a pool. Maybe we should all move in here." Oz drifts closer, still holding his dick, and he leans his head on my shoulder and bats his lashes at me.

How I ever thought I'd be able to keep my defenses in place around these guys is beyond me. I lean my head against Oz's as I find Slade and Jagger in the crowd once more.

"It doesn't matter to me. Home is wherever they are."

As the day fades into night, we all gather outside around the firepit, roasting marshmallows and drinking wine. Well, most of us.

"I miss wine," Salem says wistfully, eyeing my glass.

I grin at her. "It would be giving up coffee that would kill me, I think."

She groans. "Pregnancy is so much fun." Her shoulders slump. She looks miserable.

"Hey, what's wrong?" Zig asks, turning away from Crew and Wilder as if he can sense her melancholy.

"Nothing."

"Yeah, no, I don't believe that bullshit at all. Talk to me."

I feel like I'm intruding. I look across the pool and see Slade and Jagger talking to James, who has his head thrown back with laughter. I love how welcoming everyone is toward him.

"I'm just bored. Ignore me." I tune back into the conversation at Salem's words.

"Salem," Zig says her name softly and full of regret.

"It's fine, Zig. It's just... I've gone from being trapped in a cell to being stuck in the jungle to being trapped at the ranch, and before we know it, nugget will be here, and my life won't be my own anymore. I know all the reasons why we have to be careful. It's just hard watching my life pass me by."

Zig winces a little at that.

"Oh God, no. I didn't mean it like that. Not you and Oz. Shit, I should just shut up. I'm messing everything up." She drops her face into her hands.

"Hey now, it's fine. I'm gonna go out on a limb here and say those pregnancy hormones are kicking in."

She huffs out a laugh and looks up. "Probably. I'm fine. Just ignore me."

Zig looks at me for help, but I don't know what to say.

"If it makes you feel any better, I know how it feels. I have a

nice place purely because I spend so much time here. Maybe"—
I fake whisper loud enough for Zig to hear—"you could talk the
guys into building you a pool or a library back at the ranch."

She perks up instantly, looking at Zig, who shrugs. "I don't
see why not."

She throws herself at him with a squeal of happiness.

"Well, my work here is done," I tease, wiping my hands back
and forth together as Zig winks at me.

Salem turns to look at me and sighs. "I guess the lifestyles of
the rich and reclusive are a little different than those of the rich
and famous."

"Or rich and infamous, in my case. The only two things I've
been invited to this year are a charity ball for some foundation,
which I make a sizable donation to rather than spending two
thousand dollars on the smallest plate of food in the world and
listening to pretentious pricks compare dick sizes."

"What was the other thing?"

"Huh?" I frown at Salem, losing my train of thought.

"What was the other thing you were invited to?"

"Oh, Halloween Town."

"Say what now?" Zig asks.

I grin and sit forward. "I volunteer in the children's unit
over at a hospital about thirty minutes from here. Cassidy is an
eight-year-old frequent flier. She has been battling leukemia on
and off for the past four years. Her dad is rich-rich and,
surprisingly, really nice. He adores his daughter, and Cassidy is
obsessed with all things Halloween. So three years ago, when
they were told that Cassidy wouldn't see another Halloween, he
bought a piece of land near the hospital and built a Halloween-

themed town just for her, so she could celebrate it early. And so that all the sick children could use it long after Cassidy was gone."

"Oh, Jesus." Salem starts crying.

I shake my head. "She defied the odds. That little girl is still hanging on. If determination is the cure, then she'll outlive all of us. Anyway, every year I get invited to go to a party they throw. They had to postpone it twice because she got an infection, but she's doing better now."

"When is it?"

"Tomorrow. I have a bunch of gifts coming for the kids, and once I have them loaded up, I'll be driving down there to visit." I paste on a grin, not wanting to think about how this could be the last time I see her pretty face. Death doesn't care who it comes for. It has no issue taking a hand that's tiny or one that's weathered from time.

"You want some company?" Zig asks.

Salem looks at him, her eyes wide. "Really?"

"I want you safe always. But I can't lock you in a prison, no matter how pretty the cage is."

He looks at me. "What's the security like there?"

"I'm not sure. There are a lot of staff that accompany the children, plus parents and siblings. We have paramedics on-site, just in case, and usually one or two police officers."

He nods. "Alright, let me talk to the others, and we'll figure something out. You think your ex-detective friend would help out?"

"James? Oh yeah, for sure. He doesn't know about Salem. I wouldn't share secrets that aren't mine, but he knows about me.

He always has. And he's never betrayed my trust. In fact, he's put himself in harm's way just to keep me safe. I'm not saying you need to tell him anything you don't want to; I'm just saying you don't need to worry about slipping up. He's a good man. The best, actually."

"I'm glad you had that, Astrid," he tells me warmly, ruffling my hair before he walks over to join the others and leaves me and Salem to chat.

"Is it pathetic to admit how excited I am to go to Halloween Town? Oh, can I dress up?" She looks so giddy and happy right now that I'd never tell her no.

"I always do, so knock yourself out. There is a costume shop in town. I know the owner, so I'll give her a call. You think the guys will want to dress up too?"

"For the kids? Heck yeah. Underneath all that gruff exterior, they're just a bunch of softies."

I look out at the men, all laughing and joking, and feel something settle inside me. Something I haven't felt for a long, long time.

Peace.

CHAPTER THIRTY-THREE

Jagger

"Alright, that's the last of it." I slam the trunk shut and move to climb in the back seat beside Astrid.

"Have I told you how sexy you look today?"

"For the love of God, I wish I could remove my ears." James groans from the passenger seat, making Slade laugh as he puts the truck in drive.

"Once or twice, maybe." She grins.

"Well, it's true." And it is.

The dress she is wearing is fitted around her chest—dipping low between her breasts to give more than a hint of what lies beneath the sheer material— pulling in at the waist before falling in soft layers to the ground with a shimmering purple and blue ombré effect. Her hair is pulled over her shoulder and twisted into a fancy braid, leaving a few tendrils free around her face. On her head is a silver and crystal tiara. And attached to the back of the dress, reaching from her shoulders to her ankles, are a pair of black and purple feathered wings, the tips of which just touch the ground when she walks.

Getting in the car was a nightmare for her, but I can only imagine what the kids will think when they see her later.

"I can't believe the others won't tell me what they're going as." She pouts.

"Probably because they haven't decided yet. Salem is the only one who has picked out her costume, and she wouldn't tell any of us what she's going as. You'll find out soon enough," Slade tells her.

"I suppose. Sorry I made you all leave early, but I always take the presents to the hospital first. Some of the kids are too sick to leave, and I don't ever want them to feel left out."

"You don't need to apologize for shit. Besides, this means we can check the place out discreetly before all the kids arrive," I remind her.

She turns to look at me and smiles.

"True." Her eyes drift down my body, and she sighs.

"Have I told you how sexy you both look?" She turns the table on me.

James groans loudly.

"I'm sorry, but you can't blame me for appreciating the view. I get two 007s for the price of one," she teases, smoothing her hand down the arm of my black suit jacket—that she managed to get tailored for Slade and me this morning. Money sure has its perks sometimes. I can't say I'm into the whole monkey suit thing, but if she keeps looking at me like that, I'm willing to make an exception.

"You look very dapper, too, James."

The man in question turns to look at us, his fake teeth already in his mouth, as he hisses at Astrid, making her laugh.

"The most handsome Dracula I ever did see." She presses her hand against her chest and adopts a fake southern accent.

"Jokes aside, Astrid, this is a sweet as fuck thing to do."

Astrid shrugs and smiles shyly. "I love kids. They don't look at me like I'm a freak. Maybe it's because they still believe in magic. Anyway, I get just as much from visiting them as they get from me. I just wish I could do more, but life is rarely unfair to those who deserve it. Instead, the axe always seems to fall on the innocent."

"How did you end up volunteering here anyway? It's a little out of your way."

"Maybe, but I know what it's like to be in the hospital and have nobody to sit beside me. It's already terrifying with all the doctors and nurses around you coming in and out and using big words you don't understand. But to have no one... They just want someone to care that they're still there, fighting hard to get better. They need to matter to someone. That's all any of us want in the end, right? To matter?"

"Absolutely," I agree, sliding my hand over her thigh.

She leans her head against my shoulder. "Anyway, when I was younger, I got into a lot of trouble, and because of who my parents were, I was let off with a warning and given community service, and since I spent so much time in the hospital anyway..." She trails off, and I wrap my arm around her. "So when I moved here, I guess I missed it. One day, I was having trouble with a game I was working on and decided to take a break. I got in my car and started driving, and I ended up at the hospital. I guess it's in my blood, my parents being who they were and all. I've been volunteering there ever since." She looks up at me with a smile before resting her head back on my shoulder.

This woman... She doesn't cease to amaze me.

I pull her in tighter and kiss the top of her head before looking out the window and taking in the view outside as the sun begins to set.

"It's pretty here."

"I know."

"We meant what we said. If you want us to stay here, we'll make it work."

She lifts her head to look at me and shakes it. "I won't lie and say that just because I'm willing to work things out with the both of you, everything is miraculously fixed. We have things to work through, and they'll take time. Trust is funny like that. It's hard-earned because of how priceless it is, but once it's broken, it can never be restored to what it was before," she whispers, delivering the blow softly, but it doesn't lessen the impact.

As if sensing that, she slides her hand up to cup my jaw, tugging me until my lips are a whisper from hers. "That doesn't mean you can't make something just as beautiful from all the broken pieces. Some things are prettier because of their flaws, not despite them."

I close the distance between us and kiss her softly, pouring into it everything I can never find the words to say.

"We're here."

I pull back at Slade's words and see the hospital.

"You can park in the reserved spot marked AM, near the entrance," Astrid directs, making Slade whistle.

"You have your own parking space?"

She shrugs, looking uncomfortable. "They wanted to do something nice for me. Anyone can use it. But once the invites go out for the Halloween celebration, people tend to leave it for me."

"Well, that makes things easier. I'm an old man, so carrying the entire contents of the forty-seven toy stores you emptied was making me worry a little." James laughs.

"You think I went overboard?" She bites her lip.

Yes. She abso-fucking-lutely went overboard.

"No, not at all," I lie through my teeth.

As Slade parks, she chuckles and leans over, kissing me quickly. "Liar."

Slade climbs out and opens the door for Astrid, taking her hand as I help guide her wings out so she doesn't break her neck. Once she's clear of the car, they both wait for me and James to get out. We move around to the truck as James adjusts himself, making me snort.

"Laugh it up, penguin boy. Be grateful you don't have to worry about your costume riding up your ass."

"I really did not need to know that," Astrid states as she reaches in for a stack of gifts.

"Whoa, what are you doing?" I take the boxes from her with a glare.

"Carrying some of the gifts in?" She frowns, confused.

"Nope. Not on my watch. You have three strapping men here now to carry them in for you."

"Wait, I do? Where are they?" She looks around the parking lot, and Slade pokes her in the ribs, making her squeal.

"You'll pay for that later, pet," Slade murmurs in her ear loud enough for the rest of us to hear.

"Thank fuck we're at the hospital. I think my ears are bleeding," James states, and Astrid giggles as I nudge her out of the way.

Once our arms are full with as much as we can carry, we head inside, turning heads as soon as we step through the doors. We follow Astrid, and it takes us ten minutes to get to the children's unit after climbing about a million flights of stairs. She had told us the elevators tend to break down more often than they work, so it was better to take the stairs, and we agreed. The last thing we want is to be stuck inside one all night and miss all the fun. I could only imagine the looks on the fire crew's faces at rescuing a fairy, two secret agents, and a vampire with a chafing issue.

When we get to the right floor, a doctor is heading out of one of the rooms just as we are opening the stairwell door.

"Astrid, long time no see," he bellows in a deep voice that echoes down the brightly colored hallway.

"Hey, Dr. Denish. We come bearing gifts."

"I can see that. But why on earth did you take the stairs? You must be exhausted," he states, looking us over.

Me, James, and Slade turn our heads to glare at Astrid.

"Nah, it's fine. I have three big, strong men now. They can handle anything."

"There's no problem with the elevators, is there?" Slade sighs.

The doctor looks confused. "No. I've worked here for twelve years, and I don't remember a time that it's ever been out of order."

"You're dead to me, Astrid Montgomery. Do you hear me? Dead," James growls, making me laugh despite my aching arms.

"You're going to regret this later, sweetheart, mark my words," I warn her and grin when she shivers.

The doctor coughs. "Right, well, let's go deliver all this." He turns and leads us back the way he came, swiping his badge to open the door for us.

When the staff sees Astrid, they all walk over and greet her, but I notice that nobody touches her. It gives me pause for a minute because we're all so tactile with her. But now that I think about it, I remember her saying something about avoiding people. At the time, I thought it was because of how she was treated. I was clearly wrong.

We watch as Astrid smiles and laughs as she tells everyone about all the things we brought and about the guys coming later. By the time we're being shown in to meet the kids, she has everyone eating out of the palm of her hand.

The moment we walk into the room, I have to wonder how

my girl can possibly think she's invisible when she has this fucking blinding light that draws everyone to her.

"She doesn't see it. She's grown so much, but I still see that terrified little girl inside her. What happened to her was tragic, but it didn't stop her from seeing the good in people. It stopped her from seeing the good in herself," James tells me as the three of us stand and watch our fairy princess enchant a room full of children.

"We'll get her there. One day she'll see what we do," Slade says, watching her with a hunger bordering on inappropriate for where we are.

"And what do you see when you look at her?" James asks curiously, but it's me that answers this time, thinking about Astrid's words from before as she throws back her head and laughs.

"Magic."

He nods as if he understands exactly what I mean. And he probably does. He was the one to see something in the broken girl who crossed his path when the rest of the world closed their eyes in ignorance.

"You're right, she is, and not just because of what she can do. I mean, look at her. Look at the kids' faces—how they hang on to her every word."

"She's in her element." I smile as one of the kids laughs loudly setting off the others.

"Exactly. Kids get scared of the dark, but for Astrid she's never known anything but darkness. Somehow, she found a way to navigate it and now she's showing these kids how to do the same.

"She has witnessed the worst the world can offer, and that's all she sees. I think for a long time she considered herself bad because of it. Now, though, I think she's getting it."

"Getting what?"

"There's no bad without good. And she's good. She's the balance. And this"—he nods toward Astrid and the pile of presents surrounded by kids in hospital gowns—"just proves it."

CHAPTER THIRTY-FOUR

Astrid

"I'm going to fuck you in those boots later," Slade growls.

I grin as I hold up the hem of my dress and do a little dance in my black thigh-high boots with a billion buckles. My wings had been removed so I could slip into my leather jacket, taking me from fairy princess to biker chic.

"Why wait? There's a maze back there. I'm sure we could lose all these kids for a little while," Jagger states.

I glare at him and back up. "Oh no, mister. You keep your hands to yourself. I'm not going to be responsible for scaring any of these kids."

"Spoilsport." He pouts, making me laugh.

"Poor baby. I promise I'll make it up to you later."

He grabs my hips and yanks me to him, kissing me hard. "You better."

"Eww, Astrid's kissing a boy." A little voice breaks the mood, making Jagger laugh as I pull away from him.

I turn and look down at Emma, the six-going-on-sixty-year-old who just finished her physiotherapy on her legs after being in a car accident that took the lives of both her father and brother. Her mom clutches her hand tightly, smiling even though I can see the dark circles under her eyes. She's a reminder that, though the body can heal quickly, there is no time limit on grief.

"You are absolutely right. Boys are gross. Quick, let's get out of here before any more of them find us." I offer her my hand and glance at her mom.

"Why don't you go have a break? I hear they have the most amazing hot chocolates over there." I point in the general direction of where the food and drinks are served.

"Are you sure?" she asks, wrapping her arms around herself.

"Absolutely. We're going to see if we can reach the center of the maze before the boys." I stick my tongue out at them, and Emma copies, making us all laugh.

"Okay, thank you. I pulled a double shift, and I'm drained, but I didn't want her to miss this."

"No worries. Go relax. We'll come find you when we're done."

"Thank you so much. Be good for Astrid, baby."

"I will," Emma promises before running up and giving her mom a hug.

When she walks back over to us, we stand and wait for her mom to leave before Emma looks up at Slade. "You are very tall."

"You're very short."

She rolls her eyes, full of sass. "Of course I am. I'm only six."

Slade widens his eyes. "What? Really? I thought you were at least ten."

Emma giggles and walks over to take his hand. His eyes whip up to mine, unsure, but I just nod and smile. The sight of her small hand in his makes me turn into a pile of goo.

"Astrid!"

I turn at the sound of my name being yelled and burst out laughing. Salem is walking toward us, dressed as a giant orange pumpkin. The guys around her are in identical soldier get-ups, but more like the soldiers in *Toy Story* than the ones most of them were in their former lives.

Salem smiles as I take in her costume, and I can see that she's wearing black leggings and a long-sleeved black T-shirt underneath. That makes sense because I have no idea how she'd get in the car wearing that otherwise.

"This was not what I pictured," I admit.

"I wanted to go for something sexy, but then I saw this, and I just couldn't resist."

"You're still sexy." Zig kisses her temple, making her sigh.

"Sorry we're late. We hit traffic on the way here—some kind of accident. Plus, we dropped some things off at the hospital, too," Oz admits.

"You guys didn't have to do that."

"We wanted to," Ev pipes up, moving around Oz to give me a hug.

"I'm seriously loving this outfit. I think your next avatar

should look like this." Ev's eyes drift down to Emma, and he grabs his chest.

"You didn't tell me you knew Black Widow," he whispers loudly, making Emma giggle.

"Stop trying to steal my girl," Slade warns him, bending down to Emma's height. "I say we make this a race to see who can get to the middle the fastest. The winners get hot chocolate and popcorn. Now, as my girl, you can ride on my shoulders and lead the way if you want, and—"

Emma is already raising her arms to be picked up before he can finish, making us all laugh.

"Well, now, that's not fair. Okay, who here wants to be my teammate?" Jagger calls out. That's when I realize there are a bunch of children and their caregivers and parents watching us with smiles on their faces. A little boy in a wheelchair, who is a new addition, so I don't know his name yet, raises his hand.

"Yes, score!" Jagger calls out before running over to him. He has a quick word with the man with him, who I'm guessing is his dad, before they both lift the boy between them and move him onto Jagger's back.

"You good, little man?" Jagger asks.

"Yes. Let's kick some butt," the kid replies.

All the other guys decide they need buddies now too, so I walk over to Salem and link my arm through hers. "What would you say if I told you I knew where there was a shortcut?" I murmur into her ear.

She looks at me and laughs. "I say, lead the way, teammate."

We sneak toward the opening of the maze, fog rolling out at our feet from the fog machines inside. Just before we enter,

Salem yells, "You snooze, you lose." And giggles before grabbing my hand and dragging me inside.

We both run, laughing, ignoring the yells of *cheaters* and the pounding of feet.

"Wait, this way." I pull her in a different direction than she's pulling me. "I'm supposed to be leading you."

"Shit, I know. I panicked," she admits, making us both dissolve into giggles again.

We move through the maze, managing to only bump into Greg before we run away, screaming with laughter when he tries to follow us.

"Here," I whisper when I find the section I'm looking for. I point to a hidden opening. It's really only big enough for children, meaning we'll have to crawl through.

"I knew I should have gone with the sexy ninja costume," Salem complains as she tries to wiggle through before backing up. "Help me get this off. It will be a heck of a lot easier to get through without it on."

She raises her arms as I pull the costume off over her head, both of us huffing and puffing by the time we're done.

"Shove it through with you, or they'll find the door."

"Oh, right. Good point."

She manages to wiggle through with ease now, and I pass the costume to her before crawling through myself. We both sprawl on the ground for a second as the fog floats around us, catching our breath, before I turn my head and point toward the pavilion in the center of the maze, more fog pouring from the fake cauldron in the middle.

"We did it," Salem giggles, climbing to her feet and doing a victory dance. Now it's my turn to laugh as I watch her, feeling a little disgusted with myself that the pregnant woman has more energy than me.

With a grunt, I roll over and push up to my hands and knees, making yet another promise to myself to get fit.

"Oh, I'm sorry. I didn't realize anyone had beaten us here."

I lift my head at the sound of Salem's voice, wondering who the heck beat us, when I notice the pavilion is lit up with fairy lights. A wave of nausea rushes over me as I stare at Salem, the lights flickering across her skin as she addresses the figure clad all in black in front of her. And I realize my vision is coming to life.

Everything plays out in slow motion as the person grabs Salem and they begin to struggle. I get to my feet just as Salem knees the guy. He lets her go, doubling over in pain, and she balls her hand into a fist and punches him.

I'm running to Salem before I register it. "Salem. Run!" I yell, and she turns her head to look at me, and I watch in horror as the guy pulls a sword from a sheath at their back because what I thought was a costume sword is actually a very real samurai sword.

The sword is already on its way down by the time I make it to Salem and push her out of the way. Blistering pain explodes across my chest and stomach as I drop to the ground. Salem screams, her terror piercing the night sky like the blade had pierced my skin.

"Salem!" I hear someone roar, too far away to help.

"Fuck," the person snarls.

I sense him move, so I kick out and knock them off his feet, sending shards of pain into my lungs and stealing my breath. The night is filled with screams and tears.

As my vision fades, all I can see are the twinkling lights. It seems wrong to have something so pretty here during something so ugly.

Salem drops to her knees beside me.

"Run, Salem," I choke out, but she shakes her head.

"He's not moving. I think he landed on his sword." She reaches for me, but I scramble away, nearly vomiting from the pain.

Black spots dance before my eyes as I avoid her touch. "No. The baby," I say, tasting blood.

"I have to, Astrid. You'll die."

"Then I'll die. But your baby won't."

Salem has to take the injury on herself to heal me. With where I'm hurt, there is no way her baby would survive.

Noise to our left has Salem's head whipping up. "Oh God, help her!" she screams.

Blinking, I turn my head and find Oz's horrified gaze looking down at me. "Oh Jesus, Astrid." He rips my jacket open and curses before whipping his shirt off and pressing it down on my stomach.

I scream at the pain, everything going black as I hear Oz yelling for a medic. Everything that happens next is all a blur of noise and hands touching me as I feel myself drifting.

When the blackness fades, I turn my head and look at the man lying motionless on the ground. When he jolts, rolling closer to me, I flinch, and it takes me a second to realize someone kicked him. But that's not what has me staring in shock. It's the familiar face.

"Penn," I gasp.

Salem, who is being restrained by Greg, turns to look at the fallen man. She looks back at me, tears rolling down her cheeks. "What?"

"It's Penn."

She looks at the man again before shaking her head and sobbing. "That's not Penn, Astrid. I've never seen that man before in my life."

She disappears from my sight when Jagger appears in front of me, his face wet with tears as he wipes my face with a shaky hand.

"It was all a trick." I whimper. And that's when I finally give in to the pain and pass out.

WHEN I WAKE UP, the pain is so intense that I almost wish I hadn't. I hear the sound of arguing and wonder where I am and what's happened.

"Slade," I murmur, but even my lips hurt, so I don't say anything else.

"Sir, I'm telling you right now that if you don't leave, I'm calling security."

"Go ahead. I fucking dare you," I hear him snarl before I let the darkness take me away again.

The next time I wake, the pain is still there, but at least I remember what happened. I manage to open my eyes and find Jagger and Slade sitting beside me, talking quietly to each other.

"Hi," I whisper.

You would have thought I screamed it at the top of my lungs with how high they both jump.

"Holy shit, Astrid." Jagger leans over and kisses me on the forehead. Slade grabs my hand and holds it tightly, kissing the back of it.

"What happened? How long have I been here?"

"Since yesterday. What do you remember?"

"Everything, I think. I just don't know what happened after I passed out. Salem?"

"She's fine. Shaken up, but physically she's fine. Oz, Greg, and Wilder have flown back home with her."

I try to hide my reaction to how quickly they left, considering I'm in the hospital, but Jagger must notice.

"We forced her to go home because she kept trying to heal you."

I remember that. "I wouldn't let her touch me."

"Thank you." I turn my head and see Zig enter the room. He slides a cardboard tray of drinks onto the table at the end of the bed before walking around to my free side.

He leans over me and presses his forehead against mine. "I'll never be able to repay you for what you did." He pulls back, and the sight of his damp eyes sets me off.

"Salem surviving is payment enough."

He drags a chair close to the bed and sits beside me, looking over at Slade and Jagger with a nod. "We sent Salem home because being near you and not being able to heal you was sending her off the deep end. She always feels a compulsion to heal, but she can usually keep it in check. But with it being you…" He takes a breath. "With what you did and nearly dying and not being able to heal you because of the baby, it was all too much. She needs to rest."

"But she'll be okay?"

"She'll be okay now that I can call and tell her you're gonna be okay."

I blow out a breath and wince. That hurt. "I'm sorry."

"What the fuck do you have to be sorry for?"

"The vision was all my fault."

"How was it your fault? You can't control your visions."

I don't say anything. I know he's right, but that doesn't negate my guilt.

"Okay, how about this? You let us tell you what we know, and you tell us what you think you know. And we'll figure out everything in between. But first, let's make something very clear. You are not responsible for what happened. Okay? None of this is your fault."

"Okay," I reply. My voice comes out sounding small and fragile, which I hate.

"Before we talk, how are you feeling? Do you need any meds?" Slade asks.

I shake my head even though I fucking do. "I'll just pass out again, and I can't do that until I know what the hell is going on. What did the doctor say?"

Slade growls, making me frown.

"It's bad, huh?"

"It's not that. The sword sliced you from your right shoulder to your left hip. You lost a lot of blood, and your heart stopped. In fact, you crashed three times before your lawyer arrived with a DNR. When your heart stopped the third time, the doctors refused to work on you."

"What? But I don't have a DNR."

"I fucking knew it," Slade snaps. "James said you fired the woman and had never mentioned a DNR before, so he called in a favor from someone he knows to check in to it."

"She doesn't know she's been fired. I haven't had chance to speak to her yet."

"What the fuck does she stand to gain by lying?"

"Money. She has, or had, control of all my assets. So my inheritance from my parents, my income from my video games, which is a pretty penny, plus I have two hefty trust funds from my grandparents."

"I feel like I'm missing something." Zig looks between us all.

"My parents died when I was sixteen. Given the places they worked, they knew it was a possibility, so they made arrangements with their lawyer but updated them after the shooting—in case they died before I turned eighteen. Instead of having me emancipated and declared financially independent, they had this whole plan to make the world think they were still alive."

"I still don't understand the reasoning for it." Jagger grunts, pissed on my behalf.

"At the time, I thought they had some immortality complex. People loved them for what they did. I thought they wanted that love to go on forever. And maybe that was part of it. But now, looking at it through older eyes, I wonder if, in their own way, they were trying to protect me."

"How does lying to the world about them being alive protect you? You could have been emancipated and—" Slade shuts up and curses.

"What am I missing?" Jagger looks at Slade before frowning at me.

"There is no way I would have been granted emancipation, not after everything that happened. The most likely place I would have ended up was a psychiatric facility. I might have had the money, but they would have found me mentally unstable. Their way, I still had the protection and possible threat of their names and having their lawyer as my guardian stopped people from asking too many questions."

"Fuck, what a mess. How come you didn't tell the truth when you turned eighteen?" Zig asks.

"Because," I say, like it's a perfectly reasonable answer. But from the looks on their faces, I'm guessing not. "Because I needed to be able to hide away. I didn't want to become front-page news again. Then, after a while, it just didn't matter. I went along with it because it was easier. But after everything that happened at Apex... I don't know. I guess I was sick of hiding, of having no control over my life, and I finally found my backbone."

"You always had a backbone. You were like a hissing kitten when you first arrived. The world might have beat you down a little, but you were always stronger than you realized," Slade tells me, smoothing my hair from my face. And I smile up at him. Then I remember the kids, and my smile drops.

"What happened with the kids? Was everyone okay?"

"Everyone's fine. Scared, but they'll be happy to know you're going to be okay," Jagger replies.

I turn my head to look at Zig and reach for his hand. "I put all this in motion, and I didn't even know. If I had stayed away, she never would have been at risk."

"You don't know that. It could have still happened. Salem will always be at risk. You made the best decision with the information you had. I don't know how you and Salem navigate the fucked up shit you have to at the best of times. I know these gifts might make you seem like a superhero, but you're still just human and doing the best you can."

"You always thought I was the one who would hurt her, and you were—"

His finger covers my mouth. "Nope. You are not responsible for what happened. You are not the villain of this story. You are the hero. And if you never showed up that day, you never would have crossed paths with Slade and Jagger."

I blow out a breath and nod because I know he's right. Besides, I can't change the past.

A knock at the door has us all looking that way as Ev pops his head in. When he sees that I'm awake, he smiles widely and walks over, revealing James behind him. Zig moves out of the way so Ev can give me a gentle hug. Then Ev steps back so James can wrap his arms around me.

"You are so fucking grounded," he chokes out, making me laugh and ripping a hiss of pain from me.

"Shit, sorry, honey. You scared the fucking life out of me, though."

"It scared me too," I admit as he kisses my head and stands back up.

I look at him and Ev and brace myself. "Salem told me the man who did this wasn't Penn Travis. So, who the hell was he?"

"His name is Dean McKinney. He's a former Black Ops soldier who went MIA eighteen years ago. He was officially declared dead nine years later." Ev sighs, leaning against the end of the bed.

"I don't understand. He was the man who stopped me from killing myself after the shooting. He was the man who came to my house and sparked a vision— Fuck. The vision was never about Salem. It was about him. I thought I had it because Penn —Dean—was connected to Salem. But that's not it. I had the vision because he was the killer."

"Would-be killer. You changed the outcome, Astrid. You changed everything," James reminds me.

Then I remember him seeing the vision that I did. "Salem said it wasn't Penn's gift—seeing my vision the way he did. She thought it might have been a part of my gift. But I don't think that's it. What if this Dean person is gifted too?"

"Gifted how?" Zig is all business now. "You think he manipulated what you saw?"

"No. Maybe. His face, when he saw what I did, wasn't one of horror but of determination. He definitely used me to draw her out. He must have known where she was all along. She was just much harder to get to at Apex." I think about what happened in the maze and compare it to my vision.

"My vision wasn't the clearest. It's not unusual, but this time it was because it was manipulated. My focus when I saw it was on the victim. She was dressed all in black, something I forgot all about, probably because she started the night as a friggin' pumpkin. The attacker was dressed in black too. I thought it was a mask, but he wasn't wearing one in the maze, so I think he blurred what I saw somehow. Bastard clearly has much better control over his gift than I do. I remember watching Salem die." Tears fall down my cheeks.

"You never mentioned how, now that I think about it," Zig says, and when I look at him, he at least has the decency to look sheepish. "Right."

He coughs. "What do you remember?"

"I remember the sword. I saw it swing, and then Salem's stomach was red." I cover my mouth with my hand, feeling sick.

"Shh. Easy, baby. You're okay. Salem is okay," Slade says, running his hand up and down my arm.

"Where is this Dean asshole?"

"On the floor below us, with a police detail watching him until they can take him in."

"Why do you think he did it?" Ev asks.

I think about it all again. "Because he was after the baby," I gasp.

Zig and Ev are out the door before I can say anything else.

"Go," I order Slade and Jagger.

"I'll stay with her. I won't leave her side," James vows.

With a quick nod, Slade and Jagger follow them.

James sits beside me and takes my hand, using his other to wipe away my tears. "Calm down, Astrid, or you're gonna make yourself sick. And I don't think you want to be throwing up with all those stitches holding you together."

"I can't help it. Why would he save my life just to try to kill a baby?"

"I don't know, Astrid. I really don't."

It feels like we wait a lifetime for them to come back. When they do, I know something is wrong. "Please tell me he didn't get away."

"He's dead," Zig answers.

I sigh with relief, but the grim look on his face has my breath catching. "What? I thought you'd be relieved."

"I am. But Dean didn't die from his injuries. He was suffocated, and there wasn't a single police officer around when it happened."

"Someone shut him up," James summarizes.

"Looks that way."

"Shit," James curses as Zig's eyes move to mine.

"I need to get back to my family, but we are not leaving you here. As soon as you're well enough to travel, we're all heading back to Apex. The guys can pack up whatever you need and send it to the ranch." I nod in shock.

I'm not going because I'm being told to, though I want to go with them. I need to.

James squeezes my hand as Zig looks at him. "I'd like to extend an invitation for you to join us too. I know you care about Astrid, and I think we could use all the help we can get."

"I'd be happy to come with you. I might never let Astrid out of my sight again."

His words are barely out of his mouth when the hospital room around me dissolves. I find myself looking at a basement somewhere. James is lying on the floor with a woman leaning over him, crying his name as she presses her hands against his chest. Blood coats her skin and pools around them both.

When his eyes slip closed, she tips her head back and screams.

I snap out of it and find a bunch of concerned faces staring back at me. I turn my head to look at James, feeling my heart break, to see wide eyes.

"Something changed when you said you'd come with us."

"You saw."

"What?" I ask confused.

"I saw flashes. It wasn't clear, but I saw Astrid. I saw."

Shocked, I sit silent, tears running down my face. "Maybe Salem was right. Maybe there is more to my gift."

"What did you see?" One of the guys asks me.

"James. Lying on the floor bleeding. There was a woman there. I think she was trying to save him."

"Shh, it's okay. I can go home if you want me to." James overs me a smile but his face is still pale from shock.

"But I don't know if the catalyst is us leaving you or you coming with me."

"You know what? It doesn't matter. You've changed the outcome of your visions twice now. I trust you can do it again."

I nod, hoping to God he's right.

EPILOGUE

Astrid

The healing process is a bitch after someone tries to flay you open. The stitches are gone now, thank God, but I swear the constant itching will haunt me forever.

"Fucking, fuck, fuck. How do you always do that?" Ev curses, tossing the controller on the table.

I look away from the TV and wiggle my fingers at him. "I've got mad skills, Ev. That's all you need to know."

Slade leans down as he walks past and kisses my cheek. "You kicking his ass again, babe?"

"Of course." I smile up at him.

Ev grumbles as he stands and heads into the kitchen.

"Must you always humiliate the man?" James asks without lifting his head from the paper he's reading at the table.

"It's important to keep these guys humble."

"True that," Salem grumbles from the sofa beside me, holding out her fist to bump.

I chuckle and bump it as the croissant she has balanced on her big belly is kicked off.

"I see nugget is feeling feisty this morning."

"Morning, noon, and night. I swear, this kid never sleeps. It does not bode well for when they arrive."

"Look at all the uncles you have to help out. You'll be fine," Creed tells her, lifting her feet into his lap so he can massage them.

"Oh, dear, sweet baby Jesus. I'm so glad you guys are back. You're my favorite."

Hawk and Creed missed everything that happened because they had been working a case, and they were pissed. As a result, they have stuck close ever since, trading off jobs with Crew and Wilder.

"I thought I was your favorite," Hawk complains as he hands her a glass of juice.

Wisely, Salem doesn't say anything. The woman has them wrapped around her finger. It's hilarious to watch.

"Hey, Astrid, there's a message for you."

I look over at James, who is frowning at his phone. "Coming."

Hawk reaches out his hand to help me up, which I take gratefully before I'm pulled to my feet. After I was released from the hospital and arrived at the ranch, I refused to ask for help, and boy, that did not go over well. I was told that I was family, to stop being a stubborn brat, and to let them take care of me. I cried for an hour. I've never had that before. Since then, I take all the help they offer.

Another thing that happened was that I confronted Mandy about the stunt she pulled at the hospital with the DNR. I informed her that I would be reporting her for fraud, theft, and attempted murder. She threatened to tell the world the truth about everything if I did. So instead of letting Mandy control my past, I took control of my future, and broke the news myself. I wrote an open letter to the world, telling my truth. Slade and Jagger were beside me every step of the way.

And for once, the world heard me.

I have to say, given my history, I'm shocked at how accepting people have been. Instead of condemnation, there was praise. Where there was once hate, there is now curiosity. People from back when the shooting happened even came forward to talk about how I had tried to help and been persecuted and ridiculed for it.

Mandy lost her license to practice, was disbarred, was charged, and is now awaiting trial.

James still works the cold cases, which he is flooded with now thanks to our association—though I couldn't catch glimpses of the past, no matter how helpful that might be. We are still planning on working together, but I'm focusing on healing right now. In the meantime, with all the exposure I've had, people who believe they have gifts have contacted me.

"Think it might be someone who thinks they have a gift?"

"No clue. Here." And he hands me his cell phone.

I click on the tab and sign in to view the message. A picture pops up of a man and a woman standing next to each other. In front of them are two boys, one around five or six, and the other a little older, maybe ten. In the man's arms is a tiny baby wrapped in a pink blanket with a little flowered cap on her head.

The man smiles widely, his face familiar, but I can't place him until I zoom in. I press a shaky hand to my mouth and smile.

"What is it?" Jagger walks up behind me, sweaty from his run. The man has more energy in his baby toe than I do in my whole body.

"The trucker I had a vision about the night I left. I saw another truck crash into his, pushing him through the guard rail and catching fire. He was trapped inside."

Jagger wraps his arm around my chest and pulls me back against him. "You saved him."

"He saved himself. I didn't know if he'd listen to me," I whisper, remembering the photo of his family and pregnant wife.

"I'm glad he did," Jagger says softly.

"Me too."

I zoom back out and notice the writing underneath the photo. "Thank you. Because of you, I hold the whole world in my hands."

I blow out a breath to stop myself from bawling like a baby.

"It makes it all worth it, doesn't it?" James looks at me knowingly.

I nod and reach out my hand to squeeze his shoulder. The only shadow on the horizon is the vision I've had of him. That, and trying to figure out if Dean was working alone or not.

"Here." I hand James back his phone.

"I'm gonna take a quick shower. I'll be back, okay?" Jagger kisses my temple and pats my ass as he leaves.

The doorbell rings, and Hawk dives over the sofa to reach it, but nobody seems panicked, so I assume they know who it is.

I walk over to the island, contemplating what I want to snack on. Hawk walks back in carrying three boxes of doughnuts in his hands with his wallet balanced precariously on top.

"You, sir, are a god," I proclaim, walking over to help him.

He manages to slide them onto the island as I reach for them. All I do is knock his wallet on the floor. Bending down slowly to pick it up, I spot a photo inside—his wallet having landed open. I stare down at the older photo of Hawk and Creed with a tall, willowy woman standing between them. She has the body of a ballerina and the poise of one. She's pretty, like model pretty, and the smile she's wearing lights up her whole face. I've never seen that smile before, but I've seen that face twisted into a mask of terror.

"How do you know her?" I whisper, picking up the wallet and staring at the photo.

"Astrid?" Hawk says my name, his voice making everyone turn to look at me.

I hear movement, and then Creed is standing beside him, taking the wallet from my hands as Slade walks over and pulls me into his arms.

"That's the woman from my vision. She's the one trying to save James."

"What? Are you sure?"

I nod. "Positive."

"Holy fuck."

"What's going on?" Ev asks, looking down at the photo. "That's your wife, right?"

My head snaps up to look at Hawk as he swallows hard. "Yeah, that's our wife."

I hold Slade tighter to stop my legs from buckling because something else dawns on me. When I first saw the vision, there was something familiar about the woman, but I couldn't place her. My attention had been on James. Now, seeing that face and her honey blonde hair, I know I've seen her before, in person and in a vision.

She's the woman from the diner. The one who will shoot and kill someone without remorse.

And now, knowing what I do, I have to wonder if that person might turn out to be someone I love.

ALSO BY CANDICE WRIGHT

APEX TACTICAL SERIES

The Brutal Strike

The Harsh Bite

THE INHERITANCE SERIES

Rewriting Yesterday

In This Moment

The Promise Of Tomorrow

The Complete Inheritance Series Collection

THE UNDERESTIMATED SERIES

The Queen of Carnage: An Underestimated Novel Book One

The Princess of Chaos: An Underestimated Novel Book Two

The Reign of Kings: An Underestimated Novel Book Three

The Heir of Shadows: An Underestimated Novel Book Four

The Crown of Fools: An Underestimated Novel Book Five

The Mercy of Demons: An Underestimated Novel Book Six

The Throne of Lies: An Underestimated Novel Book Seven

The Echo of Violence: An Underestimated Novel Book Eight

Ricochet (Underestimated Series Spin-off)

THE COLLATERAL DAMAGE SERIES
Tainted Oaths: A Collateral Damage Novel Book One
Twisted Vows: A Collateral Damage Novel Book Two
Toxic Whispers: A Collateral Damage Novel Book Three

THE PHOENIX PROJECT DUET

From the Ashes: Book one

From the Fire: Book Two

The Phoenix Project Collection

Virtues of Sin: A Phoenix Project Novel

DEATH IN BLOOM SERIES

Coerce

Compel

THE CANDY SHOP SERIES

Dulce

Reese

Lollie

Sugar

SHARED WORLD PROJECTS
Cautious: An Everyday Heroes World Novel

Hoax Husband: A Hero Club Novel

ACKNOWLEDGMENTS

Pretty in Ink Creations – For my fabulous cover.

Tanya Oemig – My incredible editor - AKA miracle worker. I'm so grateful to have you on my team. You're amazing and I adore you.

Briann Graziano — Proofreading Goddess.

Julia Murray — my amazing PA and friend.

Thais, Stacey, Marie and Mallory – my sprinting crew. Most days I only make it through because of you guys.

Aspen — my weapons expert. Thank you for all the times you drop everything just to read my words. You're my ride and die and I couldn't love you more.

My readers – You guys are everything to me. I am in awe of the love and support I have received. Thanks for taking a chance on me and on each of the books that I write.

Remember, If you enjoyed it, please leave a review.

ABOUT THE AUTHOR

Candice is a romance writer who lives in the UK with her long-suffering partner and her three slightly unhinged children. As an avid reader herself, you will often find her curled up with a book from one of her favorite authors, drinking her body weight in coffee.